Daggers & Dresses

Enlighten Series, Book Two

Kristin D. Van Risseghem

Kasian Publishing
PO Box 211205
Eagan, MN 55122
www.KristinVanRisseghem.com

This is a work of fiction. Names, characters, businesses, places, events and incidents are either the products of the author's imagination or used in a fictitious manner. Any resemblance to actual persons, living or dead, or actual events is purely coincidental.

Cover design by Angela Fristoe,
Covered Creatively
www.CoveredCreatively.com

Author photograph by Jessica Krueger Photography,
www.JessicaKruegerPhotography.com

Formatting by Jaye Cox
Formatting the Affordable Way

ISBN: 978-1-943207-39-8 (Paperback)
ISBN: 978-1-943207-49-7 (Hardcover)
ISBN: 978-1-943207-38-1 (Kindle)

Other works by

Kristin D. Van Risseghem:

Enlighten Series:

Swords & Stilettos, Book One

Daggers & Dresses, Book Two

Wars & Wings, Book Three

Novellas:

Fires & Fairies, Sidelle's Story

Arrows & Angels, Kieran's Story

Short Story:

Poisons & Princes, Finn's Story

Ninjas & Nephilims, Shay's Story

Sign up for the author's mailing list
and get a FREE eBook copy of
Finn's Short Story.

Go to: www.KristinVanRisseghem.com

This book is dedicated to my family.

Last night a friend of mine rose from the dead—and I was the one who brought her back. So, I guess ... I'm an angel. Or, at least most of my friends think I am.

Even wrapped tightly in the arms of my favorite oversized PINK hoodie, I shivered. It was chilly for mid-April while I sat on my front porch. The sun was coming over the horizon, but that wasn't where the tremor had come from.

I glanced up, startled by the high-pitched squealing of truck brakes that rang above the music playing from my phone. The truck turned into the cul-de-sac and careened straight into the next-door neighbors' driveway. What made it really strange was the house had been empty since last October. I could still see the top of the "For Sale" sign on the manicured front lawn. I pulled out my cell phone to text my boyfriend, Shay.

Me: Good morning!

As I waited for a response, a gray-uniformed driver opened his door and climbed down. He walked to the back of the truck; multiple doors slammed.

"This furniture goes into the living room on the main level," a man said.

I didn't particularly want to be a nosy neighbor, but I couldn't help myself. I eased higher on the top step, hoping to get a look at the man who seemed to be in charge. His back was to me, so all I could tell was he had short blond hair. He glanced down at something, then looked back up, turned, and pointed toward a number of other, smaller trucks in the cul-de-sac's parking. More uniformed men jumped out of the smaller trucks and gathered around their boss, waiting for instructions. I had no interest in watching a bunch of people move boxes, so I just stayed on the step and waited for my best friend, Kieran, and Shay.

A shadow moved into my vision. I lifted my head and spotted someone standing on the street in front of my gate. From this angle and with the sun directly behind the person's head, I couldn't see the face, but I knew the body.

Then he cleared his throat, and I smiled. I stood and lifted my hand to shield my eyes. No wonder he never texted me back. He probably thought an in-person hello was better.

"Hi," I said to Shay. "Why are you just standing there? You can let yourself in."

He stepped forward and opened the gate, and as he came into view, my eyes traveled up his body, over the usual black boots and black jeans. A blood red T-shirt hugged his upper torso, which was odd. When had Shay added color to his wardrobe? The sleeves barely contained a notable set of muscles, and the rest of the material was unsuccessfully hiding what I knew to be an impressive six-pack. In contrast to his dark clothes, Shay had blond hair, unlike my own long, brown hair. Now that he was coming out of the direct sunlight, I was able to admire his strong chin and soft lips. Last week I'd kissed those lips on a number of occasions.

But by the time I reached his eyes, which were the most startling aqua color, an intense shiver ran through my body. The sensation was nothing new, but it felt off.

My mouth opened, ready to speak, but he beat me to it. "Name's Aiden," he said.

Aiden?

The person standing in front of me looked so similar to Shay he could have passed as Shay's older brother. *He* was going to be my next-door neighbor? *Whoa.*

"Hey, Aiden!" a shrill female voice shouted from an open window. "You still have unpacking to do! If I have to tell you one more time, I'll raise holy hell ..."

I couldn't speak. Maybe the saying "we all have a twin in the world" was true. Aiden turned and briskly walked back toward his house. I gawked at his retreating back.

Just then a gold Cadillac CTS-V screamed down the road toward me and finagled its way through the parked vehicles. Kieran usually walked with me to school since his house was only six away from mine, but the events of last week had kicked him into protection-mode overdrive. I watched him climb out of the car, wearing his usual cream-colored dress slacks, a tan, unbuttoned shirt rolled up at the sleeves, and a white T-shirt underneath. His tall, slender build was one a model would be proud of, and his wavy, light-blond hair had all the girls at school wanting to date him—except for me, of course, because well, because he's my best friend. But he's swoon worthy, or so they tell me.

"Hi, Zoe."

"Hi, K. What's up?"

When he took his sunglasses off, he revealed his bright blue eyes, but he wasn't smiling. Actually, he looked a little panicked.

"Have you been waiting here long?"

I shrugged. "No, just listening to music and texting Shay."

He shook his head and then gestured toward my neighbors' place. "New people moving in?"

"Yep. Guess they finally sold the house."

"They seem to have a lot of stuff."

"Yeah, especially for only two people. He just stopped over and introduced himself. You just missed him. It's amazing. He looks like Sha—"

"Him?"

Kieran always made such a big deal out of things. I raised one eyebrow. "Yeah. He said his name was Aiden."

Kieran's body tensed visibly. "Aiden? He said his name was *Aiden*?"

"Uh-huh. Do you know him?"

"Maybe." He rubbed his chin. "A long time ago, I knew someone who used that name."

"Why are we driving to school?" I asked as we headed toward Kieran's car.

"It's safer and faster," he said. "After last night's demon attack, you can't be out alone. *Ever*." He opened the passenger door for me, and I climbed in, a little too afraid to protest. "Your safety is now priority number one." He closed the door.

I waited for him to get in on the other side, thinking how only seven days had passed since my eyes had been opened to the Enlighten world. Last Thursday, Kieran and I had been chased by two demon knights sent by Sammael, the King of Hell. Even more amazing, as we fled the creatures, Kieran created a warehouse in the Void—an in-between place separating Earth, Heaven, and Hell where we could try to hide. When matters got really rough, I became completely surrounded and protected from the demons by a purple orb, which I apparently manufactured all by myself.

"Where's Shay?" I asked. "How come he's not riding with us?" That warehouse was where I had met a tall, drop-dead gorgeous guy, Shay Curator. He and Kieran fought the DKs—short for demon knights—and sent them back to Hell. Memories of those disgusting battle images, of black blood and decapitated heads, made me shudder.

"He's with the Archangels for a meeting, so it's just us for now."

"A meeting on what?"

"To find one of the Seraph Swords."

"Oh." My shoulders sagged. "I hope he's not gone long." Shay had rescued me at the warehouse, then explained that he was a Nephilim, meaning he's a half-angel and half-human. He had amplified human traits of super speed, hearing, and vision, which was why he's a warrior for Heaven. While I had struggled to take all that in, we happened to touch—and that's when we discovered that whenever we came into contact with each other, an electrical current ran through our bodies. Eventually, we learned that reaction meant we were soul mates. So, of course, I was concerned about him. He's the love of my life.

Just then Mom pulled into the driveway with my little sister, Stella. They both got out and hauled sports bags from the trunk.

"Hey, Mrs. J," Kieran said as he opened his door. "Let me help you with those."

"Oh, Kieran, you're such an angel," Mom said. "Thank you."

I had to snicker as I got out of the car and quickly followed him inside.

"Hi, Kieran," Stella said shyly.

"Hey, Squirt. Just get done with soccer?"

"Yup. I hate these early morning practices!"

Mom stopped at the kitchen counter. "Zoe, honey, your dad won't be home for dinner tonight until late," she said as I entered the room. "I see the new neighbors are moving in. I'll bake something while you're at school, and we can bring it over this afternoon to welcome them to the neighborhood."

"That sounds great."

"Now hurry, so you have time to stop off at Coffee Grind before school. I know how you can't function without it."

I sprinted back outside and glanced over at the new neighbors' house. Kieran stood next to me, and we watched the twenty or so movers haul the last of the boxes and furniture into the house. When they were done, the trucks drove away, leaving us to the early morning quiet.

"Earth to Zoe." Kieran poked my shoulder and motioned to the car.

"What?" I cleared the images from my mind.

"I said, what you did last night was badass."

"I know, right? I had no idea I could do that! It was awesome." I hesitated. "But something else really weird happened after my hand started to glow. I didn't get to tell you guys about it."

"Yes?"

"I heard a woman's voice in my head."

"Really?" Kieran asked. "What did she say?"

What a relief that he didn't just laugh at me about hearing voices. Then again, he was an angel, my guardian angel, so he'd probably heard them a lot.

"She said she was my *mother,*" I told him, still in awe as I slumped into the car seat. "She also said to be prepared because more sorrow and death is coming." I swallowed, afraid to hope for the impossible, but it had to be said. "And when she was speaking, I think she might have passed part of her Angel Light, what makes her an angel ... to me."

The angels believed I would join the Enlightens—the

Eternals, the Naturals, and the Ordinaries—in their mission to stop evil from taking over and destroying the earth.

"Did she say her name?" Kieran asked, apparently not fazed at all by my idea.

"Grace," I said.

"Grace!" Kieran slammed his hands on the wheel. "She's the highest ranking Seraph angel. And if she said she's your mother—"

"I know." I beamed, hopping up and down. "She basically confirmed that I am going to be an angel, too."

Angel Zoe.

When I turned eighteen in a few months, I would become the Seraph angel, of whom the Prophesy foretold. To mark me as an Eternal Enlighten, I would get a tattoo: a golden Triquetra symbol with wings.

I'd always thought of myself as an average seventeen-year-old girl. I'd never considered I might be special—or even extraordinary. But all that had changed when Grace said last night I was going to save the world.

Kieran smiled and shook his head. "Zoe, you're not just any angel. You're *the* angel we have all been waiting for. She validated that you are the one who was prophesized."

At lunch Kieran and I met in the library instead of the cafeteria. We needed privacy. I pulled out a chair, and Kieran sat beside me. I wished Shay were here. It was strange I hadn't even received a text from him yet.

Kieran nudged my shoulder. "Vash invited us to the pack's compound. We should share the information we have and get them to join us. We need them to fight."

Vash Bellator, the Beta from the Spiritus wolf pack, had told us during a late night meeting last week that the wolves could kill the Marquises demons, and that they stay dead—unlike the demon knights, who, when beheaded, regenerate in Hell and come back.

I nodded. "When do you think we should go?"

"This weekend."

"Road trip!" Sidelle squealed as she entered the room. "I love roads trips. When are we going?" Sidelle sauntered to the side of the table, her signature stiletto heels clacking on the floor with every step.

"We?" Kieran leaned against a bookshelf.

"Yes, *we,*" she replied. "You're going to need me to help you pull this off. After all I can read the wolves' minds when they let me. Besides, I'm going as the 'Summer fairy representative.'" She air quoted. "If Alpha Keegan sees me, maybe he'll be more inclined to help our cause."

Sidelle always came in like a storm, like she had when

she'd saved Shay and me last Saturday night. We went on our first date to a friend's party, where I discovered Sidelle was a Summer fairy. She had revealed herself by saving Shay and me from more demons by manipulating the weather. She created a crater to swallow up the Marquises Demons—the warriors of Hell who had crashed the party. I'd been safe, though, because another one of my purple protective orbs had encased Shay and me. He was a little frustrated by that, since it wouldn't allow him to help her, but I was just glad we were both all right.

I wondered how long this quest would take, and how long to find other Enlightens and get them to fight with us? Honestly, I hadn't even known they existed until last week. But I'd figure out how to make time. I didn't really have a choice. Besides, school was almost over, just another seven weeks to go. During the summer months, I'd have more free time.

If we were leaving this weekend, it shouldn't be a problem. I'd have to think of something to tell my parents. I couldn't be gone from school for days without them noticing. This could be difficult. Maybe Kieran or Sidelle would have some ideas on how I could do it. Or maybe we could make long weekends out of it and not have to miss school at all.

What would happen if and when we finally found these

other Enlightens? Would they even consider uniting with us if they didn't know for sure that I was the angel they were waiting for? I had no proof to show them, just a few amazing powers that only emerged when I was really scared. I'd have to get practicing, or at least figure out if I could control these powers. If I didn't at least do that, there was no way they'd believe me. On the other hand, my friends would vouch for me. Confirmation from an angel and a fairy had to have some pull, right?

"Where's Finn?" I asked Sidelle. Last night she had returned from her homeland, Fairyland, with a Winter fairy named Finn in tow to help us fight the demons.

She glared at me, tossed her head, and huffed away. Huh. Maybe that was a sore subject.

I sighed. "Okay, so let's go over this again."

"What do you want to go over?" Kieran asked.

"Last week, well, let's just say I might not have been paying close attention to everything. But now I've got to focus and understand my part in this." I removed a sheet of paper from my purple backpack, ready to take notes. "Let's start with angels. Tell me everything about them."

Looking thoughtful, Kieran leaned back in his chair, arms crossed. "Okay. All angels, including the halfs, can fly. Nephilim are the warriors of Heaven, and they carry blessed swords, which they use to dispose of the DKs.

Guardian angels—like me—are protectors, and we can create orbs around ourselves, but not around others. On the other hand, Archangels can create them around others along with themselves. They can also suggest Ordinaries to do things. It's called Persuasion. Sort of like mind control."

I nodded and continued to scribble.

"Seraphs, well, we don't know a whole lot about them, because they're reclusive," he continued. "They've never set foot on Earth. What I *do* know is that they are the keepers of the Seraph Swords. And when the time is right, you will be blessed with one. It will be there when you need it the most."

I stopped writing and frowned at him. "How am I going to know when the time is right? Don't you think I need it now? I mean, I *am* being hunted. It'd be kinda nice to have one sooner rather than later."

He chortled. "I know. We could use it now. Truth is, I'm not sure when you'll get it. I guess you'll know when you know. They're custom to the individual, like the Nephilim Swords and—"

"The Seraphs Swords are powerful, too." Sidelle reappeared at the table, smiling smugly. "Yeah, see the Marqs, when they're killed, they don't regenerate. When they die, they die for good. Which is a good thing. The Prince of Hell and the King, Sammael, rarely venture out of Hell, but my guess is one or both will ... and soon. Especially when Sammael is released from his cage because of the prophesy." She pointed at me. "Which will be when you turn eighteen in six weeks."

"Maybe you should try a Mind Walk and find out more of what's going on in Zoe's head," Kieran suggested.

"Wait," I said. "Mind Walk? What's that?"

"Fairies can read Ordinaries' and Naturals' minds," Sidelle said. "We watch their memories play out like a movie. We just grab it out of your brain."

I remembered. "Oh, yeah, you told me about that, but you didn't call it Mind Walk. Did you ever figure out why you can't get a read on me? Could it be a Seraph thing?"

"Maybe." She frowned. "But you're still an Ordinary for a few more months. I should be able to."

"I'd assume an angel thing since we can keep fairies from reading us," Kieran agreed. "I think the protective orbs are, too—how you can project them around yourself and others just like the Archangels can. And if I was a betting angel, I'd also tell you that you will get all the enhanced abilities the Nephilim have, like increased speed, strength, hearing, and sight."

"You think so?" I asked.

"You'll get other cool things, too. Things no other angels can do."

I practically vibrated with anticipation.

"So, when is this road trip?" Sidelle asked. "Like, for real? I'll need to dig into it more as to why I can't Mind Walk you."

"This weekend," Kieran suggested. "The sooner, the better. Zoe, will your parents let you sleep over at my house for the weekend?"

"Probably. But why both nights if the pack lives only thirty minutes away?"

"Just in case we need more time to persuade the Alpha."

"Oh." I drew in a deep breath. "Where will we be staying?"

"They'll probably have us stay on pack land with them. If they don't, we'll find a hotel or something. Don't worry about it."

"Who's all going?" Sidelle asked. "Just the three of us?"

"Yes," Kieran said, lifting an eyebrow. "Is that a problem?"

"I'm just wondering. Okay, *Boss*?"

"Should I ask Shay to come?" I asked.

"He's not in Minnesota at the moment," Kieran said. "He'll catch up with us later. I'm not sure how long he'll be gone. Let's just go meet the pack."

"Tell me that Shay's okay." I rose; lunch was almost over.

"Yes, he's fine. It's hard to focus on school but come on. We gotta cruise." Sidelle blew me a kiss. "See ya later, Sweet Pea."

"Mom, I'm home," I said, walking through the back door and checking my cell for any texts from Shay.

Her voice drifted out from the kitchen along with the aroma of freshly baked brownies. "How was your day?"

"Good." I shook my head to clear any bad thoughts on why Shay hadn't answered me. "Can I spend the weekend at Kieran's?"

"You guys don't want to come to the cabin instead?" Mom was digging through a cabinet when I walked in. "Remember all the fun times you and Kieran had when you were younger? I forget that you're not little anymore and don't want to hang with your folks. What are you guys planning to do instead?"

Kieran and I did have many fun summers at our lake property in northern Minnesota. Back then we spent every waking moment together swimming in the lake, catching turtles, and eating ice cream. My parents thought of Kieran as the son they never had.

"It's not that we don't want to spend time with family ... We just ... we plan to cause as much trouble as we can. So, it's no difference if we were here or at the cabin." I draped my backpack behind the kitchen chair, and then reached for one of the hot treats cooling on a plate.

"I have no doubt about that." Smiling, she lifted a white cover and then fit it over the platter. "What are you going to do if you stay there?"

"Not much. Just watch movies, go swimming, maybe get ahead of school work and stuff. You know, the typical summer activities."

"All right. What time are you going over there, and what time will you be home?"

"Later tonight, and I'll be home Sunday afternoon. Sound okay?"

"Well, I guess you are old enough to stay here. Please keep your phone on at all times, so if we need to get a hold of you, we can." She opened another cabinet. "We're leaving in five minutes to go meet the new neighbors. I wonder if they have children your age?"

Crap. I'd forgotten all about that. "Um, there's a guy a little older than me. He stopped over to introduce himself already. I was sort of spying on them in the front yard." I crammed the brownie into my mouth.

"Does he have a name?"

"Aiden," I mumbled through a full mouth.

I headed to my bathroom and gawked at the messy

reflection in the mirror. I brushed my teeth, combed the rat's nest out of my hair, and applied some light makeup. I didn't want to appear like I was trying too hard, but I didn't want to look like a total disaster, either. Sprinting into the walk-in closet, I pulled out a pair of Miss Me jeans with sparkles on the back pockets and paired them with a light purple, button-down shirt that had little white polka dots.

"Zoe?" Mom called from the hallway. "Are you ready?"

"I'm coming."

"Okay. Stella and I will meet you downstairs."

I rechecked myself in the mirror and figured I looked as good as I was going to get. Back in the kitchen, Mom held the covered plate in one hand and my sister's hand in the other. I fidgeted with a shirt button, feeling nervous for some unknown reason.

When we arrived at the neighbors' red front door, the windows were open, so it was hard to miss all the clanking and shuffling sounds going on inside. Mom smiled at my sister and me, then I knocked. My hand was slick with sweat. *Calm thoughts, Zoe.*

The door opened and a younger woman—maybe in her early thirties—stood in front of us. She had short blond hair, light green eyes, and wore jeans with a short-sleeve shirt. Her appearance said "California," and she was the most beautiful woman I'd ever seen. Sidelle was pretty, but the lady in front of me screamed elegance—with a hint of danger.

"Hello," Mom said, giving her the full, welcoming

smile. "My name is Jackie. These are my daughters, Zoe and Stella. My husband, Kevin, is still at work." She signaled to the left. "We live in the yellow house next door. Welcome to the neighborhood!"

"Hi." The gorgeous woman smiled and shook our hands. "Sarah Mors. Come on in. Please excuse the mess. Just arrived today from California." She motioned for us to follow her into their living room, and we sat on their black leather couch. "Sit down. Make yourself comfortable."

"We brought this for you and your family." Mom handed her the platter. "Just return the plate whenever you get a chance."

"Thanks, Jackie. That's kind of you. And they look delicious. I'll make sure to save some for later."

"Do you have kids?"

"No. It's just my brother and me." Sarah turned to me. "You must be the young lady Aiden mentioned."

Aiden told her about me? I snapped my mouth shut.

"He's in his room unpacking. I told him he needed to get some of it done before school on Monday. Head on up if you want." She glanced at Mom. "Oh. If you would prefer she stay down here, I can go get him."

"Oh, no," Mom said sweetly, sounding nothing like herself. "If he's busy unpacking, Zoe can go upstairs."

I stared at her, speechless. Who was this lady sitting next

to me? If I'd thought my mouth had hung open before, it was now on the floor. My mother had given me permission to go into a guy's room—*alone.* She smiled and nodded.

Okay, you don't have to tell me twice. I have enough questions swirling around in my head that my mom doesn't need to overhear.

I headed for the staircase, leaving Stella to sit next to Mom.

"Last door on the left," Sarah called cheerfully.

"Thanks," I replied.

I could barely contain my excitement. I had to force myself to take one step at a time when all I wanted to do was to run and pepper him with questions. At the top of the stairs, I drew in a deep breath, letting it out before walking the short distance to the end of the hall. His door was open, and I lingered in the hallway so I could watch him. He sat on the floor, unpacking boxes of movies and books.

Eventually, I knocked on the doorframe, but he didn't look up from the stacks of boxes. I knocked a little harder, and this time his head snapped up. His eyes locked with mine, and we stared at each other for a few moments.

He broke the silence. "Hello."

"Hi, Aiden. Your ... your sister said I could come up here," I stammered.

"Sure." He motioned me in, his eyes intent on me. In that instant I experienced a strange, uncomfortable feeling. Like I was prey being stalked by a lion. Could this be the same Aiden that Kieran knows?

The previous owner had used this room for her quilting, sewing, and other projects. It looked very different now that it was Aiden's. He hadn't gotten far with unpacking. His bed was made, but most of his clothes still lay in opened boxes.

"Sit ... or whatever." He waved his hand at the bed, and never took his eyes from me.

I chose the floor, and his eyes widened slightly with surprise at my choice. Neither of us spoke. I mean, what I was going to say? "Hey, did you know that my boyfriend looks like you?" How crazy would that sound? I wasn't sure why he wasn't talking, though. Maybe he was shy, or maybe he was nervous about having a girl in his room. Somebody had to soften the atmosphere, so I spoke up.

"Do you have a lot to unpack?" I asked.

"What you see is what I have." He pointed to the pile of movies and books in front of him. "It's mostly clothes once I get these sorted. It's Zoe, right?"

Had I told him my name? "Would you like help?"

He shrugged. "Sure, if you want to." He pushed a stack of movies toward me then pointed at the tall bookcase next to his bed. "Alphabetize these and then put them on the lower shelf."

"Um, would you like them sorted into genres then alphabetized?" Lowering his head, he hid his mouth.

It was a bit weird that he wanted them alphabetized, but whatever. I lifted a few plastic containers to show him what I meant, taking advantage of the opportunity to look him over more closely. Now that the initial shock was over, I could study him. There was a definite similarity to Shay. He looked about the same age, maybe a year or two older, but with the same aqua eyes, hair color, and build.

He chuckled. "Sure. I wasn't going to ask you to do that. I thought you'd think I was weird."

"That's how I would do it," I said. "What's the point if I alphabetize them now, then you have to redo it all into genres?"

He howled, and his whole body shook with it. Oh, he was beautiful. *Knock it off. You have a boyfriend.*

"What?" I sort of snapped at him.

"Nothing."

"No, it's *not* nothing. You keep doing that, laughing at me. What's funny?"

"You. You're what's funny."

Was he being mean? I started to stand, uncomfortable. He didn't need to laugh at me.

Seeing me move, he jumped to his feet and nearly tripped over a stack of movie cases. "Wait! Why are you leaving?"

I glared at him. Was he that dense? "You just told me you thought I was funny. I offered to help you, and you laughed at me. I don't need to take that. Especially from a stranger."

"Oh, hey. I'm not laughing at you. The situation is just funny. I thought it was cute. Most people wouldn't ask if they should sort into genres first and then alphabetize them." He stood and reached for my hand but then lowered it. "And then for you to go on a little tirade about it, well, that's what I meant was funny. Okay, so maybe funny wasn't the correct word. I'm sorry. I thought it was cute ... your behavior, I mean."

Okay. Totally *not* the jerk I'd thought he was being. For one, he'd just told me I was cute—twice. So that might be a little stretch; he thought my *behavior* was cute. And two, he apologized. *What guy apologizes without being prompted?*

I sat back down and returned to sorting and alphabetizing the movies. He did the same with his stack of vintage vinyl records. We worked in silence, and when I was done, I scooted over to the bookshelf and placed my pile on the lower shelf as he had asked earlier.

"Hey, I'm sorry," Aiden said, tilting his head. "I didn't

mean to offend you. Can we start over? So, you live here all your life?"

I smiled back, only too happy to break the uncomfortable silence. "Okay, apology accepted. Yes. Your sister said you just moved from California. Where in Cali?"

"Santa Clara."

"Cool. And it's just you and your sister? No parents?"

"I see *Dad* every now and then when I make a point to see him."

I could take the hint he didn't like talking about his father, so I changed the subject. "Are you going to Trinity High School? You seem older than a high schooler."

"Yeah, I will be. It's a long story why I'm not in college," he mumbled. "You like it here, in Minnesota, I mean?"

"It's all I know. I haven't traveled outside the state yet." I shrugged. "If you want, you can ride with me and my friend, Kieran, on Monday morning."

He visibly flinched when I said Kieran's name. *What's that about?* They definitely know each other. But what could Aiden have done to make my loveable Kieran not like him?

"Thanks, but no thanks. I have a car. I'll drive."

"You know it's only six blocks to school from here, right? No pressure or anything. And we always stop at a coffee shop on the way, in case you're into that sort of thing."

One eyebrow lifted. "Ah, no. Men don't drink coffee. Not unless they're old or something."

"What? Men do *too* drink coffee! And not just when they're old. There are always guys in there."

"Yeah, but they're *with* ladies. They're only there because of them. They are either married, with their girlfriend and they want to keep them happy, or they're trying to pick up a girl."

"Wow. That's so stereotypical," I exclaimed. "Real men do drink coffee. Maybe it's just you who can't man up."

I fisted my hands. Why was I letting him get flirt with me? After my tirade—as he called my outbursts—I noticed him smiling at me. *Was he teasing me?* I narrowed my eyes, and his smile grew larger.

"Are you baiting me on purpose?"

"Maybe. I'm not trying to, but you seem to rise easily to the occasion. Sorry. You have something to say to everything, don't you?"

"Whatever. I'm not even going to dignify that with an answer. So you said you have a car? What kind is it? My dad's into old classics, but I like the new models."

"An Audi."

Something tickled in the back of my mind, but at that moment, Mom called from the bottom of the stairs to let me know she was going home.

"I should go and let you finish." I stood. "So, um, I'll see you later."

"It was nice to meet you, Zoe," he said quietly.

I glanced back at him and then looked out the window. I spotted my room directly across from his. Instead of leaving his room, I walked over to the sill and stared. Yep, I could see directly into my own bedroom. *I need to keep the blinds closed.* When I turned, Aiden was standing behind me, and having him so close made me nervous. My body prickled.

"Is that your room?" he asked.

I nodded.

"Looks nice, from what I can tell. Is that a walk-in closet?"

I adored my room. I was always happy to talk about it. "Yes, I have my own bathroom, too. I love it. When my parents would ground me, they sent me to my room, but I have everything in there I need. And Stella doesn't come in. It's my own space in the house, away from my family."

"I can't imagine your parents would ground you often. Then again, maybe that mouth of yours gets you into trouble."

I turned to face him, and he was smirking. I punched at his arm, but he stepped back, making me look a bit silly as my fist sailed through the air.

"I should go and leave you to your unpacking," I muttered again. He hadn't moved, so I looked up into his eyes. I didn't move either.

"You already said that."

For a few more seconds, we just stared at each other. Eventually, I walked around him toward the door. "See ya later," I called over my shoulder.

"Until next time, Zoe. It was definitely nice to meet you."

Then I distinctly heard him whisper, "Finally."

As I walked back to my house, my mind was busy with questions. Had I heard him correctly? Had he really said "finally," or had I just imagined it? Chills ran down my spine.

4 Zoe

I opened the front door and walked straight to my bedroom in a daze. Aiden was so different from Shay, but he looked similar, and he had the same taste in movies. Plus, he was *hot* like Shay. And there was a dangerous edge to Aiden that didn't exist in Shay. I walked to my window and zipped the blinds closed. I looked between the slats toward Aiden's room, and was taken aback to see him standing there, looking back at me. He raised his hand, so I opened my window and sat on the sill.

"Howdy, stranger. Long time no see," he said.

"Aren't you supposed to be unpacking?"

"Yeah, but it can wait. It'll still be there when I get to it."

Gravel crunched on my driveway, and we both turned

our heads to see my dad pulling in. After he parked, he waved at me, and then looked toward Aiden's house.

"Hi. I'm Kevin," he called to Aiden. "Zoe's dad. You just move in?"

"Yes, sir. Name's Aiden. My sister and I arrived this morning."

"Ah, welcome to the neighborhood." Dad turned toward the door, but before he went inside, he looked up at me and whispered, "Zoe, be careful." Then he winked and walked into the house.

Was he telling me to be careful because I was sitting on the window? Or was it because of Aiden? It was strange. Just like Mom, he didn't seem to be acting like himself. I swore aliens had taken over my parents' minds.

"Your dad seems nice," Aiden said, breaking into my thoughts.

"Yeah, he is. He'll ask you a bunch of questions about your car, if you get him on that topic."

"You don't have a car? Do you have a license?"

"I have a license, but no car ... yet."

He hesitated. "If you could have any car in the world, which would you pick?"

Hadn't we already had this conversation? *Oh wait, that was last week with my boyfriend.* Boys and their toys.

"Bentley convertible."

"Nice. Nice pick."

"And you?"

"I already have her."

"You have a name for her?"

"No."

"Zoe," Dad said from my doorway. "Do you need to pack for the weekend? Mom said that you're going to Kier—"

"Oh crap," I said. "Yes." I turned back to Aiden. "I gotta go. See ya."

"Bye, Zoe," Aiden said. "For now."

I waved again, closing my window and feeling more than a little unsettled.

I found a duffle bag from the walk-in closet and started sorting through potential clothes to wear to Vash's, but I wasn't sure what to bring. After all I'd never been to a pack's territory. I dug around the bathroom cabinets and found a small, pink cosmetic bag I'd forgotten about, and I loaded it with soap, shampoo, conditioner, and makeup.

When I stepped back into my room, my heart just about stopped. Sidelle lay sprawled across my bed. I still hadn't gotten used to her poofing in and out, which she seemed to be doing every chance she got now that her cover was blown, and I knew she was a fairy.

"Hey, Zoe? Whatcha packing?"

I took a deep breath, trying to get my heart rate back to normal. "I thought you said seven. I grabbed some stuff, but I'm not actually sure what to bring for clothes."

"I know. I'm early." She played with a strand of her short black hair. "Just bring whatever you wear on weekends."

"Okay." I dug out my cell phone and checked the weather: sun, ten percent chance of rain, and seventy-nine degrees for the weekend. Warm for St. Joseph in the spring. I returned to the closet and selected two pairs of Miss Me jeans and a couple of hoodies. I stuffed them and my undergarments into the backpack.

"Uh, no, Zoe. You can't meet the Alpha of the Spiritus pack in jeans and a hoodie," Sidelle said.

"You said to bring what I would wear on the weekends. That is what I like to wear."

She shook her head. "Maybe I should have clarified. Bring what you would wear to church. Like the shirt you have on."

"So no jeans, then?" I jutted out my lower lip.

"Bring the jeans if you must, but also bring two dresses. Maybe one should be a little more formal, like a little black one." She waved her arms in the air. "Oh, and bring some heels. And let me see the makeup. And—"

"Sidelle, do you just want to pack for me?"

"Yes. I thought you'd never ask! Now move over." She pushed me out of the way. "Dump out everything."

I did as she asked; she grabbed the empty bag and disappeared into my closet. I hadn't thought she'd actually take me up on the offer, but hangers clanked and drawers opened and shut. Every now and again, she gasped or muttered something unintelligible. I could just imagine what she would pack for me, but it wasn't like I could complain about it.

A few minutes later, she emerged from the closet and handed me the backpack and a duffle bag. "Now don't look. I want it to be a surprise."

"You better have packed me decent clothes to wear, and not just a hodgepodge of stuff."

"No worries," she said with a wink. "It's all good. I would *not* embarrass you in front of the Alpha. Now Vash, maybe."

Her eyes took on a familiar glassy look, and I knew she was listening to something. She shook her head as if to clear it. "Kieran says we should leave soon."

"Okay, I'll go let my parents know. See you in a bit."

Then Sidelle disappeared from the room.

I walked in on family time. Mom and Stella were telling Dad all about our new neighbors.

I learned that Sarah had told Mom that Aiden had some

problems in the past, and she hoped this move would straighten him out. She didn't elaborate on what the "issues" were, which made me wonder. Besides his being a little mean by laughing at me, he'd seemed nice enough. Then again, how could a person get to know someone in a day?

Oh, wait. Silly me, I could. It had only taken me four days to fall head over heels for Shay. Only one day after that, I'd declared my love for him. I must've been crazy. But can one mess with the powers that be, who'd made us soul mates?

"Uh, Zoe?" Dad asked, lifting one eyebrow.

I sat at the table across from him. "Yes?"

"I know you must've noticed it because I sure did." He crossed his legs, looking proud of himself.

Ah. The elephant in the room. "Yeah, I know."

"What's going on?" Mom asked.

"Did you meet Aiden?" he asked her.

"No. He never came downstairs."

"Mom," I said. "Aiden looks like Shay. They could be brothers."

Her eyes widened. "Do you know if Shay has siblings?"

"No—or at least he never said anything. Besides, he only *looks* similar. Personality-wise, he's nothing like Shay." I shrugged. "They say we all have a twin someplace in the world." I glanced at the clock. "Sidelle will be here any minute, so I'll see you guys on Sunday."

"I thought you were going to Kieran's?" Mom asked.

"I am, but we're grabbing dinner with Sidelle first."

"Okay." Dad nodded.

I picked up my bags and checked the front window. Sidelle arrived exactly at seven in the driveway. I mentally started to check off things I'd packed, and then remembered she'd packed for me. *Lord, help us all.*

Sidelle's house was the envy of the block: a cute, little green ranch with a beautifully landscaped front yard. Explosions of flowers in all shades surrounded the house, all of them in full bloom.

Kieran arrived shortly after we pulled into Sidelle's driveway, followed by Cali's Honda Civic. *Why was she coming with us?*

"Um, where should I put my stuff?" Cali asked. "Zoe, are we staying with Kieran's friends?"

When we went prom-dress shopping yesterday afternoon, everything went well, but when we returned to my house, DKs and Marqs attacked us. During that attack, Cali was strangled to death. Cali was the friend I'd brought back to life last night.

I'd bent over her body, not wanting to leave her side. Devastated and sobbing, I'd brushed her hair out of her face, resting my hand against her still-warm cheek. When I lowered my forehead to her chest, my whole body started to tingle, sending warm energy coursing through my mind and into my hand. It was an incredible feeling. When I raised my head and opened my eyes, my hand glowed purple. Even more amazing was how Cali's torso suddenly shot up. She inhaled and her brown eyes opened, wide with wonder.

When I didn't answer, Kieran said, "Yep, and I'm driving."

"Hi, Cali," I said, helping her with the bag. "I didn't know you were coming this weekend. Hey, K, pop the trunk, so we can put everything in there."

"Sidelle invited me. That's okay, right?"

"Sure is." I slung my arm around her shoulder.

"Zoe?" Kieran eyed my two bags, lying like small islands on the ground. "Are you going for a week or two days?"

"You're such a dork," I replied. "It's not like I packed these bags, anyway."

"I'd hate to see how much you'd pack for a week of travel. We'll have to hire a trolley just to carry all your stuff."

"Why hire anyone when I have a strapping young man to do it for me?" I beamed at him.

"I can take the hint." He bent down, picked up the bags,

and tossed them over his shoulder as though they weighed nothing. "Sidelle, are you ready?"

"Have to grab my stuff," Sidelle told us as she sprinted toward the door. "I'll be right back; then we can go."

Cali walked over to Kieran's car and hopped into the back seat, letting Sidelle ride shotgun. I lingered outside by Kieran's side.

"Why do you think Sidelle invited Cali this weekend?" I asked.

"She always has a reason for everything she does. We'll find out soon enough, I'm sure."

A few minutes later, she sauntered out leading one tiny rolling suitcase. Kieran watched her suspiciously then glanced in my direction. I giggled. I knew what he was thinking.

"Oh, my gosh. How can she have enough stuff for two nights?" Cali whispered when I crawled into the back seat. "I mean, we're coming back on Sunday, right?"

"Some people know how to pack." Kieran snickered. "Good thing you girls are small, because you'd have to share space with Zoe's luggage in the back seat if she'd brought any more stuff."

I smacked his head. "Shut it, K. I don't want to hear anything more from you."

Kieran and Sidelle chatted quietly in the front while Cali

and I talked about school. I also laid out the groundwork for a little scheme I had for Cali.

"So, Cali," I said. "About last night—"

"That was so much fun, dress shopping," she said. "Too bad I didn't find one. Better luck next time, right?"

"Yeah. Next time." I poked Sidelle in the back of the head, trying to get her attention. She flipped the passenger mirror down and glared at me. I cocked my head, and she shrugged.

"So after we got back to my house, what do you remember?" I asked Cali.

Her forehead creased as she thought back. "You know what? That's the funny thing. I kinda remember arriving, then you doing my hair, and all of us having a fashion show for your sister." She turned to face me. "But everything's a bit fuzzy after that. I must've gone home though, because I remember saying 'hi' to my parents and then going to bed."

So someone—Sidelle—had wiped her mind of last night's events.

"Are you and Vash dating?" I asked.

"I'm not exactly sure. I mean, he's cute, and I like him, but ... "

She looked confused, so I helped her along. "Maybe I'm reading him totally wrong, but he has a certain look in his eyes when he looks at you, Cali. You should ask him out." I let her ponder that. "Hey, K, have you met Vash's dad before?"

"Yes. Don't worry; he's nice. You aren't a threat to him or his family. And let's face it, Zoe, you can't hurt a fly."

I screaked, a little nervous, but then I saw Cali had no idea what he was talking about. "What's that supposed to mean?" I joked, hoping to ease the tension. "I hurt plenty of mosquitoes!"

We all whooped. It was true, though. Usually, I was a weakling when it came to anything physical. Being on the track team kept me fit, but I hated conflict.

Yet, strangely enough, some prophesy written before I was born marked me as the person destined to lead others into battle to prevent Armageddon.

Twenty minutes later we wound our way down a street that led to a dead end and ended at a massive wrought iron gate. To the left I spotted a guard shack—or a small house. A dozen or so well-built men stood inside, talking with each other, while others worked a control panel and kept an eye on the monitors. When our car approached, one of the burly men stepped out with a clipboard, and Kieran lowered the window.

The guard leaned in to get a better view of everyone in the car. "Name, please."

"Kieran Auduro. Vash is expecting us."

He flipped through the pages, tapping his finger on the clipboard. "Yes, I see your name on the list. Have you been here before?"

"Yes."

"Okay. Go ahead to the main house." He motioned us forward.

"Holy cow, Kieran!" Cali said, glancing out the back window at the guards. "What does Vash's dad do for a living? I mean, who has a gate like that with so many guards?"

"He owns Bellator Construction Company and Bellator Enterprises. They design and build commercial buildings, and they also dabble in investments. They do pretty well."

"Pretty well." Cali ran her hands over her jeans. "I feel underdressed."

"Don't worry about it. Whatever you packed will be fine. You probably won't even see his dad."

We drove through the massive property, following a road lined by gnarly old oak trees and rolling green hills. Off in the distance, I could make out a lake, and every so often a house would appear. I wondered who else lived in the gated community. The rest of the pack? I knew Vash's immediate family lived in the main house, where we were headed. The trees eventually gave way and revealed a huge marble mansion. The three-story building, with its five white pillars, reminded me of a southern plantation house in Georgia or the Carolinas. We pulled into the half-moon driveway, and a man stepped out of a booth by the front door.

"Mr. Auduro and company," the valet said politely, greeting us. "Leave the keys in the vehicle, please, and follow me."

We all got out, and Kieran popped the trunk so we could grab our bags.

"We'll bring them in for you," another man assured us.

We did as we were told, leaving our bags and following the first man toward the house. The wooden doors swung open as we approached the final step, and a doorman stepped aside so he could let us in.

"Welcome to Bellator Estate," he said. "Please wait here for—"

Running footsteps crashed down the stairs, and muscular legs came into view above us. The body belonging to those legs rode the banister down the last flight of stairs, and Vash landed in front of Kieran. He threw his arm around his shoulder.

"You guys made it!" Grinning, he dropped his hand and turned to look at each of us individually.

This was a whole new side of Vash. When we'd met last week, he had been quiet and reserved. *This could be a fun weekend after all.* Cali and I looked at each other and smiled. Vash stood a few inches taller than Kieran, had brown hair that hung a bit beneath his earlobes, and light-brown eyes. His body was extremely muscular like an NLF runningback.

He extended his arms. "Where are my manners? Welcome to the Compound."

"Hey, Vash," I said.

"Hi," he said and then picked up Cali's hand and kissed it.

"Hi." Her face turned bright red. Vash was mated to Cali, but wasn't able to save her from death. Once the fighting had started, my protective purple orb had encased my bewildered school friends, my little sister, and myself. I'd watched Kieran fight stoically, and my heart broke when a demon blade sliced Shay's arm. And that was the first time I'd seen Vash turn into his wolf form. Kieran and Shay had appeared, shining their Angel Lights to diminish some of the Marqs' darkness. The fairies distracted the Marqs, so Vash could kill them.

When I saw Vash tiring, I knew I had to fight. When I joined the boys' circle, my purple Angel Light exploded out and knocked everyone off balance, finally giving Vash the upper hand he needed. He'd killed the rest of the Marqs except for one, who high-tailed it out of there. We all assumed he was off to give Sammael a full report.

"And how lovely to see you again, Sidelle," Vash said,

giving her a slight bow. "Come on. Let's make the most of this visit. We can just hang out until my dad gets home." He started to head back to the stairs, but then he stopped. "Your bags will probably be brought up to my room," he said. "We can sort which rooms you want. You're staying the weekend, right?"

"That's the plan, as long as your dad is okay with it," Kieran replied.

Vash smirked. "It'll be a nice change of pace for him to have civilized folks around here rather than the bunch of animals he's always hanging around with—myself included."

We followed him up to the top of the third flight of stairs, and I glanced back down at the foyer. I scanned the whole grand room, letting my eyes linger on the centerpiece. I hoped Vash would take us on a tour of his home, because so far it was gorgeous.

"This is my wing of the house," Vash told us, turning left down a hallway. "I get this half of the third floor, my parents have the other half, and my younger brother and sister have the second floor."

"Wow. You have a whole wing to yourself?" Cali asked.

"Yeah, it's one of the perks of being the—"

Kieran cleared his throat and shook his head.

"—oldest child in the family," Vash continued.

Nice save. We'd have to pull Vash aside—and soon—so we didn't have another slip-up. Cali had no idea about the wolves or the real reason why we were here.

Vash showed us into a living room with brown leather couches and chairs. The largest television I'd ever seen spanned the wall opposite the windows. Off in a corner, I spotted a small kitchen with a full-size fridge, a sink, and a microwave. *And I thought* I *had it good when I got grounded and was sent to my room.* Cali and I looked around the large area in awe. Her family had a big house, too, but it wasn't nearly as impressive as this. Sidelle looked out the windows into the backyard and took in the spectacular view. From this high up, I could see the lake, the flower gardens, and a few of the other houses on the property.

Vash pointed at the door on the right. "Through that door is my bedroom, a private bathroom, and a closet. Through that way," he said, pointing toward the opposite wall, "is another bathroom and a study."

"This is nice, Vash," Cali said, walking around the room and admiring the nature paintings hanging on the walls. "I don't ever want to leave."

I made my way over to Kieran and leaned in so I could speak quietly. "We need to tell him that Cali doesn't remember anything, and we'll have to keep things on the down low."

He nodded.

"Must be nice to be an Alpha's son," I whispered.

Cali completely ignored the rest of us and hung on every word Vash said. Vash followed her around the room, telling her about each painting and artist, and explaining why he liked it.

We were interrupted by a polite knock, and then the butler made his way into the room and set all our bags on the floor. Fortunately, Cali hadn't noticed that one guy had just carried six bags and a suitcase up three flights of stairs all by himself, and he hadn't even broken a sweat. He nodded to Vash when he entered and lingered in the doorway for a bit after his task was completed. Vash bobbed his head once; the servant left.

Someone's cell went off, and we all dug around in our pockets, checking. No one had called or texted me, though. When I looked up, Vash was staring at Kieran. Without a word, he nodded.

"It's mine," Vash said, holding up his phone. "My dad's running late. He said he'll be by later this evening, and we should have dinner without him."

"Were we waiting for your dad to have dinner with us?" Cali asked.

"Kieran's dad and mine go way back, and he likes to meet all my friends," he explained. "When I told him

Kieran was coming over this weekend, he wanted to have dinner and catch up."

"Sounds great," she said, smiling up at him.

"So ..." Vash forced himself to look away from her gaze and over at us. "What do you guys want to do while we wait for dinner? It'll probably be in another hour or so."

"Should we pick out rooms and go on a tour of the estate?" I suggested.

"Great idea," Vash said. "I don't want any of you getting lost and withering away without food or water, so I'd better show you around. Plus, Mom'll have my hide for not being a good host if I don't."

We picked up our bags—Kieran helped me with mine—and followed Vash back out into the hall and down to the second floor. As we passed some of the open doors, he told us what the space was and what they used it for. Across from his sister's bedroom were three other rooms that Vash told us we could choose from. He said we could our own rooms, or we could share, whichever we preferred. We took turns opening every door and looking inside, admiring how each room was vastly different from the others, with its specific color scheme. Nothing was gaudy. Between the lavish artwork, the plush carpets, and thick, quality furniture, each room felt elegant and rich. When we opened the last door, which was in gold and white marble,

I knew instantly the girls and I would share that room.

"We should use this one," I said.

My girlfriends agreed, and we walked into the room, leaving the two boys in the hallway. I felt like I was staying in a fancy hotel suite for the weekend. We laid our bags on one of the couches, and I glanced back at Kieran and Vash. I hoped they were having the conversation about Cali.

"Oh, my gosh!" Cali exclaimed. "Hey, come look at this view of the lake. We even have our own private balcony."

Sidelle and I joined her by the door, peering out. She was right. It was magnificent.

"Hey, Kieran, look at that view," Vash said, chuckling behind us. "Looks good from here."

We turned back to the boys and realized Vash was not looking at the lake; he was staring intently at Cali, and we all blushed.

"Hey, look," Cali said, turning back to the window. "Is that a wolf out there?"

Vash was instantly at her side. "Yes. Actually, a pack of wolves lives on the land. My father says we should co-exist."

"Aww, it's kinda cute. Like a big dog."

Vash had an amused expression on his face. He caught me smiling at him and looked away, but I thought his reaction was adorable. I turned back to the window and saw more wolves loitering outside. I wondered how many of them were out there, and how many were in the pack.

I nudged Sidelle with my elbow, catching her eye. I looked pointedly at Cali, and then Vash, and she immediately picked up on the hint.

"So, we should unpack some of our stuff and get organized," Sidelle said. "Meet you back in your room, Vash?"

"Sure, if that's what you want. Kieran and I can hang out for a while, right, Kieran?"

"Yep, we can find some trouble to get into," he said. "We'll come back to get you for dinner."

I wandered around the room looking at the furniture and items in more detail. Everything was white with golden accents, including the door and window knobs, the pillows on the couch, and the area rugs. Vases in varying shades of gold decorated the room. I opened the French paneled dividers to the bedroom, which revealed a large California king four-poster bed with a gold comforter and pillows. Through another door was the ensuite bathroom, and inside it was a huge white porcelain Jacuzzi tub and shower, trimmed with gold handles. The vanity knobs and faucet and mirror were all gold.

After one look at all the marble, I would've thought the whole place would feel cold, but it was the opposite. The rooms were comfortable and welcoming.

I walked back out to the main room and grabbed my bags. "Hey, guys. The bedroom has an enormous walk-in closet. We can hang up our stuff in there."

I set both bags on top of the bed and unzipped them one at a time, and then I withdrew the first item: a little black dress still on its hanger. Sidelle watched me, a smirk plastered on her face. The next item was a deep brown sundress with white eyelet trim. So far, so good. The third and fourth items were also dresses in pastel colors. Then came a short-sleeve button-down shirt and two skirts. I glanced at her, curious. Hadn't she packed *any* lounge clothes for me? I dug around the bottom of the bag and found nothing other than undergarments, heeled shoes, and my requested pair of jeans. What the heck?

"Uh, Sidelle? It looks like I'll have to borrow a few items from you, so I hope you packed enough for both of us," I informed her. "I cannot wear dresses the whole weekend."

"Oh?"

"Sidelle! You didn't even pack me any jammies or lounge clothes. What am I supposed to wear at night?"

"I guess I forgot about that part. Sorry. I have stuff you can borrow if you need to." She giggled. "You didn't really look at anything I packed for you."

"Why? Is there something special about them? You

found them in my closet, so more than likely I've worn them before."

"Why did Sidelle pack for you?" Cali asked.

"I didn't have enough time, and she was over at my house, so I asked her to throw some stuff in a bag. I guess she only grabbed dresses."

"Well, if you need to borrow something, I packed plenty," Cali said, glancing at the dresses I'd hung up.

"Thanks, but I'm too tall for your clothes." I shook my head as I reached for my cell. "Has anyone else had any problems with reception? I haven't received a single text from Shay today."

"Mine seems to be working fine."

"Same here." Sidelle smiled, looking completely innocent. "So Cali, anything you'd like to share with us?"

"Uh, no. Why? Am I supposed to share something?"

Sidelle and I exchanged a glance and giggled, but Cali shook her head, confused. With a shrug, I finished hanging the dresses in the closet while Sidelle laid out the clothing from her little suitcase, a never-ending stream of shirts, shorts, pants, and dresses. It reminded me of a clown car where people kept emerging, and you never knew how many were crammed in there.

"Really?" she asked Cali, who hadn't seemed to notice Sidelle's endless suitcase.

"What?" Cali asked.

"One word," Sidelle said, wiggling an eyebrow. "Vash."

Cali blushed. "Oh, that."

"I saw how you looked at him. So? You gonna ask him out or what?"

"I'm staying out of this," I declared. "This is on you, Sidelle. I'm going to clean up a bit before dinner."

She shot me a dark look.

I took the brown dress to the bathroom and turned on the shower, quickly stripped, and stepped into the steaming hot water. I hadn't realized my body was so tense—probably from not knowing how tonight would go—and the shower felt wonderful. I still needed to figure out how we were going to have a meeting now that Cali was in the room since she had no idea what was going on. I stepped out of the shower and dried off, and then I slipped on the dress and tugged my wet hair up into a messy bun.

"Hey, is anyone else taking a shower?" I yelled. "I'll keep the door closed so the warmth doesn't escape the room."

"Yeah, I will," Cali answered.

I hurried to clean up the bathroom, and stepped out to let Cali pass. "All yours," I said, stepping out of the bathroom to let Cali pass.

Sidelle was still sprawled on the bed, apparently deciding which dress she'd wear that evening. I sat on the edge of the mattress and ran my fingers over one of her dresses. It was the softest silk I had ever felt, and I knew the deep, emerald green color would perfectly accent her light green eyes.

"How did you get all that in your luggage?" I asked. A dozen more dresses, five pairs of shoes, two pairs of jeans, and multiple yoga pants were set out nearby.

She checked the bathroom door before she responded. "Glamour. I just think of something, and then I can pull it out of the luggage. It actually comes in quite handy. You should try it sometime."

I shook my head, laughing at her casual suggestion. "After dinner we should try to get Cali outside with either you or Kieran. You can walk the grounds while I talk with Keegan and Vash." My fingers skimmed over one of the cashmere sweaters. "You didn't think that part through, did you? I mean, when you invited Cali to come with us this weekend."

"Sure I did, but your plan will work."

Kieran and Vash knocked, and we invited them in. Both noticed I had changed, and when I looked at Sidelle, she wore the green dress I had admired earlier. *Wow, that was fast.* I'd love to have that power.

"My father arrived earlier than he planned," Vash said, "so dinner will be served in a few minutes. He's anxious to meet you, Zoe." His eyes scanned the room. "Kieran told me the shortened version of you coming over today, and I already talked with my father and asked him not to discuss too much over dinner because of Cali." He grinned. "Speaking of which, we're here to escort you ladies to the dining hall."

"I thought I heard voices." Cali emerged from the bathroom and stopped dead in her tracks. Vash stared at her so intently I was sure an atomic bomb could've exploded, and he wouldn't have noticed. Or maybe he would have, but he wouldn't have cared. The only person he saw was her, wearing a blue and white striped skirt and a pink T-shirt. An instant later, he walked to her side and extended his arm to escort her to dinner. They continued to stare at each other as they walked out of the door and down the hall.

Kieran, Sidelle, and I looked at each other with wonder. The air swirled with emotion. Maybe that was where the expression "love in the air" was taken from. We had witnessed something spectacular.

"So, K," I whispered. "Sidelle and I thought that after dinner you or her could take Cali for a walk outside or someplace so I can talk with Vash's dad."

"We won't have to do that." He peered around the doorframe to watch the lovebirds leave. "I'm pretty sure Vash will want to take her for that walk. Besides, Sidelle and I should both be with you when you talk with Keegan."

I nodded. "Kieran, I'm worried about Shay. He hasn't answered any of my texts today." I checked my phone again. "Do you think something happened?"

"No. I'm sure he's fine. The angels will let me know if something's wrong. Don't worry about it. Shay can take care of himself. He's a good fighter for a Nephilim, but don't *ever* tell him I told you that. He has a big enough head as it is." He tugged on my hand. "Come on, let's go eat. Let me know when you hear from him. Okay?"

"I will."

We strolled out of the bedroom and followed Vash, Cali, and Sidelle down to the first floor, passing the grand foyer again. We made a left after the staircase and walked into a dimly lit hallway, which had floor-to-ceiling windows facing the backyard. On the adjacent walls hung more original nature paintings depicting wild animals and wooded scenes. We stopped in front of a thick oak door with an intricate wilderness scene carved into it. It was so beautiful and realistic I had the urge to run my fingers across its ornate surface.

Vash pushed the heavy door open and presented the enormous dining hall. The room was dominated by a huge oak table, long enough to seat at least thirty people.

Even though the room was large, it felt warm and inviting. Green, orange, and brown rugs and wallpaper stretched throughout the room, and tall, crystal vases overflowing with blooming flowers sat on the buffet table off in the corner. Antique chandeliers hung from the ceiling, and matching sconces lined the walls. The lighting they provided felt romantic but pleasant. The southern wall of the room was made entirely of windows that overlooked the backyard and the lake, providing a gorgeous view.

"I hope you like steak and potatoes," Vash said. "That's what the chef made."

The heavy door opened, and a tall, muscular man with dark brown hair and eyes appeared in the archway. He wore a black, expensive three-piece suit over a crisp white shirt. His vest was open, the top button unfastened. So this was the Alpha. It was uncanny how much he resembled an older Vash. Then again, when he strode over and I saw him more closely, I realized he actually didn't look all that much older than Vash. He could pass as an older brother.

"Hello. I'm Keegan," he stated as he approached us. "Welcome to our home. I expect Vash has been a good host, and you have felt welcomed? Unfortunately, my wife, Lilli, and our other children will not be joining us for dinner tonight, but she will return home later, and you may meet her then." His dark eyes slid between us, studying us. "I'm sorry I'm late. Work has been a bear lately. Come sit down and introduce yourselves ... please." He waved a hand toward the high-backed oak chairs with mocha velvet cushions, while he took the seat at the head of the table. Vash sat to his right, Kieran on his left, and I sat next to Kieran. Sidelle took the chair on my other side, and Cali sat next to Vash, which seemed to make them both happy.

"Hi, Mr. Bellator. I'm Zoe."

"Sidelle," my fairy friend said with a nod.

Our host's eyes moved to Cali and Vash. "Nice to meet you, sir. My name is Cali."

His smile was warm. "No need for such formalities. Please call me Keegan. It's been a while, Kieran. How are your parents?"

"They're well, thanks for asking."

Keegan relaxed against the back of his chair, seeming pleased. "We haven't had such lovely young ladies at the dinner table in a long time. Most often it's just my immediate family or the extended family. And when we all get together, it can be like a pack of dogs eating. No manners at all." He shook his head. "Your well-mannered influence should make this meal a treat."

Multiple servers waltzed in through a side door I hadn't noticed before, carrying plates of Greek salads, a pile of sizzling meat, and mounds of red potatoes. I ate my salad and a few pieces of steak, but eventually I was so stuffed I could barely walk. After the hearty dinner, we moved to a room that was much cozier than the formal dining room. It was richly decorated in reds and browns, and I wondered if Keegan's wife had done the decorating or if it had been professionally done. A floor-to-ceiling hearth with a mantle was the centerpiece of the room, and two brown leather couches sat before it. Behind each couch stood matching mahogany sofa tables, which held large red vases and lamps.

"I'm so full," Cali said, patting her stomach. "Dinner was fantastic, but I need to walk around for a while. Could we go outside and look around?"

Vash shot out of his seat and extended his arm. "I'll escort you if you'd like to take an evening stroll." He looked to the rest of us. "Anyone else?"

This was perfect.

"I'll pass. Thanks for offering," I told him.

"I'll skip it, too," Sidelle said. "Too comfortable to exert myself right now."

As Cali and Vash left the room, I heard Cali asking about

the wolves and the potential danger of getting too close to them. I hid my smile. I didn't hear Vash's full response as they walked farther down the hall, but he said something about how the wolves wouldn't bother them as long as he was with her. If she only knew how true that statement was.

I waited for someone to speak ... then realized everyone was waiting for me. I squeezed Kieran's hand for support, and he nodded encouragement. When I was ready, I looked Keegan squarely in the eyes and took a deep breath.

"I'm not sure how to say this, so I'm just going to come out with it." I glanced at Sidelle, who nodded, so I faced Keegan again. "I'm the Redeemer who was prophesized. The Seraph angel, Grace, confirmed it last night. I'm not sure if you'll believe me without any actual proof, and I can't provide you with any evidence until I turn eighteen in a few months and receive Heaven's Mark. I can only tell you who I am in hopes that you'll trust I'm telling the truth. If you can't, I guess we'll have to wait until June, but that may be too late."

When no one said anything, I leaned forward, determined. "Keegan, the world's in trouble, and more bad things are happening. I'm afraid even now we may be too late. Evil has been spreading and running unchecked for a while. Too many countries are at war with each other; too many natural disasters have been happening, and the world is no longer safe with so many demons allowed to be loose on the streets causing all this."

"I agree," Keegan said. "My pack and the others around the world are doing what they can to curb the evil that's spreading, but the demons outnumber us. We can only do so much. Trust me when I tell you we don't want more evil in the world. Our goals are the same as yours."

He stood and linked his hands behind his back, eyes on me. "It took great courage for you and your friends to come here today, and I commend you for doing so, even without proof. You're taking a huge leap by telling me who you are. I believe you are the Redeemer. I can feel it deep within my bones and in my heart. Also, you've had protectors for many years, which means the angels must've known something. Otherwise, why send Kieran?" He looked at Sidelle and tilted his head. "*And* a Summer fairy."

"You know I'm a fairy?" Sidelle asked. "How?" Her eyes flattened to slits.

"You smell like rain, pine trees, and wildflowers," he said casually. "When I first entered the house this evening, I thought my wife had gone overboard with flowers and decorations. But the rain smell threw me off. It hasn't rained here for days." He shrugged. "So, I knew one of you ladies had to be the fairy."

"I thought it was going to take more to convince you and your pack to help me fight," I said, feeling unbelievably relieved.

He held up one finger. "I didn't say I would help you fight, Zoe. I merely stated the packs are not idle right now. Yes, you told me who you are, and I believe in you, but there are many more packs to convince. I'll do what I can. I will speak with the other Alphas, but some of them may not be so eager. They will want proof. They may want to see your tattoo or the sword."

"I don't have a Seraph's Sword yet." I blew out my breath. "So, if the other packs won't acknowledge who I am, you won't fight if called upon?"

"I have to discuss it with my pack. I realize what you're asking and what's at stake here, but this is not only my decision to make. Yes, I am Alpha, and ultimately my word is law, but I also believe each member of my pack should have an opinion on the matter." He shifted so he stood directly in front of me. "When are you planning to leave here?"

"We're staying the weekend, if that's okay with you," Kieran said.

"You're welcome to stay here for however long you want," Keegan said. "I'll call a pack meeting for tomorrow night, and I'll let you know the outcome before Sunday." He turned to leave, then hesitated and looked back at me. "Vash and my other son, Jackson, will accompany you back to St. Joseph. They'll help guard you and report back to me." He left the room, and we sat in silence again.

Huh. That was not how I'd thought the meeting was going to go. First, I didn't think he'd believe me. I'd figured I'd have to beg and plead my case. Second, he didn't confirm whether or not the pack would fight. He had been surprisingly diplomatic about it, letting the pack as a whole decide its fate. I'd thought if they were on the side of good and had taken the oath, they would fight against evil. But maybe the wolves didn't take oaths. Maybe that was just something the Eternals did.

And ... what was all this about other packs? Was I expected to get *them* on board, too? How was a seventeen-year-old girl—who didn't have a car—supposed to travel around the world, persuading packs to fight? No one had said anything about that until now. How was I going to get money for a world tour and get the time off school? Oh.

boy. Someone was going to have to find me a money tree and soon.

"What are you thinking, Zoe?" Kieran asked from his place on the couch. "You look a little lost."

I paced the room. Then it dawned on me. *Fairyland*. I'd have to go there, too. I knew the Summer King wouldn't be as diplomatic as Keegan. King Oberon might possibly even want me to grovel. At this point, I wasn't planning to visit Queen Mab of the Winter Court, though I'd have to think about that. Maybe I could do both in the same visit, but more than likely, they'd have to be separate trips. If Sidelle didn't come with me, I'd have to figure out how to get into Fairyland. Another problem for another day.

"I am." I turned toward him. "I'm surprised at how different the meeting went from how I'd thought it was going to go, that's all." I looked to Sidelle. "Are we going to go to Fairyland soon? Are we visiting only Oberon? Or Mab, too?"

"I'm not sure," Sidelle said. "I'd say we should visit Oberon for now and see how that goes. It'll depend on how long we are in Fairyland, because your parents would notice you being gone longer than a weekend. We'll have to do some more thinking about that trip. Maybe over summer vacation if it can wait that long, but I think we're going to have to skip some school. I know you don't like to ditch—"

"Yeah, but this is important. Like earth shattering, major stuff that I have to do. So if lying to my parents for a while is what it takes, then that's what I have to do."

We heard Vash and Cali giggling and whispering in the hall before they appeared in the doorway, arm in arm. I took that as a good sign, but I'd ask her about their walk later.

I jumped at the sound of a loud *crash* then heard male voices bantering back and forth, their voices echoing up the staircase. We left the sitting room and looked over the railing, down into the foyer. While we watched, two massive boys and a little girl with sandy blond ponytails pushed their way into the house, sidestepping a fallen vase.

"You're in big trouble if you don't clean that up!" the girl exclaimed. She looked to be about eight years old. "Jackson, if Mom catches you and finds another broken vase—"

"She shouldn't keep them so close to the door," he replied.

"Well, if you both didn't try to walk through the door at the same time, it wouldn't happen."

"Go play with your chew toys, Era."

"I don't play—" She sniffed the air. "Strangers are in the

house."

The boys froze and inhaled, fanning out into a triangle and stepping in front of the girl. Their bodies tensed.

"Hey, Jackson," Kieran said.

Six dark eyes swiveled to meet ours.

"Kieran?" Jackson asked, breaking into a broad smile. He led the others up the staircase. "What are you doing here? I didn't know you were coming. Vash only told us that Father was having guests this weekend."

Kieran grabbed my hand, surprising me. "It's an impromptu visit."

"Who do we have here?" Jackson gave me a once-over and then admired Sidelle. He took her hand, kissed it, and bowed. "Waterfalls surrounded by beautiful flowers dancing on the golden rays of the sun do not do you justice. And you are?"

"Corny pick-up line and I'm too good for you, puppy," Sidelle said.

One dark eyebrow shot up, but he was still smiling. "Hey, now, no need for name calling ... yet."

"Jackson," Vash said. "Knock it off."

Kieran cleared his throat. "This is Zoe, and that's Sidelle."

"And this is Cali," Vash said, stepping in front of her.

"Zoe?" Jackson asked, his stare instantly on me. "The

same Zoe who Vash was sent to—"

"Yes," I said quickly.

"Come on, Jacks," his buddy said, continuing up the stairs. Unlike Jackson, he looked bored with the visitors. "Let's go play some Xbox. Let Vash play host tonight."

"Yeah, okay," he said reluctantly. "I'm coming."

The little girl smiled up at me. "I'm Era. Don't mind my brother or his jerk friends." She poked Jackson's shoulder as he passed. "He has no manners at all. Are you staying the weekend?"

"Yep," I said.

"Awesome! It'll be nice to have some more girls in the house." She jerked a small thumb at Jackson's back. "They're just a bunch of stinky beasts most of the time." She glanced at Kieran. "Sorry, K."

"No apologies needed." Kieran laughed. "How ya been?"

"Good. Been practicing chang—" She glanced between Sidelle, Cali, and me, alarmed that she might have said too much.

"I think we're staying on your floor of the house," I interrupted, saving us all.

She brightened again. "Really? Which room did you pick?"

"The gold one."

"That's my favorite. What are you doing while you're here?"

"Not sure yet."

"Ooh, wanna come see my room?"

"I'd love to, but—"

"Hey, Short Stuff," Sidelle said. "I'll come see it."

Era grabbed her hand and hauled her up the stairs. I had to smile. Era reminded me of Stella, my little sister.

Vash said something about beating up his brother and his friend before he led Cali to the game room. Kieran and I lingered in the hallway, finally alone.

"That went well, right?" Kieran asked. "With Keegan?"

"I guess." I leaned against the banister and sighed. "But he wasn't clear if the pack will fight or not."

He shrugged. "He'll do what's right in the end."

"I hope so because we need them."

I walked to a window and looked out onto the vast property. It truly was amazing. So beautiful. In a way, I wished I could just stand here all day. I took a step away from the window, but stopped as an unexpected shiver ran down my spine. I turned back and squinted into the shadows of the trees, but I didn't see anything. Vash had said the property was protected, and I couldn't imagine anything being brave enough to attack the wolves' den, but ... no. It was nothing. I was sure. *I'm just jumpy after last night.*

Kieran must have seen something on my face because he stepped over and squeezed my shoulder in reassurance.

"Come on," I said. "I wanna change clothes; then we can go find Vash and Cali."

We went back upstairs. By the time we headed back down, loud male voices echoed throughout the house over the bass drum that vibrated the windows.

"Sounds like Vash was serious about the beat-down," Kieran muttered.

When we arrived at the game room, a full-on brawl was underway. Loud, heavy metal music blasted from the surround-sound speakers, and I heard some sort of battle cries over the grunting. Vash was indeed taking on his brother and his friend, dressed in a helmet, black gloves, and kneepads. His arms swung through the air while his legs kicked, but his opponents weren't anywhere in the vicinity. Jackson and his friend were on the other side of the room, wearing the same gear Vash had on. Confused, I turned to Kieran, who pointed at the TV where four figures were duking it out. A simulator! *That could be handy.*

On screen, Jackson and his friend had Vash cornered in a vacant alley. Their images were so lifelike I was amazed. I sank down onto the couch beside Cali, staring.

"They've been going at it like this since we got here,"

Cali said.

On-screen Vash turned his head. "Hi, Zoe. I'm glad you came to watch the end. I am just about to—"

"You're letting down your guard!" Jackson shouted as his screen version ran and drop-kicked Vash. The real Jackson ran in place and made the identical move with his legs.

Chuckling, Vash dropped to the floor, and Jackson missed. "You think you had me? Focus!"

Jackson fell. His friend lunged at Vash while he was occupied, but Vash was faster. He rolled to the side and blocked the punch. He kicked his opponent from behind before turning to fight Jackson. The whole thing reminded me of Thursday night's fight against the demons, with three beings moving against one.

"Hi, boys!" Sidelle sauntered into the room. "What am I missing?"

Thrown off by her sing-songy voice, Jackson hesitated. Vash took that second to knock him out of the game with an uppercut to the head.

"Lesson number one, Jacks: never let a female distract you." Vash removed the helmet. "That's game for now."

"Oops. My bad." Sidelle pouted. "Sorry."

I rose from the couch and pointed at the helmet in Vash's hand. "What is this?"

"A video simulator called Silico. We use it to learn and maintain certain skills."

"Plus, it's fun," Jackson said.

"It's really sophisticated," Cali said, joining me. "I've never seen anything like it before."

"It's something one of my dad's companies developed. It's still in testing mode."

"And on that note, I'm leaving." With a grin, Jackson waved and headed toward the door with his buddy. "See ya tomorrow night."

"What's tomorrow night?" I asked after they'd gone.

"We're having a bonfire out on the beach," Vash said. He walked me over to the wall, opened a cabinet, and selected two smaller black helmets. "Wanna try this? Here. This should fit you." He gave the other one to Cali. "You girls probably are about the same level: one."

"What about Sidelle?" Cali asked, glancing back at the couch.

"Oh, I don't do that sort of thing." She winked at me. "Helmet hair is not my look."

"So the first lesson—" Vash said.

"—is not to be distracted." Cali beamed.

"Yes. That's right." He helped her with her helmet, gloves, and kneepads. "Keep your mind and eyes focused at all times."

Kieran placed the mitts on my hands and the pads on my knees then tapped my head. "Ready." He walked me to a mat and pointed at the footmarks, while Vash did the same with Cali. We waited while Vash went to the cabinet to do something.

"I'm going to create your avatars to load into the program, so hang tight for a minute," he said. While we watched, he took out a controller and punched in a series of codes. A round disk dropped from the ceiling and emitted a blue ray, creating a circle of light around us. The beams flickered then scanned each one of us from head to toe.

"There. That should do it."

A few more taps on the console, and our images appeared on the TV.

"This is so cool," Cali exclaimed. "I've never done anything like this before."

"Whatever movements you make, the program will make on the screen. So don't worry. You aren't actually hitting the other person." The screen showed a large, white mat with a black edge. "Okay. So this is only Level One: Part One. Your view is a little different from what we see, because inside the helmet, you see the outer edge. It's marked in red."

Cali and I nodded.

"If you step off the mat on the screen," he continued, "the red line will blink inside the helmet. I'll load the instructor, so you can get basic stances and maneuvers. Don't go all out or anything. This program is intense. Trust me, you'll be sore tomorrow."

The blaring music stopped when thevideo started, and a nondescript sensei appeared. We walked through the ten basic stances of karate, mimicking the instructor. Cali and I had just had a karate lesson in gym class the other day, so this wasn't entirely new to us. My body followed the movements easily. Then we started doing small combinations of the different stances. My mind went to *The Karate Kid*—"wax on, wax off." I glanced at Cali, and she didn't seem to be having any problems, either. As the simulator progressed, the series of blocking and kicking became longer and harder to remember, but I was determined to finish the program. Thirty minutes later the video stopped, and we were still standing.

"Great job, you two." Vash lifted the eye shield from Cali's helmet. "You're naturals."

Cali and I grinned at each other. I rolled my shoulders and tilted my head. I didn't even feel sore ... yet.

"Can we do that again?" I asked. "Or go on to the next level?"

"Hold on, Zoe-san." Kieran cackled. "Why don't you

give your body a rest? We can come back another day."

"It's early," I insisted. "Unless Vash has something else planned for tonight?"

"Nope," Vash said. "We can do some more. I'll reset the program."

A few hours later, and after Cali changed clothes, she and I made it into Level Two, Part Two. We then watched Vash and Kieran take each other on in a street fight. This was the third time I'd seen Kieran brawl. The first had been in the warehouse last week when we'd been chased by the two demon knights. The second was last night at my house when more DKs and Marquises demons tried to kill me. Up until then, I hadn't known he could hurt a fly, let alone kill someone.

Sidelle, Cali, and I sat on the couch watching the boys, and eventually the rhythmic thudding of the hits lulled me to sleep. I felt my eyelids closing, and Kieran's warm hands wrapped under my legs and arms as he picked me up. I faintly heard Vash's deep voice saying again how well I'd done using the fight Silico.

"Maybe unnaturally so," he said.

My Friday morning started like any other. I lay in bed, thinking about last night's events and wondering what they might mean for me.

Zoe.

I knew she was the Redeemer. I felt the solid truth of that in my bones and in my heart. And I loved her. There wasn't anything anyone could tell me that would change my mind about her. We'd somehow overcome the fact that she could never be with me. She was an Eternal. I was a Natural. We would always be fighting against the powers that be that said we couldn't be together. We'd find a way. Over the years I grew to admire her. But when we finally met, I realized I loved Zoe. And I would stand by her until the day I died.

What I'd watched her become last night had been awe-inspiring. When the purple Angel Light had poured from her into me, something inside me broke. From that moment I knew that I'd follow her anywhere.

A quiet knock pulled me out of my daydream.

"Son? Are you awake?" Gabriel asked through the closed door.

I groaned in response.

"The Archangels need you to come with them today," he told me.

"Does Kieran know?"

Gabriel opened the door. "Yes, he's aware of the situation. He'll take care of Zoe."

I sat up. *I* needed to be the one to protect Zoe, not Kieran. "But—"

"You are one of the warriors of Heaven, Shay. You must do your duty. Kieran and the others will protect her."

"I understand." Rolling out of bed, I grabbed black jeans and a T-shirt from the floor, sniffed them just to be sure it didn't smell too disgusting, and then dressed. "I'll meet you downstairs."

I was always startled by the appearance of my father, of his glorious gray wings, and the unearthly feel that washed over me whenever he was nearby. I got my blond hair from him, and I suspected my silver-colored wings were from him, too. But to this day, I hadn't figured out where my aqua eyes had come from. My mother's dark brown eyes and his blue ones could never produce the color of the ocean. Then again, I couldn't say never. Maybe that was just what God wanted for me.

Sighing, I laced up my combat boots and left the room. Down in the kitchen, Gabriel stood with his back to me, talking with Michael.

"Where are we going?" I asked.

"We have a lead on a Seraph Sword," Michael said. "So grab some food and weapons, then we'll go."

On the table lay a map of Florida, specifically the Orlando area. I didn't want to go to Florida seeking out a sword. I wanted to be with Zoe, looking after her. But being a Nephilim was my duty; her being soul mate came second. I headed to the fridge and flung it open, letting my emotions get the better of me. Michael and Gabriel glanced at me with eyebrows raised, but I shrugged off their stares. Both of them knew what I was feeling anyway.

"Do I have time to make breakfast, or are we in a hurry?" I grumbled.

"Here, let me." Gabriel waved his hand over the table, producing scrambled eggs, bacon, and a stack of buttered toast. "There you go."

"Thanks."

I shoveled food into my mouth, all the while listening to Michael and Gabriel. They said to take my time, but I knew that was code for "hurry up." I grabbed some jerky off the counter and stuffed it into my jean pockets before I left the kitchen. I walked down the hallway and pressed my palm against the code reader. An invisible Triquetra symbol become visible and glowed on the wall, and a door appeared.

The walls of the room were lined with racks of weapons. Guns, ammo cartridges, and swords of varying lengths were stacked high on the shelves. I selected two holsters, crisscrossed them on my chest, and took two .45s from the display. I placed a couple dozen clips into my pants and jacket pockets, tucked them into the waistband of my jeans, and slid some into the custom-designed side pockets of my boots. Before leaving the room, I grabbed a dagger and strapped it onto my boot. When I thought of my blessed Nephilim Sword, it appeared in my hand, along with its scabbard. I sheathed it across my back.

"Are you stocked with supplies?" Gabriel asked when I emerged. "If you need anything else, one of the Archangels will get it for you. I'm not sure how long we'll be gone. I've already taken care of notifying the school of your absence."

"Okay. Let's go. You can tell me the plan on the way."

Gabriel laid a hand on my shoulder, white Angel Light glowed, and we disappeared from Kieran's house. I was vaguely surprised when we landed outside the gates of Disney World's Magic Kingdom. Michael appeared by my side, and all three of us opted to remain unseen.

"So the word is one of the Seraphs hid their sword here, in plain view," Gabriel said, "but we don't know if that's true or not." He frowned, obviously disapproving. "I'm not sure why an angel would leave their sword lying around. I would've kept it with me, like the Nephilim do."

"This is a good cover, though." I meandered through the crowd, careful not to bump into anyone. When I was invisible, I couldn't touch people. They'd feel me—unlike the angels, who could pass right through people. "Tons of people, lots of Disney stories, which often have a sword as a character's accessory, *and* it's the happiest place on earth. Demons would never think to come here."

"Where should we start to look?" Michael asked.

"Let's split up so we can cover more ground," Gabriel suggested. He pointed to the carousel. "We'll meet back there in an hour. Shay, don't go off to the different parks. We need to stay together."

"Fine. Do either of you sense any demons around?"

Both closed their eyes, then opened them and shook their heads.

"And if we run into any Marqs?"

"Point taken. You and I will look over there," Gabriel said. One of them had to stay with me since I couldn't produce an entryway into the Void. He pointed to the right. "Michael, you search the other way."

Michael's blue wings sprang from his back, and he glided into the sky. When the coast was relatively clear, Gabriel took his hand off my shoulder and became visible. My jaw dropped, and I had to fight back laughter.

"What? Is this not appropriate attire?"

He wore jeans and a red Mickey Mouse sweatshirt, with a camera strapped around his neck. I looked around and realized everyone was decked out in mouse-themed clothes. Since I was dressed in all black, I stuck out. But I was *not* about to wear mouse ears.

"Come on. We have a lot of ground to cover if you're going to look like that." I waved him forward, chuckling.

We glanced in every souvenir store, bathroom, and food cart, but didn't find anything out of the ordinary. We definitely didn't find any swords, play or real that could've been a Seraph's Sword. Gabriel and I even rode every ride in the section, so we could honestly say we'd cleared it. Michael met us at the designated time and place, and he hadn't found anything on the left side of the park either. Together, we searched the middle area and found a few swords outside of Gaston's Tavern, inside Peter Pan's ride, and in the pirate section of Peter Pan's merchandise store, but none were angelic in the least.

Zoe would've loved it here since she was a huge Disney fan; *Tangled* was her all-time favorite movie. I was tempted to text her, to ask where other swords might be in this make-believe world. Then my eye caught a flash of light and someone grunted. When I focused on the source, I realized people were taking pictures in front of an anvil ... with a sword protruding from the center. *The Sword and the Stone*. I should've known!

We ran to the line and waited, but it didn't take long. Gabriel must've used his Persuasion because people started leaving. Michael ran his hand over the sword, but nothing happened. He bent down and inspected it while Gabriel shot picture after picture, playing the part of an avid tourist. Every once in a while, he'd show me a photo. Some were close-ups and some were farther away.

"This isn't it." Michael shrugged, looking disappointed. "I guess this whole trip was a bust."

"We had to track down every lead," Gabriel said. "And you never know. This could've been—"

A gut-wrenching scream filled the air. Our heads turned in the direction of the shriek, hearing shouts and chaos coming from there as well. A crowd ran from the same area, bumping into each other as they fled whatever it was.

Gabriel became invisible as his gray wings extended, and he and Michael flew to the spot while I barreled through the panicked throng of people. When I arrived, Michael had already created the Void's passageway, and Gabriel was backing the DKs into the Void's edge. I scouted the area, highly suspicious. Where there are knights, Marqs usually followed.

A dark shadow passed by a tree.

"The wall has to be extended!" I shouted above the pandemonium. "Over there."

I pointed toward where I'd seen a dark trail and Michael nodded. He stretched the outer wall to encompass the Marqs, who grew out of the grassy location, but soon there were more black-robed Marqs rising from the lawn than Michael and Gabriel could fight.

I had my hands full with controlling the Ordinaries still lingering in the area and managing the DKs. Thankfully, the humans couldn't see what was happening. As soon as the last human was outside the Void boarder, I unleashed my true power. One hand gripped my Nephilim Sword, cutting and slashing at the demons, while my other hand shot the gun. The DKs were easy targets, especially with my enhanced human reflexes. With one hand on the gun, I fired round after round while knights fell to the ground like dominos. Then using my sword, I cut off the fallen knights' heads and sent them back to Hell. I reloaded until I was down to my last clip.

But the demons kept coming. I didn't have time to look to see how Michael and Gabriel were holding up. Both were experienced Archangels and could easily handle three or four Marqs, but there were way more than that. We'd soon be outnumbered.

Colored rays streamed down from the sky, and relief settled over me. More Archangels were on their way to help us, which meant Michael or Gabriel had sent a distress signal. Brightly colored wings dropped from the sky, renewing my energy in the fight. I couldn't kill a Marq, but I sure as hell could try. No way the wolves should get all the fun.

The last DK fell, and I sliced off its head. I turned toward the nearest Marq and lifted my sword when I was yanked from behind. My feet shot out but didn't connect with anything.

A wave of sadness washed over me.

Zoe doesn't love you.

Thoughts of hopelessness crept into my mind.

You can't win this battle; you're nothing.

I shook my head, trying to clear away my doubts, but they bombarded me.

How could she possibly love you when she could have a Guardian angel? You're nothing but an Ordinary with enhanced skills. Eventually you'll die, leaving your soul mate, who will go on and live forever. Without you.

Grief rocked me to the core. Suddenly weak, my arm lowered, and I dropped my sword to the ground. More Marqs surrounded me, touching my chest and head, while others grabbed my arms, legs, and clothes. Blackness enveloped me, and ribbons of darkness surrounded my mind and heart. One last surge of power flashed briefly in my mind. *They won't take me without a fight!*

But they did.

On Saturday morning I awoke to a girl's light snoring, which reminded me of Shay and the first time he had spent the night in my bedroom. I wondered what he was doing with his dad and Michael, and then I pictured the worst possible thing: his death. To ease my mind, I pulled out my cell to text him to find how his mission was going.

Me: Everything ok?

I looked over at Cali's sleeping body. Sidelle was awake and staring at me, so I waved her over to my bed but pointed at our sleeping friend. She silently *poofed* and reappeared next to me.

"Morning, Zoe-san," she whispered. "You sore today? You did a number on that program."

"I feel great, actually." I rolled my shoulders and head, checking.

"You know, Vash told Kieran that you and Cali mastered Level One, and neither of you should've done so well."

"I guess we're both naturals, like Vash said." Maybe joining the cross-country and running clubs had helped my coordination and stamina.

"She is." Sidelle tilted her head toward Cali. "You aren't. You're an Eternal, which may be why you did so fab, too."

"Can we do some more training today with the Silico?"

"Probably not a bad idea. The more practice you get, the better. Maybe Vash has another Silico we can take with us, and Kieran can keep it at his house. Then you can keep on going with training."

"How come Cali doesn't remember what happened Thursday night?" I whispered.

"I wiped hers, Rena's, Quinn's, and your sister's memories of everything after the fashion show."

"You can do that?"

She looked unsure. "Cali was a little harder, and I'm not sure if it'll stick with her. She already has her paw mark, so my glamour might not work."

I'd forgotten about that. Her paw mark was similar to the tattoo I would eventually get, marking me as an Enlighten. But hers meant she was marked as Vash's mate.

Cali stirred, stretched, and then gave a loud yawn. As soon as she opened her eyes, she blushed and put her hand over her mouth. "Oops. Sorry. I forgot where I was."

We giggled. "No worries," I said. "Good morning."

"Hi," she said. "Have you guys been up long?" She peeked through the curtains. "Looks like the sun's already out. You should've woken me earlier."

"We've only been up a few minutes." I threw off the covers. "I'm going to shower before we eat."

"Wonder what's for breakfast," Cali said. "I hope they have apple juice."

"After last night's three-course dinner, I'm sure chef will have anything you want."

Ten minutes later I stepped out of the bathroom with my hair and body wrapped in towels, just in time to hear a light tap on the door.

A pony-tailed head poked through. "Morning." Era pushed the door open farther. When she saw everyone was awake, she walked over to the window and threw open the curtains. "Did everyone sleep well last night? Breakfast's ready. The chef will keep most of the cold foods out until lunch time if you don't want to eat now."

She plopped onto my bed, and waited for Cali and me to finish getting ready. Then the four of us, led by Era, meandered down to the first floor and stopped at a long kitchen table loaded with platters and bowls of breakfast foods. The chef stood over the commercial-sized stove, making omelets for the boys, who were perched on bar stools.

"How are you girls feeling?" Vash asked. He stood and pulled out a chair for Cali. "Are you sore?"

"Nope," I said. "Totally fine. I could go another round."

"I'm okay, too," Cali said. "The first day of cheer camp was harder."

"If you guys want to continue, we can do a different program after we eat," Vash suggested. "We'll do balance stuff until our stomachs settle."

"Sounds great." Cali laid her napkin across her lap.

We stuffed our bellies with eggs, bacon, and hash browns, washing it all down with milk and orange juice—plus, apple juice for Cali and steaming hot chai for me.

I borrowed another yoga outfit from Sidelle for the day's exercise program, and then Vash and Kieran led the way back to the game room where they helped Cali and me put on the equipment.

A gymnastics beam appeared on the screen with an instructor.

"This program isn't like the one from last night," Vash explained. "It strengthens your core but also helps with balance."

We mirrored the stances. This was easy enough. One foot on the beam, the other suspended a few inches in the air, and then high-step marches to the end and back again.

For the first thirty minutes, it was easy, until random objects flew toward our bodies. The first shoe that soared past my head made me lose my balance, and I stepped off the beam. I had points deducted, but when the couch pillow got lobbed at me, I was ready. Then the program changed. We were no longer on a balance beam in a gym, hovering over a safety pad. Now, I stood on a tightrope wire. My mind knew we weren't suspended over the Grand Canyon, but try telling that to my body. I had to adjust my footing, another point lost.

I didn't know how Cali was doing it. She stood like a statue; nothing bothered her.

The wind on the screen picked up, and a real fan or something else above my head made my hair move, and the thin wire beneath my feet swayed back and forth. My arms began to pinwheel, and I knew I was about to plummet to my fake death.

The word "Pause" flashed on the screen.

"Here, Z," Kieran said. "It's not fair if you move into this Level without the proper equipment." He handed me a long, slender balance pole.

"Thanks." I clutched the smooth rod and regarded the perfectly still Cali. *If she can do this, I can, too.*

Kieran pressed, "Play."

Now that I had an object in my hand, I regained my

balance against the breeze. The program went on like that for a few more scenes before we were back in the gym and on the balance beam.

"Now," Vash said, "the object to this next level is to knock your opponent off the beam. Here. Let's exchange the poles for shorter ones so you don't actually poke someone's eye out." He handed us padded batons, and Cali and I each got our own mock challenger on the screen. "Remember everything you've learned so far ... and begin."

This time it got even more complicated. Not only did we have to remember to balance, we had to recall the offensive and defensive stances from last night. After a while the screen changed yet again, and we were suspended over a mountain pass on a narrow wooden bridge. Wind and snow were factors now, and the stupid fan actually spat tiny ice particles onto our heads. Hours passed, but Cali and I pressed on. We were both really into the simulator, and we were both competitive.

"Let's take a break," Sidelle eventually suggested, taking the batons from us. "You've been doing this for three hours. You should eat to keep your energy up."

"But I'm not—" Cali started. Her stomach growled, and she blushed. "Okay, I guess I am a little hungry."

Vash smiled. "Come on. Chef Victus probably made sandwiches or something."

"What are you guys going to do today?" Era asked as she sauntered into the game room.

"I'm not sure," I said. "When's the bonfire?"

"Not until after dark," Era said.

"What did you have in mind?" Cali asked as she headed for the door.

"I don't know. I was maybe thinking you guys could drive me to Minneapolis, and we could go shopping," Era suggested. "Our school is having a Spring Fling Dance in a few weeks—"

Cali stopped, hand clutched on the doorknob.

"Cali?" Sidelle asked. "What's wrong?"

Cali's body remained frozen.

"Cali?" I whispered, stepping toward her. "Is everything all right?" I glanced at Sidelle. "What's wrong with her?"

Cali's shoulders slumped before an ear-piercing scream escaped her lips. Her hands flew to the sides of her head, and tears streamed down her face as her small body slumped to the floor, her head narrowly missing the door handle.

Vash dashed over to catch Cali. He lifted her arm, and it hung from his hand, limp as a noodle. My mind went back to two nights ago, to when she was being choked to death by a demon. *Oh, God, could I bring her back to life again?*

"Cali," Vash coaxed, gently shaking her. "Wake up." He looked at Sidelle, dark eyes pleading. "What's wrong with her?"

Sidelle knelt beside Cali. "Maybe she remembers what happened Thursday. I tried to wipe her memory, but I'm not sure it worked. She's your mate, Vash, and because of that, glamour doesn't always work."

"She's your mate?" Era asked. "That's so cool! I'm sure she's not de—"

Vash glared at his sister as he lifted Cali's slender body and held it safely against his chest. With a delicate touch he moved some of her hair to the side, revealing a dark tattoo that matched his own: an intricate leaf design wrapped around a brown paw print. I'd seen it Thursday evening as we were getting ready for the prom-dress fashion show, but it wasn't prominent. Kieran and I looked at each other helplessly. Sidelle was probably right; Cali was in shock from suddenly realizing what was going on. The brain could only handle so much, and this was probably Cali's way of processing the information. She lay still in Vash's arms, her silent tears trickled down her cheeks, but she didn't wake. Vash carried her out of the room and into our bedroom. We followed close behind and waited while he laid her on the bed.

"She should rest," he said. "I'll stay with her until she wakes up." He brushed the hair away from her face and glanced at Sidelle. "She will wake up, won't she?"

"I'm sure she will when she's ready," Sidelle said softly. "And of course we'll stay with her."

"Era," Vash said, his eyes back on Cali, "why don't you leave and let us—"

"No. I'll be quiet. I won't get in the way," Era assured him, her feet planted firmly.

"We'll take turns." I sat on the bed and looked at Sidelle.

"What do you think she remembers?"

"I don't know but my guess? All of it." She joined me on the bed. "I can try to Mind Walk her to see what's going on inside her brain, if you want."

"Do it," Vash decided.

"Wait," I cried. "Kieran? Can you heal her?"

"I'm not sure. If glamour doesn't work on her, I doubt Angel Light will."

"But we should try it before Sidelle invades her mind, right?"

"Okay, move over." Kieran placed his hands on the sides of Cali's face, and white light filled the room. A pulse of energy lasted a few beats then faded. "Sorry, Zoe. It didn't work."

He stood to let Sidelle lean in, and we waited in silence as she touched Cali's face with the palm of her hand. A pale green light glowed from her fingers, and she closed her eyes in concentration. No one moved. Minutes passed before Sidelle's eyes opened again.

"It's a mess in there," Sidelle muttered, rising. "And yes, she remembers everything. I couldn't get a good read on the minutes before she died, though. So either she doesn't remember that part, or she's blocking me."

"When will she wake up?" Vash asked.

"When her mind is ready to come to terms with what it

saw Thursday night."

"Is that how Ordinaries normally react when they find out about the Enlighten stuff?" I asked. "Or is something else going on?"

"It could be because I tried to wipe her memory," Sidelle admitted. "It's a lot to take in, you know? Seeing demons for the first time and watching them get killed, then her coming back to life ..."

I knew the feeling well.

"Okay," Vash said, reluctantly backing away from the bed. "I'll go scrounge us up some food from the kitchen and bring it back here."

"I'll help you," Kieran said. He patted Vash's back. "Don't worry. She'll wake up. Give her some time."

The boys left, and I motioned for Era to join me on the bed because she hadn't moved since she entered the room. I didn't know if she'd ever experienced anything like this. Sidelle paced the room and started moving things around. I'd never seen Sidelle out of sorts before. She was always the calm, cool, and collected one.

Eventually, Vash and Kieran came back with sandwiches, but no one ate anything. For a long time, no one said anything either. There wasn't anything to say. Both Sidelle and Vash paced the room, and I couldn't take it any longer.

"I need to get out of here," I declared. "Anyone want to go outside?"

"Okay," Kieran said. "We don't all need to be in here, hovering around her."

"I'm staying," Vash said. "I need to be here when she wakes." He took my place on the bed.

"Okay," I said. "We'll be outside. Call our cells if you need us or if she wakes."

He nodded. I waited for a response from Sidelle, but she just shook her head then disappeared from the room.

I hesitated by the door. "Era?"

Tears had formed in the corners of the little girl's deep brown eyes. "This is my fault," she murmured. "If I hadn't said anything about going shopping, she'd be okay."

I placed my hand on her back. "It's not your fault. You didn't know. Don't beat yourself up. Do you want to come with us for a bit?"

She shook her head, so Kieran and I left.

Cali remained in her coma-like state for the rest of the day. Sidelle didn't return to our bedroom after the episode. Vash never left Cali's side, leaving Kieran and me to find our own entertainment. There was nothing we could do for Cali, so we opted to hang out with the rest of the pack members.

As dusk fell I changed into my jeans and a borrowed

hoodie. Then we made our way outside toward the lake for the bonfire. Groups of people emerged from the woods in small numbers. Everyone gathered around a massive pile of wood stacked on the beach. A half-moon shone over the glassy water. Someone used a torch to light the bonfire, and the powerful *whoosh* made me take a step back. I cringed away from the intense heat and stayed close to Kieran.

"Have you heard from Shay?" I asked. "Because I texted him when I woke this morning and a few times after school yesterday. He still hasn't said anything, which isn't like him."

He glanced away. "No, I haven't."

"I'm starting to worry. Do you think something could've gone wrong on their mission?"

He led me back to the fire, and we sat on a fallen log. "The angels would tell me if—"

"Would they? Are you sure?" I snapped. "I'm sorry, Kieran. I just ... with Sidelle gone, Cali out of commission, and no sign of Shay, I feel completely useless."

"Hey, don't." He shook his head and embraced my shoulders. "We *are* doing something. I'll go find out. Would that make you feel better?"

I threw my arms around him. "*Yes.* Would you?"

"Of course. Anything for you. You know that."

"When? When will you go?" I bounced on my legs.

"Now?"

He smiled. "Yes. I'll be back as soon as I can. In the meantime, I'll get word to Sidelle to see where she went off to, and tell her to get back here ASAP. You stay in the compound until my return, okay?" He tipped my chin up. "Zoe? *Okay*?"

"Yeah, fine. I won't go running off. Since I don't know where Shay is, you don't have anything to worry about."

"I'll be back soon."

Kieran's gold wings emerged from his back as he sprang into the air. My neck strained to watch him until he became a dot in the sky, then nothing. With him gone, I sat completely alone despite the crowd of people. I stared blankly into the dancing flames, letting the hushed voices around me soothe my nerves. Eventually, I blinked and noticed most of the pack members staring at me. Some looked at the sky.

"Most of us haven't seen an angel with their wings out before," Jackson explained, settling into Kieran's spot. He was grinning. "We've only read about them. But to see one right before our eyes? That was cool." He nudged my shoulder. "So I'm on Zoe detail now. Vash sent me."

I nodded.

"Are you mute?"

"I have a lot on my mind."

He chuckled. "I bet you do since you're the one who will unite us. Must be a big task. Are you up for it?"

"Let's hope so. Right now, I'm seriously having doubts."

"Everyone second guesses themselves. Especially when tasked for something as momentous as this. But from what Vash tells us, you'll figure it out." He grabbed my hand. "I'm on board with you."

"Even if it's against your father's and pack's wishes?"

Jackson's eyes dropped.

I snatched my hand back. "Are you saying you will because of Sidelle? Because she kinda has a—"

"Don't say it." Jackson turned to face me. "I know perfectly well that Enlightens need to stay within our own Order. Fairies are Eternals, and wolves are Naturals. I just ... " He gave me a lopsided smile. "Well, she's hot."

I couldn't help smiling back. "Don't let her hear you say that, because she won't let you live it down."

"Where is she, anyway?" He scanned the area. "I thought she'd be out here with you."

"Long story," I muttered.

"I'm listening."

I figured since he was assigned to my detail now, he should be caught up, so I explained to him what had happened two nights before, covering everything from after our dress shopping, to the DKs and Marqs showing up, and the moment when Cali had died. He listened intently when I explained how I'd used Angel Light to bring her back, and I told him all about Cali's episode earlier this afternoon.

While the rest of the pack mingled and gossiped, Jackson and I sat in silence, thinking. A parade of food came from the main house, and most of the others gathered around the table to graze. Almost every age group was represented in the crowd. Some were obviously still in grade school, some were college age, and others probably had nine-to-five jobs. I watched all the interactions between the members; briefly wishing my life could be simple again. But that'd be a cop-out. I had been chosen for this role. It was time for me to stop wallowing in what could've or should've and just *be*. I had to get over it, stop whining, and figure stuff out.

Something brushed my arm, as if someone was next to me, but when I turned, no one was there. On second glance, Sidelle *poofed* next to me.

"Jeez!" I yelled, slapping my hand over my heart. "Don't *do* that."

"I heard someone say my name." She leaned forward and stared at Jackson. "Was it you?"

Even in the firelight, I could see his cheeks flush.

"Kieran told me where he'd gone," she told me, "so I came—"

"And where did *you* go?" I asked.

"I had fairy business."

I glared, waiting.

"All right. If you must know, I went back for an audience with the Summer King and told Oberon about Cali's situation. He agreed that we need to wait it out. She'll wake when she's ready. Anything we try will be useless."

"Did Kieran say anything else about where he went?"

"No, but he said he'd be back tomorrow."

"Tomorrow?" I stood and crossed my arms. "Something's going on, and you're both keeping me in the dark. What's happened to Shay?"

"Why do you think something's happened?" Jackson asked. "He's the Nephilim, right?"

I nodded. "Because neither Kieran nor Sidelle have been direct with me all day. They've been dodging my questions, and that's not like either of them." I punched Sidelle's shoulder. "So spill. I'll knock it out of you. I won't win or even hurt you, but I'll try. He's my soul mate, and if something's happened—"

"Fine. Okay. The thing is ..." She drew in a deep breath.

Oh, this was going to be bad.

"Gabriel, Michael, and Shay ... they ran into a little problem." Sidelle twirled her hands nervously. "They fought against a lot of Marqs and ..."

God, no! My mind leapt to the most horrible possible scenario: a gruesome battle with black blood, horns, ... and Shay's dead body sprawled on a street somewhere.

"The Archangels held their own," Sidelle said carefully, "but Shay, well, they were outnumbered and—"

"Is he dead?" My eyes stung with tears. "Just tell me, Sidelle."

"I can't say for sure. I don't have all the information. Kieran is blocking me, so I can't get a good read on the situation." She scooted closer, cleared her throat, and whispered, "Shay was captured."

"What?" My body launched off the bench, and I took a few steps toward the house before Sidelle grabbed for my arm.

"There's nothing you can do about it, Zoe."

"Yes, there is." I slapped her hand away. "There has to be. They'll kill him. I can't let that happen."

"We don't know where they took him. All the angels are out looking for him. Let the Angel Trackers do their job, find him, and form the rescue team. You can't travel between the Void levels yet, so there isn't anything you can do."

"But it's *me* they're after." I threw my arms in the air. "I have to do something."

"You *are* doing something," Jackson said. "You're gaining allies."

That was no comfort to me. I stormed back to the wooden bench in front of the fire, but I couldn't sit still.

"Sidelle, I want you to find out as much information as you can. There has to be a reason why they took him. I want to know who did it, where he is, and if he's alive. Can you do that? If you need to track down Michael or Gabriel, do it."

Without a word, she nodded and disappeared.

Unfortunately, taking charge of the situation hadn't calmed me one bit. Why had they taken Shay? To get me mad? To throw me off my game?

Well, they'd succeeded at both. I would make them regret it.

I paced around the bonfire, waiting for Sidelle's return. In my mind, I couldn't stop seeing a battle scene featuring tangled arms and legs, swords, and demons' black blood. I tried unsuccessfully to block out the fact that some of those limbs could belong to Shay, some of the blood could be his. He *had* to be alive. What would I do if he weren't?

With envy I watched the youngest pack members roast s'mores, laughing as the marshmallows browned, burned, and dripped into the flames. A few of the kids ran around with chocolate smeared across their faces, and it reminded me of the many times my sister and I had made the treats at our cabin in northern Minnesota. Eventually, the parents corralled the younger children to send them back to their homes, and the older members made a tight circle around the fire.

A hush fell upon the group as Keegan approached. The Alpha nodded and looked around at all the faces. "Hello, everyone. At least one representative from each family is here?" His eyes landed on Jackson. "Good. I'm going to tell you something, and I want your sacred vow that you will keep this knowledge a secret." He stretched out his arm toward me. "Let us welcome Zoe Jabril to our home. She has come here to request the pack join her in the ultimate battle against Sammael and his demons."

Jackson squeezed my hand, and I waved with my other one.

"Is she the one we've been waiting for?" Keegan asked. He didn't wait for a response but spoke directly to the pack. "We all know the prophesy:

Glory!
Babe born.
First and last.
Heaven and unto Earth
Receives the highest in jubilation.
Enlightens will unite; they shall band.
Triumph be if darkness is driven back.
Help found who love, the world will stand."

He studied the eyes of each pack member. "What proof does she offer? None. Just her word. Will I accept that as enough? Well, it's not completely up to me. As the pack leader, I will give you each a voice. Ultimately though, I will decide what is best for all."

He crossed his arms, and I was in awe of the command he wielded. Not one face looked away from his. "We all know what's at stake: Earth's destruction and that of the other realms. It's always been our mission to stop this evil. It's what we were created to do. I fear troubling times will be upon us all soon, and we must follow our calling. Is Zoe the one? I ask each of you to reflect on what your heart tells you." He drew in a deep breath. "Search within and reflect seriously. We will convene tomorrow at the house, so come prepared to explain your positions."

"Tell us a story," a teenager shouted.

Keegan grinned, his teeth reflecting the shine from the firelight. "Ah, yes. I know which one to tell. There are a lot of demon myths and legends I could choose, but I will tell my favorite."

Keegan glanced around for an open chair, but decided to sit on the sand with his back to the lake. The others rose from their lawn chairs and sat on the ground beside him, though a few remained on the other side of the fire.

"This is a story from my youth," Keegan said, his voice

low. "Our own Chanhassen Dinner Theater was built on the site of a home that had burned down, trapping and killing a woman inside. Her spirit is said to haunt the theater, along with the ghost of a former actress who'd been bicycling home when she was hit and killed by a car. Of course both the theater and the Chaska Historical Society deny the hauntings, but we all know what happened on that night in the early 1960s."

A few of the adults nodded.

"The veil thinned earlier than expected," he continued. "Demons managed to get through, and they entered the Earth's realm. The pack was waiting, but we hadn't anticipated the numbers, so we weren't prepared. A bloodbath ensued, and many of our brothers and sisters died. We tried to save the Ordinary woman, but a Marq took her hostage. She fought back but was powerless. When we wouldn't let the Marq escape the property, he killed her then set the house on fire to cover his tracks. Her restless soul refused to pass into Heaven because of her brutal death.

"The young actress who was killed while riding her bike? She never met up with a car. She ran into a lone DK and was a victim of being at the wrong place at the wrong time. This second death marked the land as an unholy place." He shrugged. "We had to tell the authorities something, and ghost stories were a nice way to cover up the ugly truth."

I'd never known that about the dinner theater. My parents had taken my sister and me there a few times over the years.

Murmurs spread through the circle after the story ended, as clusters of teens and young adults had their own conversations. After a moment Keegan stood, and all whispering stopped.

"I'll leave you to your party."

The pack watched their Alpha turn and head back toward the house, and I noticed a movement on the third floor. I squinted for a better view and recognized Vash. He stood with his head bowed at the window with the curtain peeled back. If he was still up there, then Cali was not better. I waved, hoping he could see me. I wanted him to know he and Cali were still on my mind. Seeing my movement, Jackson turned and nodded when he saw Vash.

The party atmosphere resumed. Some people returned to the tables of food, some took a stroll by the water, and others remained by the bonfire. Conversation and laughter bounced through the night air. A dark cloud floated over the moon, casting shadows across the land, and I shivered. The feeling suddenly intensified. The tiny hairs at the back of my neck stood at attention, and uneasiness grew in the pit of my stomach. I clenched Jackson's arm, digging my nails into his skin.

He gasped with surprise and looked at the half-moons I'd dug in his arm. "Zoe? Are you okay? You don't look so good. Your face is as white as a full moon. Maybe you should go inside and lay down or something."

I shook my head, my vision swimming. "I feel—"

A *boom* shuddered through the night like a cannon firing. Something crashed into the water, and a massive wave rolled over the beach. A black figure rose from the middle of the lake, its soaked robes flapping heavily in the wind. Before anyone could move, the figure had floated over the lake toward us, reaching for something behind its back. As soon as the cloaked figure closed half the distance, an identical body emerged from the same spot in the lake, followed by another and another. Before long, a steady stream of creatures had materialized and headed our way.

"Jackson!" I screamed. "Those are Mar—"

Someone howled and chaos erupted. People scrambled, the food tables were flipped onto their sides, and the bonfire blazed intensely after more wood was thrown on to brighten the beach area.

"How did they get into our territory?" Jackson roared. "Everyone stay calm. This is what we are meant to do." He grabbed my hand and jerked me behind his body. He looked for his little sister. "Era? Era, get back to the house and find Dad."

"I'm on it, Jacks!" came a high-pitched shout from across the yard.

"I didn't think the Marquises demons could come here," I yelled over the screams. "Kieran said—"

More and more demons rose from the water's surface, lifting their swords as they glided onto the beach. The pack transformed into their wolf forms, and each took an opponent.

"They've never been able to before." Jackson tugged me toward the house. "Come on. You have to go inside. You'll be safer in there."

"Will I?" I demanded, digging in my heels. "Because they're here on your land now. I won't be safe anywhere."

"Do as you're told, Zoe."

Vash ran out of the house and grabbed my shoulders, squaring them. "Go watch over Cali for me. Era's in there with her now." He gave me a shove toward the house before joining in the fight.

With no other choice, I sprinted through the foyer and up the stairs, stopping momentarily to glance out the picture window. More Marqs rose from the lake, except now they carried something on their backs. As soon as their forms cleared the water, they flung whatever it was onto the beach. The packages rolled ... then stood.

Great. They'd carried DKs with them.

I flung open the door to Cali's room. Era already sat on the bed, guarding her, so I ran to the window to watch the battle. The DKs added to the disorder, though they were easy to pick off. They died like humans, and once they were decapitated, their bodies returned to Hell to regenerate.

The wolves raced all over the property, killing the demons, but there were too many. More than the pack would ever be able to handle. Beside the raging bonfire, I spotted a lone wolf lying on the ground, not moving. He didn't get back up.

"Is it bad out there?" Era asked softly. She sounded close to tears. "I want to join them, but the Alpha and Beta told me to to stay here. But ... but I can feel the call of my pack. They need help, and I can't do a thing."

I didn't bother turning to look at her. "Yes, it's bad. And I know exactly what you mean."

All at once the moon's rays flooded the grass—or at least I *thought* it was light from the moon. Then I saw a stream of white light circling onto the ground, just outside the fighting. A figure stood within the ray, golden wings extended.

"Kieran!" I slammed my fist against the glass. "Kieran's back."

Era bounced off the bed and stood next to me. "He must've heard my prayer."

At least fifty demons had risen from the water, taking on only twenty wolves, but now we had an angel. Watching Kieran fight was like watching a ballet. His movements were graceful but deadly. His Angel Light obliterated the DKs.

"There's my dad." Era pointed toward a massive white wolf running from the house into the fight. As we watched, Keegan slammed into the nearest demon. Without stopping he rolled, and was back on his paws, running again. He headed for the cluster of Marqs who had landed on the beach, where he joined Vash. I knew Vash's dark chocolate-brown fur from two nights ago when he'd helped defeat the Marqs at my house.

The groups of Marqs had thinned. We were making a dent, or so I hoped.

"Look," Era cried, pointing at the lake.

The water pulled back from the shoreline as the lake formed a wave. Sidelle now stood in the spot from which the demons had emerged, her arms waving high above her head. She sent the water crashing onto a small cluster of demon knights, sending them to their watery graves.

Now, we had a fairy on our team.

Sidelle could hold a few of the Marqs at bay, but she

couldn't stop them. During battles the Marqs were usually left to the Archangels, so she concentrated on the DKs. With her help, more demons were disappearing, which evened the score. Glancing down, I noticed a smaller, tan-colored wolf lying on the ground in a pool of blood. With a pang of fear, I wondered if it could be Jackson.

"It's not," Era said.

"What?"

"It's not Jackson."

"Can you read my mind?" I asked, frowning at her.

"No. I just saw you staring and made the connection. I'm worried about him and my family, too. You're probably—"

A shadow moved across the door, and my heart raced. "I hope you know how to fight," I whispered to Era. "Because it looks like you're going to get your chance."

Era turned and as she did, she fell to the floor. In her place stood a beautiful white wolf, the size of a husky, with a brown spot covering one eye and the tip of her tail. Era howled as she launched herself at the Marquises demon standing in our doorway. The creature stood before me in all its deathly glory, strands of long, black hair whipping from under his hood. Hollowed spaces stared at me instead of eyes. Era stopped him from entering the room, and I ran in front of Cali's sleeping body to protect her. I wasn't sure what I could do, or how I would stop a Marq, but I sure as hell had to do *something*. How had he managed to slip through the barricade of wolves?

Normally by this time, a purple, protective orb would have formed around me. For some reason it hadn't. *I could sure use one right about now.*

The snarling Era was no match for the demon warrior. She tried her best, but she was only a pup. The Marq easily lifted her body and threw her across the room. She stumbled onto her paws and charged the demon again, determined.

I couldn't ask her to lay down her life for mine. I didn't have a protective orb this time, but I wasn't helpless. I knew it was in me somewhere: the Light that made me a Seraph angel. I left Cali's side and advanced on the demon, determined that Era and I would take it down. Stupid move? Maybe. But as soon as I joined the fight, the demon stopped trying to slice Era in half with its sword. With my head held high, I summoned every ounce of Light I could find within me. I thought of the other night, of everything Cali had gone through today, and of the wolf whose body lay still outside.

A spark of purple light showed in my mind. *There*. Now I just had to call it, force it out, and find more. But in the split second it took to summon the Light, the demon had advanced the few steps to get to me. Its sword lashed out, and a yowl of pain filled the room. Era's white fur was stained red, and she limped toward me, still doing all she could to protect Cali and me. I had to do something. Era wouldn't stop fighting back.

"No," I screamed. *"You will not kill us."*

My palms thrust outward, and purple light shot out of them. The black color drained entirely out of the Marquises. Vaguely, I remembered that this was how Kieran had helped defeat the demons. The fading color of the demon meant its powers were weakened. The light pulsed once more, and then an explosion came from the room. I flew backward from the force, thankfully landing on a soft bed, before scrambling to my feet. I scanned the room for the demon, but it was no longer with us; however, its empty black cloak lay heaped on the floor. I ran to Era's side and lifted her paw, checking it. She slowly rose.

"You stay here." I told her. "I'm going outside to help."

She shook her head frantically, but I ignored her and bolted for the door. Something huge and furry blocked my path. Vash.

"I thought I told you to stay in the room." I stared at him, dumbfounded. He was still in wolf form, so he couldn't speak, but I could *hear* him in my mind. I'd never been able to hear the wolves before. I swallowed my amazement and

got back to work.

"You did, and now I'm leaving." I tried pushing past the huge brown wolf, but he didn't budge.

"There's nothing you can do out there."

"Why are you here? Shouldn't you be out there?"

"I heard an explosion and came to check on you two."

"Don't worry. I took care of the Marq, with Era's help." The spotted wolf was licking her paw. Her brown eyes flickered when I said her name. "And now I'm going outside to help you. Move out of my way. You'll have to bite me to stop me." I sidestepped past him and sprinted down the stairs.

"You know I can't and won't do that," Vash said as he trailed behind me.

The battle outside was chaotic. Sidelle flung trees, dirt, and debris at any demon, and rays of Angel Light shot through the sky. Howls and metal clanks filled the night air, but I could see no more knights; they must've all been sent back to Hell. A few Marquises demons still stood on the beach. Seeing them, Vash ran ahead of me and joined the Alpha wolf, as well as a dark gray one.

As I came across the bodies of dead wolves, I paused at the shock of seeing the bodies slain, but grief only fueled my rage.

I stopped where the grass met the sand, and Kieran

landed softly at my side. Sidelle appeared on the other side. We watched for a brief moment, wanting to assess where we could help the most. The wolves seemed to be holding their own with the remaining demons. Kieran opened his mouth to speak, but I raised my hand to stop him. I had a plan. I searched within and found my Angel Light again. I grabbed both my friends' hands. With our linked fingers, I knew we would be strong enough to handle whatever came our way. I drew on that knowledge.

Then I saw the body of the white wolf—the Alpha—lying on the ground, a silver sword protruding from his stomach.

A purple haze filled my vision. As I felt my body's power growing, a scream cut through the night, coming from inside the house. We turned toward a shadow in the third-floor window: Cali was awake, her hands pressed desperately against the window.

A dark purple hue emitted from my palms, unlike anything I'd produced before. Because of our joined hands, it amplified and created a star-like effect. Kieran and Sidelle blinked down at our linked fingers, then at me. Without a word, they both took a step back. In that instant, purple light shot out from every part of my body that wasn't covered by clothes. Even then, you could still see a glow from underneath. The power felt stronger than it had the other night, when I'd drawn on Kieran and Shay's Light.

This was a beast all its own.

My head tilted back, and I let out a gut-wrenching roar, so loud and fierce I thought my head might explode. I thrust my hands forward, and the dark purple light streamed out like whips, slashing the black cloaks and reducing the Marqs to nothing. They disintegrated on the spot.

12
Zoe

The lake had sucked back all the demons' cloaks when my purple light destroyed them. A calico-colored wolf bolted from the house, running full speed toward the beach. She dropped to the side of the white Alpha and desperately nuzzled his neck, but the white wolf didn't move. After a terrible moment, her head tilted to the sky, and she let out a lone, mournful howl that twisted my heart. In that call I could feel all her heartache and loss. The other wolves congregated around us and lowered their heads in respect of their fallen Alpha and all their brave comrades.

Then Cali's form appeared in the doorway of the house. Her hands held onto the threshold. Vash, still in wolf form, ran to her side, beating me to her. I wanted to pull her into a tight hug, but someone grabbed me from behind. Strong arms held me back.

"Wait," Jackson, now back in human form, whispered. "Let Vash. She needs to hear it from him." I tried to shake him loose, but his grip was like a vice. "You should be dead. No human has ever gone up against a Marq and lived. No one." He hung his head. "I need to go be with my parents. Let them do their thing."

"What's going on?" Cali asked, her voice trembling with fear. "Who are you?" She stood as if in a trance, staring at the huge wolf, and then she shook her head. "No. This makes no sense. How's that possible? How can you be Vash? You're a *wolf*." Her eyes grew huge. "And how are you speaking to me in my mind?"

"Let it out," I heard Vash say. *"I know you feel the animal inside, melt into it and feel it. Let go. It's safe, just let go."*

Her body shuddered, and her knees buckled. "I can't. What's going on?" she cried.

"Relax. Trust yourself."

Her blue eyes pleaded with mine. "Zoe. Help me."

"I'm sorry." I tried to pull free of Jackson, but he held me tight. "You need to do this without me. Vash is here to help you. He's—"

Her body convulsed, and she rolled onto her hands and knees. She screamed as her back arched, and her clothes started to disappear. Tears streamed down my face, and I looked away, helpless. Bones audibly cracked then broke, and white fur sprouted between Cali's skin and what remained of her clothes. Her nose and ears elongated in a process I couldn't bear to watch, and a tail grew on her backside. Within a minute a beautiful wolf stood before us, her coat glistening as white as a freshly fallen snow. Confused blue eyes looked at me.

"Zoe?"

Cali's soft voice spoke to me in my mind. I looked at Kieran and Sidelle, but their attention was on her wolf form.

"Yes?" I silently answered.

"Can you understand me?"

"Yes."

"I'm a wolf?*"* Cali lifted her paw and examined it. *"Why ... how ..."*

"Zoe?" Vash's voice echoed inside my head. *"How is this possible?"*

"I don't know what's happening either. Could it be an angel thing?"

"Angel thing?" Cali asked. *"What's going on?"*

"Cali, don't freak out or anything, but I have a lot to tell you," Vash said. *"Right now, though, I'm needed on the beach."*

I watched the snow white wolf swish her tail, examine

it, then wrap it around herself. I imagined it would be somewhat daunting to learn that you're a wolf. I sort of understood what she was going through—except for the learning to walk on four paws part. Without another word she marched behind Vash, turning to look at the tan wolf's dead body as she passed.

"Hey, K?" I said.

"Yes?" Kieran and Sidelle both replied.

"I can talk to and hear the wolves."

"How?" Kieran asked.

I shrugged and continued on to the beach without answering. There wasn't anything I could do to stop my powers from emerging, so I decided to go with it. When I glanced back, I noticed they were still standing with their mouths hanging open like fish out of water. I ran to catch up with Cali.

"Hey, you're taking this well," I told her. "I thought you'd freak out or something."

"It's still early," she replied.

When we arrived, the calico wolf's body lay over the white one. I suspected she was the Alpha female, Vash's mom, Lilli. She barely lifted her head, but she glanced at her sons and daughter—all in wolf form—as they approached.

"Vash," she whispered. *"Your time has come, and you will*

be a great leader. Listen to your heart to know what's right. When you falter, seek guidance from your mate. She will need you as much as you need her. Now, more than ever. Be strong, my son."

The rest of the wolves stepped forward, creating a semicircle around the group. For a moment I was confused. Why did she look so weak? So ... resigned? Then I remembered a conversation I'd had with Vash not long ago. He'd been explaining to me about the wolves' soul mates, and I hadn't thought it fair at the time.

"So you only get to find love once?" I had asked. "What happens if you don't find her, or if one of you dies?"

His explanation had been matter-of-fact. "Usually, fate seems to work it out that we find each other. A force draws us to find each other. But if you die after you are mated, your mate will follow. One half of the soul cannot live without the other."

It certainly wasn't fair now.

Lilli's eyes went to Cali's. *"I'm sorry I didn't have a chance to spend any time with you, to introduce you to our world. But my son will be a great Alpha with you at his side. Behind every pack leader is a strong, capable female. He will need you now more than ever. Pack, listen to your new Alphas. Encourage them. Respect them. Support them."*

She took a deep breath and nuzzled her husband again. *Alpha Vash and Cali, Era, Jackson, my pack ... remember me as I will always remember you.*

Her last breath died on the wind, and a white flame flickered out from both their mouths. The fires joined together and traveled as one into the sky and out of sight.

The members of the pack bowed their heads for a minute then turned to look at Vash. The brown wolf sat quietly next to a small, white one. His head bowed over his parents' still bodies. A long, low howl filled the night. Small white paws stepped forward, and Cali nuzzled the fallen Alpha pair. She stepped back to join Vash, and together they howled again. More members joined, mourning with them, and paying respect to their dead leaders.

"I can't believe Vash's parents are ... dead," I whispered, looking at Kieran and Sidelle. "Did you hear what Vash's mom said as she died?"

They both nodded.

"That was beautiful." Then I thought of something. "How did you hear? Can you hear the wolves?"

"When they allow me to," Sidelle said.

"And I hear Sidelle, so she translated for me," Kieran said.

We left the wolves to their grieving, and as we passed their bodies, I paid my respects to the fallen. Silently returning to the house, I wanted to talk about all that happened, but some images were too fresh and painful in my mind. I went back to our bedroom and flopped onto the bed, burying my head in the pillow. How would the wolves move on? Some of them would be old enough to remember a time when Keegan hadn't been their leader but the young pups? The change would be hard on them. I had no doubt that Vash would be a great leader, and with Cali by his side ...

Oh, Cali. Would she continue with high school? *She has to. She only has one more year.* Would she move here to the mansion? What would she tell her parents?

"Hey, Zoe." Sidelle leaned against the doorframe. "Wanna talk about tonight?"

"Yes," I mumbled into the pillow. "No. Maybe." I shook my head. "I don't understand how the demons got here. Keegan said we'd be ... safe here." Just saying Keegan's name made my nostrils flare, and I fought back tears. My fist hit the bed. "He said they'd never been here. I don't understand. This is all my fault." The first traitor streaked down my cheek. I couldn't stop them as the floodgate opened.

"None of this is your fault, Zoe," Kieran said softly as he walked into the room. "You didn't make the demons come here, and you didn't kill anyone." He moved to sit next to me on the bed, and rubbed small circles on my back. "Well, except for the Marqs at the end, but this isn't your fault."

"That was really badass, Z," Sidelle said, grinning. "I've never seen anything like that before. Those purple streamer thingies were super cool. How did you do that?" She settled in on my other side.

"Jackson said, ... he said that no human had gone against a Marq and lived. Is that true?" I asked in between sobs.

"Yes, as far as I know," Kieran said.

"So how's that possible?" My eyes burned; my cheeks felt flushed.

"Another angel perk?" Sidelle suggested. "But first we need to figure out how the demons invaded the wolves' sacred land. That should be our priority."

"Agreed." Vash stood in the hallway, holding Cali's human hand. They walked into the room, but Jackson and Era lingered at the threshold. "The demons forced our hands," he said, looking directly at me. "Zoe, my pack has agreed to help you. We will join this fight. Tomorrow's Sunday—" He checked his watch, realizing the time. "Rather, *today* is. I've decided Jackson and I will attend your high school for the rest of the year, so Cali can complete her junior year, and I'll come home on weekends to make sure everything is taken care of here. Jackson will stay at Kieran's house." He turned to his brother. "Start packing. Whatever you can't bring, Kieran can get."

His eyes went to his sister, who still waited in the doorway. "Era, I need you to stay here and make sure everything runs smoothly while I'm gone. You'll be the lady of the house while Cali is away. She'll need you to step up and—"

"Yes, sir," Era shouted. "I'll do everything, and I'll make sure it happens. Don't worry about a thing. I'll make you proud. And mom and dad."

He held in a smile. "If you need assistance, call Timber. She'll be here to guide you. Or call me if you have any questions. I'm only twenty minutes away."

"Okay." Era stalked out of the room. "All right, you guys, listen up!" she shouted. "Vash said I'm in charge, and we're going to ..." Her voice faded as she bounded down the stairs, headed for another room.

"I can't believe you left her in charge," Sidelle said, frowning at Vash. "Isn't she kinda young to run a house this size as well as all the other houses on the property?"

He shrugged. "I just told her that so she has something to do. Keep her mind focused on a task. Timber will be the one who'll actually run the household stuff. She's my mom's right-hand wolf and her best friend." He clenched his fists. "*Was*. Anyway, she already knows how everything is done around here." He frowned at us. "Now, any ideas on how the demons got onto pack land—"

"Vash," I asked. "How are you doing?"

"I'm fine."

"You can't be. Your parents died in front of you."

"Yes, but I have to be the strong one now. If I'm weak in front of the pack—"

"It's not being weak to show emotion. It means you care. I didn't know them long, but look at me. I'm a hot mess." Tears streamed down my face. "They were your parents. And now they're ..."

"I know, Zoe. But seeing death is part of life. At least it is for the pack. Our existence is much easier and less complex than an Ordinary human's."

"Well, if you want to talk about it or anything, just know I'm here when you're ready." I shook my head. "I didn't think demons could come here."

"I don't know, but we'll find out," Kieran replied. "You should have some members scout out along the shoreline and see if they find anything strange. In the meantime, I'll search the lake." He disappeared from the room.

Vash went to start the pack's search, while I felt helpless ... again. The energy to do anything had been sapped from my limbs, and my body wouldn't move from the bed. I turned my head toward Sidelle.

"Did you find out anything about Shay? Please tell me something good, because right now I don't know if I can handle any more waiting."

"Sorry, babe. Nothing."

"Kieran didn't tell you anything?" My voice came out harsher than I meant. "Sorry."

"No. I understand you're on edge. We all are. Especially now."

I let out a long breath. '"On edge doesn't even begin to describe how I feel."

Late Sunday morning Cali rode back with Vash and Jackson, and Sidelle dropped me off in my driveway. I lugged my clothes up to the front door, my mind and heart as heavy as the bag. The pack's search of the grounds had produced nothing. Kieran's look in the lake hadn't answered any questions either. And I still hadn't heard from Shay, which really bothered me. If we were true soul mates, shouldn't I feel him somehow?

I trudged through the empty house, dragging my stuff behind me, relieved my family wasn't there to pepper me with questions, though I wasn't sure where they were. I had a lot to reflect on. For starters, Keegan was dead because of me. The demons were after me and if I wasn't there ... But no one blamed me for the Alpha's death. He hadn't denied me as the Redeemer, but now the pack was preparing for battle, with Vash as the leader.

I dumped my luggage into my closet and walked over to my window, remembering at the last moment that I should close my curtains. Before I did, I peered outside. I wasn't completely surprised to see Aiden sitting on his sill, jamming to music. He motioned for me to open the window.

"Where have you been, Zoe?"

"Who are you, my dad?" I snapped.

He looked taken aback by my outburst. "Nope. I'm definitely not your dad." He smiled. "You did something different with your hair? It looks nice."

I looked down, ashamed of my outburst. He hadn't deserved that. He had no idea what was going on in my head or my heart. "Sorry I snapped at you," I muttered. Then I touched my hair. I couldn't believe he'd noticed that I'd styled it in an up-do today. "And thanks."

"I've missed this." He waved his hand back and forth. "You know, us, sitting out here, talking."

At first I didn't know how to respond, so I started to shift back inside, feeling a bit creeped out. "I have a ton of homework—"

"How was your weekend?"

"Good. We went and hung out with some of Kieran's friends."

"Oh? I thought it was just going to be you girls and Kieran."

Had I told him that? "It was, but then he got a phone call from one of his buddies, and we decided to hang." I shrugged. "What did you do?"

"Were you there all weekend?" He completely ignored my question.

I decided I didn't like his tone or this line of questioning.

"At his friends' house?" he pressed.

"Yeah." I crossed my arms. "What did you do?" I asked again.

"Oh, this and that. Unpacked the rest of my stuff. I helped my sister around the house most of Saturday, did yard work, that sort of thing. Today was pretty laid back. Kinda boring, actually—until now."

"So, you didn't go out with anyone? Find a party?"

He thought about that. "I took a stroll to that coffee place you told me about, Coffee Grind? Anyway, I met some people there. One said her name was Rena, and later I met ... what's her name? Oh, yeah, Morgan. Did I get those names right? They both said they knew you."

Ugh. Morgan, the Captain of the Bitch Squad. "What'd you guys do?"

He shrugged.

"I see," I said shortly. "You can hang out with my friend Rena, but I can't be with my other friends for a weekend without getting the third degree?" *Why am I getting to mad?*

"I didn't say that."

"That's what it sounded like to me."

I rose, slammed my window shut, and closed the curtains. I couldn't believe he was quizzing me about my weekend, but he wouldn't tell me any details about his own. At first I'd thought he was flirting with me—and maybe he had been—but he'd moved right on to something that seemed very close to an accusation. I wasn't under any obligation to clear things with him.

After digging around for my backpack and pulling out some school books, I decided to tackle my homework in math, English, and chemistry. I hated math. It was my absolute worst subject. I wasn't going to grow up to be a mad scientist or a mathematician, but I still tried to do well, though all I really cared about was passing the class. Plus, if I didn't understand it, Kieran would help me. He was great at everything. In fact if he kept on his present path, he would graduate valedictorian. I was determined to graduate with honors.

With twenty formulas to do, I was pleased I was able to do most of them, though I left three because the questions didn't make any sense. I'd have to call Kieran later about those. Grabbing the chem book next, I read the assigned chapters, but my eyelids grew heavy. Maybe it was because of the boring assignment, or maybe it was the exhausting weekend, but I soon fell asleep on the book, leaving a crease on the page. Eventually, I peeled my face from the pages, hoping it hadn't left an imprint on my cheek, and listened for movements in the house. I hadn't heard my family come home, but the clock told me it was dinner time. Pots and pans clanged in the kitchen, and my parents voices floated up the staircase. Someone had checked on me because my bedside light was turned off. Any minute I expected my door to fling open with my little sister chattering on about her weekend at the cabin. But thankfully she never showed.

I had English homework left to do, so I flipped through the pages of the novel we were supposed to read. I could pound out a two-page summary easily on the five chapters. I just needed to focus and get it done.

You'd think that would be easy, right? Wrong. As soon as I looked at the blinking cursor on my laptop screen, my mind wandered back to the Enlightens. How was I going to get the leaders of the Orders to follow me into battle? I imagined when I told them the world would end if they didn't join me, they would get on board real fast. To convince them, I would need Keegan—No, *Vash*—and his pack, they'd vowed to be with me. If Sammael started sending more Marqs after me before I had my special Seraphs' Sword.

I couldn't control my powers, didn't really understand them, and would have to practice to be any sort of help. What if I couldn't fulfill my task? What would happen to the world and everyone?

No. I'd cross that bridge if we ever found a sword.

Tink. Tink. Tink. The sound pulled me out of my endless line of questions, and I whipped my head around my room, looking for its source.

Tink. There it was again. With my heart full of hope, I got off the bed and walked over to the blinds; Shay had done this exact same thing to my window last week. *Shay?*

But it was Aiden. He sat on his sill, throwing something at me, motioning to open the window. I hesitated, still feeling a creeper vibe from him. But that's not the Minnesota way. I should give him a chance and be nice. After I unlocked the latch and struggled to crank it open enough to hear him, he lobbed something and yelled, "Quick. Catch!"

I dodged, and the missile sailed right past where my head had just been. Grinning, he threw another.

"What the heck?" I ducked again. "Stop that. You could

poke my eye out with whatever you're throwing."

"I highly doubt that." He laughed. "They're M&Ms. I'd be surprised if you actually sustained an injury from one of these."

I glanced at a red M&M on my floor. Then I picked it up and launched it back at him. Gross. The five-second rule did *not* apply. I was not about to eat that. The candy hit him squarely between the eyes, and he was a little taken back by my direct aim. I was, too, but I flashed him a huge, smug smile as if I'd totally planned that.

"What're you doing?" I demanded. "Besides throwing candy at me like I'm a zoo animal, I mean. You know, they don't like it when you taunt the animals."

"Ha! That's funny, Zoe. Nice aim, by the way. You play softball or something?"

"No. I'm on the track team."

"You are? Cool, we should go running sometime. I usually go every morning before school, but I'm not sure if I'll be going tomorrow being my first day."

I ignored his invitation to go running. I probably shouldn't go with him, even though I needed the exercise. Kieran told me I needed to be with him when I went running since Shay wasn't here. Plus, tomorrow would be a long day if I got up earlier to run, go to school, and then attend a meeting with everyone at Kieran's house.

"Do you want something? I'm busy," I said.

He shook his head. "I just noticed your light was still on."

That seemed harmless enough. I settled onto the sill. "Are you nervous about tomorrow?" I asked, assuming he must be. "Don't worry. Most everyone is super nice. A few aren't, but that happens everywhere, right? I'm not going to tell you who they are. You've already met one," I mumbled the last sentence.

He shrugged. "People are people wherever you go. Some are nice and some aren't. They'll either like me or they won't. I bet you have a bunch of friends."

"I guess so. I hang out mostly with Kieran." I pointed toward the white house. "He lives in that house, near the entrance of the cul-de-sac. When I'm not with him, I'm hanging out with my girls."

He looked at Kieran's house for a long time. "Is he your boyfriend?"

"Who, Kieran? No. He's my best friend. I've known him since kindergarten. He's like a cool older brother, ... even though, um, we're the same age," I blurted, trying to cover my error. "He always acts way older than me. He's way more responsible." I drew in a breath. "Do you have a girlfriend back in California?"

"Had one, but she was taken ..." His eyes pulled from

mine for a split second. "Nope." He popped the "P," looked directly at me, and smiled. "I am *free* and *available.* Why? You askin' to be mine, Angel?"

"Ah, no. I ... I was just wondering." I looked away. Something must have happened to his girlfriend. "What happened to her? She was taken, like as in kidnapped?"

Had he just called me "Angel." *Probably just a term of endearment.* Yeah, that's what I decided to go with. Neither of us spoke for a long time after that awkward moment. When I finally glanced at my bedroom clock on the nightstand, it was close to ten-thirty. Wow, time had passed quickly. It didn't feel like ninety minutes had gone by. Shay would've stopped by if he ... I held in tears and faked a yawn. *I hope you're safe, Shay, wherever you are.*

"She went missing for a while. I couldn't handle it. I ditched out on school, flunked out of my junior and senior years, got into drugs and alcohol. That's more than you probably wanted to hear."

Missing? Like Shay.

"Anyway, cops thought I had something to do with it, but I didn't. She had some mental health issues. Met her through some other people I hung with, who weren't good for me."

"Were you together long?"

"Couple years. She turned up eventually, but it wasn't

the same. She was different. Anyway, time for bed. It's a big day for me tomorrow." He smiled, but it didn't reach his eyes.

"Yep. You could meet the girl of your dreams," I teased, wanting to see him really smile. "You'll want to look your best. The key is getting enough beauty rest. Oh, um, not that you're not beautif—" Too late. My face was burning. I needed to crawl into something and shut my mouth. "Whatever. You know what I mean."

"You think I'm beautiful?" He smirked. "I prefer to be called handsome."

I rolled my eyes. "Like you don't know what you look like. Have you seen yourself?"

He cackled. "I know what I look like. We do have things called mirrors in California. In fact I bet we have more of them there, and we use them more frequently than they do here."

"Gah! You are so frustrating." I threw my arms into the air.

"So, going back to the fact that you think I'm beautiful—"

"I did *not* say you were beautiful. You said I said you were beautiful. Totally different."

"Well, whoever said it." He smiled. "Let's go back to that."

I shook my head, but I had to give in. "All I'm saying is that you'll be the talk of the school tomorrow. You know, being from California and all."

"Ah ha. And you'll be the talk, too, since I'm your new neighbor. Lucky you." He wiggled his brows.

"Oh, geez. Conceited much?"

"Nope," he said, again with emphasis on the "P." "I'm not conceited. I'm confident. As you said, 'totally different.'"

He was mocking me now. I didn't sound like that, did I?

"Yeah, well, ... whatever. I'm going to bed. Good night."

I closed the window and whipped the curtains shut. *So there.* I stormed off to my bathroom for my nightly ritual and washed my face too vigorously, splashing water all over the sink. Scrubbing my teeth and hair with too much gumption, I finished and slammed the hairbrush onto the countertop. I stalked into my walk-in closet and selected my jammies and threw myself onto the bed.

He was so frustrating, but I had no idea why I let him get to me like this. I was mad at him, and for what? Little jibes that my friends also used? *Stupid.*

I flipped off my bedside light but continued to toss and turn, still upset about Aiden and missing Shay, since it had been two days without any word from him. I tried to calm my breathing and relax, but it just wasn't going to happen. I flipped onto my back, then got up, and walked to the window, picking up a few M&Ms still lying on my floor. When I drew back my curtain, I saw his bedroom light was off. It had only been thirty minutes, so he probably wasn't asleep yet. I tossed one M&M straight up into the air and caught it, before I breathed a heavy sigh and went back to bed.

Now I felt bad, but it was more because of my behavior than my words. I lay on my back for quite a while, just thinking.

"I'm sorry," I eventually whispered into the darkness.

Monday morning, I rose earlier than normal. I hadn't slept well. Throughout my tossing and turning, all I could envision were eyes. Some were aqua, some were black, and some would never blink again.

I rose from my bed and took a long, hot shower. I scrubbed my body clean, brushed my teeth, and dried my hair. Using the curling iron, I curled half of it then tied it into a loose ponytail. For makeup, I applied black eyeliner and pink lip gloss. After I dropped all my books into my backpack, I headed down to the kitchen. Both my parents were already up and moving about.

"You're up early," Dad noted, peering over his cup of coffee.

"Yeah, guess so," I said. "Early bird catches the worm."

"This early? Hmm. Someone is definitely trying catch something," he teased. "How was your weekend? Do anything exciting?"

Ignoring his comment, I grabbed a bowl from the shelf and dumped cereal and milk into it. "Nope, nothing exciting." We ate breakfast in silence after that. What would I tell him? I saw one of my best friends turn into a wolf, I witnessed wolves die from the hands of demons, Vash became Alpha of his pack. Oh and I used some sort of kickass angel powers.

When I was done, I cleaned up and went outside.

Kieran stood next to the driver's side door. "Are we stopping for coffee this morning?" he asked.

"Why wouldn't we?" I slung my backpack into the back seat of his car.

He shrugged. "Maybe you wanted to get to school to see the new student."

"Aiden? I already know him. Mom, Stella, and I went to his house before you and Sidelle came on Friday. I helped him unpack some movies and stuff."

"Stay away from him. Word is this guy got caught up with a bunch of bad people when he lived in California."

"How do you know that? Is he the same person you used to know?"

"I'll see him today and let you know. But Zoe, you need to stay away from him in case he is the same."

"Maybe we don't have all the facts about him." I frowned. "He seemed to know you, though. When I mentioned that you and I were friends and that you lived down the street, he got all tense. Oh, and guess what? He kinda looks like Shay. They have the same aqua eyes, hair color, build—it's like they could be brothers. But Shay doesn't have any siblings, right? I thought he was an only child."

Kieran clenched his teeth. *What's up with that?* "No. No, he doesn't have any siblings."

When we arrived at Coffee Grind, I ordered my usual chai tea latte then looked around. Lots of other early risers were already seated in the alcoves. I grinned when I spotted Cali, Vash, Jackson, and our other friend, Quinn, sitting off in a corner.

"Hi." I waved, putting on my upbeat attitude. "Ready for the weekend yet?"

"It can't come soon enough!" Quinn exclaimed. "Another weekend past means another weekend closer to summer. I wish the weather would get warm so we could start going to the beach." She fanned herself. "I want to wear my new bikini in front of Caden. Make him drool a bit."

"Yeah, I'm ready for the weekend, too," Cali said. "But no parties at my place. My parents canceled going out of town because they're still a little mad about the last house party. Someone broke one of my mom's favorite vases, but if you ask me, everything in the house is her favorite. It wouldn't really have mattered what was broken. Anyway, they told me I can't have any more parties for a while."

"Hey, we should get going to school," Quinn said as she checked her phone. "Do you want a ride, Zoe?"

"No thanks. Kieran drove us."

"Okay, see you guys later."

Our drive to school was quiet. Kieran kept looking over at me, but I didn't want to talk. I'd open up to him eventually, but I was still fuming mad at Aiden after last night's talk. Misdirected anger? Yes. And the fact no one had informed me about anything new with Shay.

"Did ..." Kieran hesitated; then he dove right in. "Aiden. Is this about him?"

"No." God, I missed Shay something fierce. Someone better know something soon or I'd crack.

"I see."

"Anything?"

"They're still looking."

As we waited in line for parking, I noticed a red car in the far corner of the parking lot. If all the upper classmen had driven to school, there would be about a hundred vehicles in the lot, and the flame-red vehicle stuck out like a sore thumb. I'd never seen anything like it, which was odd. I knew most of the vehicles the kids drove and what some of their parents drove as well. From this far away, I couldn't tell if anyone was sitting in the car or not.

After we were finally able to park, Cali and Quinn strode up, laughing about something. Quinn quickly retelling a story, about how she thought she'd been a ninja in a past life. We all whooped again, and not only because it was a ridiculous idea. The truth was, Quinn was one of the most uncoordinated people I knew.

"See ya later, girls." We parted ways when we entered the school, and I nudged Kieran's shoulder. "Hey, K. You have to help me with math. I left three problems."

"Sure."

We approached my locker, and I noticed Sidelle wasn't at hers yet. At Sidelle's request to the administration, our lockers were next to each other's again this year, directly across from the cafeteria. It was strange not to see her there. I dropped my backpack on the ground and tried my locker combination. To my surprise, it opened on the first try—again.

"I wonder where Sidelle is."

Kieran shrugged.

"Maybe she's hanging around with Jackson," I said. "Showing him the ropes."

"Did Aiden say he would be coming to school today?" Kieran asked in a hushed voice.

"He said he was, so we'll see. I offered for him to ride with us, but he declined, said he wanted to drive." I looked around but didn't see him. "He's probably in the office getting his class schedule."

As soon as I finished my sentence, Aiden strode down the hall toward us. He was dressed in black from head to toe, except for a red T-shirt. His eyes were on the sheet of paper in his hands, and he occasionally glanced up at the locker numbers. He hadn't noticed me. Everyone he passed turned and gawked.

And casually hanging on his shoulder was my rival, Morgan. She snapped her gum and waved like royalty at onlookers as they passed.

Kieran was frowning, which was not a good look for him. I elbowed him in the stomach.

Aiden and Morgan stopped next to us, and I realized he'd been assigned the empty locker at the end of the row. Just my luck. He glanced up, noticed everyone in the hall was staring at him, and then noticed me.

"Hey, there, Zoe," he said, trying to work the locker combination.

"Hi."

Morgan sneered in my direction. "Poor Aiden. You're in the slums," she said. "I'll have to see if we can get your locker location changed so you can be closer to mine." She looked me up and down. "You don't want to be in this part of the school."

Aiden's eyes were on Kieran. "We haven't met officially." He stuck out his hand. "Name's Aiden."

Kieran drew in a deep breath, and then slowly shook Aiden's hand. "Kieran."

That done, Aiden smiled back at me. "Looks like we'll be locker neighbors, too."

"For now," Morgan said, sniffing with disdain and glaring at me. "Don't get used to seeing him here."

"See what I mean, K?" I said to Kieran.

"We'll talk about it later," he muttered.

"Zoe," Cali called as she and Vash ran up to me. "Oh, Sidelle's not here yet?" Her eyebrows wiggled. "She and Jackson must be taking the *long* way. Hi, Morgan." She dropped her school bag on the floor before noticing Aiden. "Oh, hello. I'm Cali. You must be new."

"Yep, just moved over the weekend. From California."

"Well, welcome to lowly St. Joseph, Minnesota." She turned toward me, making sure Aiden couldn't see her face. "He's hot," she mouthed. Then she peeked at Kieran and shrugged. "Sorry," she whispered.

When I heard the distinct clicking of stiletto shoes, my heart stopped, fearing it would be the other two sides of the Triangle coming to harass me since their leader was standing in front of me, but I was relieved to see Sidelle walking briskly down the hall, with Jackson trailing in her wake.

"Hi ya'll. What's happenin'?" she called as she approached. "You're new," she said, circling a slender index finger toward Aiden. "You all remember Jackson, Vash's younger bro?"

Jackson walked over to Vash, who stood in a protective stance next to Cali.

"You're handling this well." I pulled Cali in for a hug.

"Handling what?" Cali asked.

I cocked my head, obviously not wanting to say anything out loud in front of other people.

"Oh, *that*. Right. Vash told me everything, so I'm up to speed about you. Now me?" She shook her head, smiling wryly. "I'm still adjusting to that."

Both boys shook their heads, seeing us talking. "Are they always like this?" Aiden asked. "Cryptic, I mean?"

"Yes, always," Kieran replied.

"So what do you have for classes?" Sidelle asked Aiden. She grabbed the sheet out of his hands, not bothering with introductions, then nodded slowly, one eyebrow raised. "Ah. Looks quite similar to Zoe's schedule, actually."

It did? I grabbed the paper out of Sidelle's hand and quickly looked down the list. It wasn't similar; it was *exactly* the same schedule. How could that have happened? There had to be a higher power working here. I handed Aiden his schedule, my eyes narrowed.

"And don't get used to that either, Zoe," Morgan hissed. "He's changing his schedule, too."

"Whatever, Morgan." I smiled at Aiden. "I guess you're stuck with me today. I'll show you around, if you want."

"He doesn't need you." Morgan stepped forward. "I'll take him wherever he needs to be."

"Whatever."

I turned back to my locker, still confused about Aiden's schedule. This couldn't be a coincidence, right? There had to be a reason why he had all the same classes as I had, but I couldn't guess at any. Oh, well. For whatever reason we'd see each other a lot, which would give me a chance to get to know him better.

"I'm off to class, Z," Kieran said.

I grabbed my books and turned to go. A crowd had started to form at this end of the hall, mostly made up of giggling girls ogling Aiden. Seriously? Was this elementary school or high school? Eventually, they walked on, especially after meeting Morgan's dead stare.

Rena came bounding up to Cali, Sidelle, and me. "Hey, girls. We have a new student here." Apparently, she hadn't noticed Aiden standing behind her.

I giggled.

"What?" she asked.

"He's standing right behind you," Cali informed her.

"Oh, God. He is?" Rena slowly turned around. "He is." Her face turned bright red, but she still gave him a once-over. "Hi, again," she said, sticking out her hand. "We met yesterday afternoon at Coffee Grind."

"Yes, I remember. How could I forget?" He shook her hand, and she beamed.

The first bell rang.

"I guess that's my cue to leave," she said, sounding genuinely apologetic. "Nice seeing you again. You'll have to join us at lunch."

"Um—"

"Not today he won't. And not the next either," Morgan said. "He'll be sitting with me and the *better* people."

Rolling her eyes, Rena walked away with Cali. Vash and Jackson trailed behind them. That left Aiden, Morgan, Sidelle, and me alone at the lockers.

"You'd better hurry off to class, Zoe," Morgan said, sneering. She leaned into Aiden and placed her chin on his shoulder. "A goodie-goodie is never late."

I grabbed my backpack and left without comment. Whatever. If Aiden wanted to date Morgan, the leader of the Triangle, so be it. I refused to stay and watch them suck face.

"Come on, Zoe," Sidelle said. "Let's get to class."

"Don't you think Aiden looks like Shay?" I asked as we walked toward my first class.

She shrugged. "No, not really. You're just missing Shay so much that you're seeing him in everyone."

"Any word on his whereabouts? Kieran has assured me that the angels are looking. But you have to admit, though, they have the same color eyes, right?"

"You're still on that? Shay's are more teal. Aiden's are a little bluer. Not the same."

"What about the hair color?"

"Different, too. Shay's is a bit blonder. Aiden's is browner."

I still thought they looked similar.

When Aiden entered the room, the teacher glanced up from her desk and waved him over. "Hello. I'm Ms. Hart. Do you have your schedule?"

Aiden handed it over, and she quickly read it, confirming his enrollment in her class. She pulled a history book out of the cabinet for him, then opened a drawer in her desk, and pulled out the seating chart. She perused the diagram, tapping the paper with her finger.

"Ah, Aiden ... this seat is open. It will be your assigned seat for the rest of the year. You don't really have to sit here every day; I don't actually care where you sit. Just be here on time. If you do that, we won't have any problems."

"Yes, ma'am."

"Great." She looked at me. "Zoe, go ahead and take a seat, and we'll get started. Class, may I have your attention, please? This is our new student, Aiden Mors. Please give him a warm welcome."

All eyes followed Aiden as he took his seat. Thinking he might appreciate a familiar face, I motioned for him to sit next to me, but he chose another open desk. History class was a required course, so it was full, unlike some of the elective courses. Once he was settled, Aiden looked around and nodded to people who were openly staring at him.

Caden turned around and introduced himself. "Hey dude. I'm Caden. Aiden, right?"

"Yes," Aiden said.

"Rumor is you're from California."

"Not a rumor. True statement."

"Cool!"

That ended their conversation. I guessed boys didn't need to know much. Class got underway, and I couldn't help but notice Aiden occasionally glancing over at me. I tried not to return the look since I needed to pay attention in class, but I couldn't resist. I was caught—twice. When class was over, some of the students rushed over to introduce themselves. Aiden had met a fourth of our grade in one hour, and it wasn't even lunchtime.

As soon as we left the history room, I noticed Morgan leaning against a locker. Just great. What did she want now? I kept walking.

"Hello again, stranger," I heard her purr to Aiden. "I'll walk you to your next class. What is it again?"

"Physics," he said.

"Boring."

"You got that right, babe."

"Did you miss me?"

Her pouty little question made me feel ill. I tried to ignore them both.

I'd planned to arrive a little early since I wanted to maybe get at least one missing math problem done, but the halls were filled with students trying to get a glimpse of the new guy. I pushed my way through and into my classroom, then sat in silence for a few moments, waiting for Kieran.

"What's his problem?" Kieran asked, walking into the room and jabbing a thumb back at the hall.

"Ah," I said. "You must have passed the exhibitionists."

"Yep."

"Do you see it?" I asked. "Sidelle didn't."

He frowned. "See what?"

"Aiden's resemblance to Shay. I swear they could be brothers."

"I guess I'm not seeing what you see. Then again, I haven't stared into Shay's eyes as much as you have."

I punched his shoulder.

Noah strolled in with Aiden a few minutes later. "I'll introduce you to my friends," he offered. "I'm on the basketball team, and Coach likes all the players to sit together. Says it's a 'team building' thing. We can always make room for one more."

"Thanks, man."

The second period bell rang. Aiden wandered back up to the front and handed Ms. Miller his schedule. She barely glanced at it before waving him off. He shrugged and found an open seat in the second row.

"Have you figured anything out yet?" I whispered to Kieran. "I mean about Aiden. It seems so weird that he has all the same classes as me, doesn't it? And our lockers are together? I don't know. Maybe I'm being paranoid, but—"

"No. There's ... he's hiding something, but I can't figure it out."

"He's been nice so far, at least when Morgan's not around. Is he the same person you knew before?"

Kieran wasn't convinced. "I want to know what he's hiding. I should ask Sidelle—see if she can get a read off him. He doesn't look the same, so it can't be him. Hmmm ..."

Ms. Miller got to her feet. "Class, let's break into groups of three or four and go over the homework assignment. Aiden, you can join any group and just listen for now, since you didn't have the assignment."

Kieran and I immediately pushed our desks together while Aiden slid his desk over to Noah's group, right next to us.

"I'm co-captain of the basketball team with Caden," Noah informed Aiden. "You probably met him in your history class."

Aiden nodded. "Yep."

"So how's it been going so far? Heard you were from California. You liking it here?"

"Not too bad, I guess." He turned his head, making sure I was listening. "I have a neighbor who likes to have food tossed at her like a zoo animal, though."

I wasn't about to let him talk about me behind my back. "Hey! I do not. You threw candy at me. I had nothing to do with it, and I didn't eat it."

"Wait. Zoe? You're the neighbor?" Noah asked, looking surprised.

"Yeah, he moved in next door to me."

"That's cool."

"Class," Ms. Miller said. "More math, less socializing, please."

"What was California like?" Noah turned his attention back to Aiden.

Aiden's casual smile was dazzling. "Oh, you know. Warm, sunny ... babes wearing bikinis and short shorts, and loads of wild parties."

"Maybe I should move out there," Noah said. "Sounds like my kind of place."

"It was a little piece of heaven." He watched me a moment, and then he winked at Kieran.

What was that? Okay, now I knew he was trying to send me or Kieran some sort of signal. Why else would he look directly at me when he said the word heaven? Was he trying to gauge my reaction to the word? I looked at Kieran, but his expression didn't give anything away.

Since we couldn't talk about anything remotely pressing—like what had happened over the weekend, where we would go from here, or about my powers—Kieran and I spent the rest of the class chatting and not reviewing the homework assignment. Noah and his group seemed enthralled with any story Aiden told about California. He obviously had a man crush on him or else one was forming. But I understood it in a way. What *wasn't* there to like about Aiden? He was tall, mysterious, funny, from California of all places, and hot as hell.

Morgan stood outside the classroom, waiting to escort Aiden to his next class. When he walked through the door of our PolySci class, I immediately took my seat, leaving

Aiden at the front of the room. I sort of felt bad for him. I could only imagine what it'd be like, being the new kid in school at almost the end of the year.

"So, the new guy?" Quinn leaned over and whispered to me.

"He just moved from California. I watched him and his mom move in."

"You watched them move? Which house did they buy?"

"My next-door neighbor's. Remember the snow birds? Their house."

"Wow, lucky you. You get to wake up next to that."

"I have a boyfriend, Quinn."

In that instant, Aiden's eyes locked onto mine. Then his eyes moved to the desk next to me and focused on Quinn. She was, well, Quinn was adorable. Skinny little Quinn had long blond and brown highlighted hair, a cute little face, and she stood only about five foot three. She wore a size two. We all hated her ... but loved her, really. She ate whatever she wanted and never gained a single pound, and she was always cheery. She kept us laughing.

Right now, she was staring back at Aiden, wearing a googly-eyed expression. This apparent connection would be bad if Morgan found out.

Mr. Bell made his entrance and asked the students to settle down; then he welcomed Aiden and told him to take any seat. "Here," he said, handing him a book. "You'll need this."

Aiden took the seat on Quinn's other side. "Hi," he said smoothly. "Name's Aiden."

Something stirred in me, and it was a feeling I did not like. Was I jealous? No. I'd much rather see him with one of my friends than with one of the Triangles. What was I feeling then?

When Aiden looked the other way, Quinn turned and mouthed, "Yummy," at me.

I nodded. What else could I do? Aiden and Quinn stared at each other during the whole long hour, and I tried not to pay attention to them. Eventually, I gave up and doodled in my notebook, grateful when class finally ended. It was actually making me nauseated, looking at them. I was anxious to get to biology and talk with Sidelle.

As I stood to leave, I caught the tail end of a conversation between Quinn and Aiden. "Yeah, okay, sounds fun," he said.

Then I saw her slip him a piece of paper with her phone number on it, meaning they were making plans to do something together. Just great.

"Bio's next," I informed him. "If you care."

"I don't, but lead the way." He glanced back at Quinn, who was looking at him with longing eyes. "Morgan won't be in the hall," Aiden told me quietly. "She said she has something to do."

"Lucky for you," I muttered.

"Hey, Aiden," Quinn said. "Save me a seat at lunch."

He and I walked out of the classroom and into the hallway.

"I see you're already collecting digits."

"She gave me her number," he admitted.

"Don't tell Morgan. If you're dating her or whatever, she'll claw out your eyes, so you can't even look at another girl. And I don't even want to think what she might do to Quinn."

"Oh, I can manage her."

"Whatever."

He stopped walking, grabbed my sleeve, and forced me to stop. "Are you mad at me?"

I crossed my arms. Was I? "No. Hard to be mad at someone who doesn't say but two words. Just don't lead Quinn on. She's my friend, and she deserves better than that."

Even though I'd said I wasn't angry, I turned and stalked away as if I was. After a few feet I stopped, looked back at him, then motioned for him to hurry up so we could get to class. This whole Aiden thing was making me crazy. By the end of the school day, I was going to be a basket case.

"Oh, my gosh, Zoe, what's wrong?" Sidelle tugged me to the back of the biology room, then glanced back at Aiden. "Sorry, babe. Gotta steal her for a bit. Girl chat."

"What are you talking about?" I asked her.

"You. You're a mess. What's going on?"

"Is it that obvious?"

"No. Just to me. You look upset. Are you going to cry? Please say no. I can't stand crying people. I just don't know how to handle them." She glanced back at Aiden, who was busy talking to girls from the junior class. Then she put her hands on her hips. "Spill."

Oh no, I was *not* going to cry at school. But I had to talk to Sidelle about what I was feeling. Where could I start? How was I going to explain this to her so she would understand? Especially, since I didn't really understand it myself.

"How can someone who looks like Shay be so nasty and hook up with Morgan?" I quietly blurted out. "Quinn gave him her number, and I flipped out. I'm on an emotional roller coaster and can't rein in my feelings. I just miss Shay so much. I'm worried about him, and my brain is giving me really bad images."

Her eyes were all sympathy. "Oh, honey. You have got to pull yourself together. We'll find Shay—and he won't want to kiss someone with snot running down her face."

My hands went to my cheeks. "I have snot on my face?"

"No, I'm just saying. You have to do better than this."

"Aiden likes Quinn. You should have seen them last period together. It made me sick just watching them. Is that what Shay and I look like? Sidelle, you have to help me."

"First of all, forget about Aiden for the time being. You need to have your head on straight for this weekend, Zoe. After that we can tackle your man issue."

"Why? What's this weekend?"

"We're going to try to get into Fairyland. We'll need extra time off in the regular world since time passes differently there."

"Extra days off? How's that going to work?"

She grinned. "I just created them. I suggested to the principal that he should send some of the teachers to a two-day conference in Minneapolis."

"Is there a conference?"

"No, silly. The teachers are actually staying home since I suggested to them that they needed extra time off. Memos will be sent to the parents today, reminding them of the days off. Of course the letter will be backdated."

"Oh. Of course."

We took our seats, and I was happy to see the lights blink off then on, indicating we were going to watch a video during class. Nap time. The teacher motioned for Aiden to come with him to the back of the room while he prepared the video. It was the only empty seat left, and it happened to be next to Sidelle. Not daring to text her openly during class, I quickly tore out a sheet of paper from my notebook, scribbled a message to Sidelle, then handed her the sheet: *Mind Walk.*

She glanced at the sheet and nodded at me. I smiled, relieved. Now, I could nap. I laid my head on my desk but still watched the video, letting my mind wander. It was a good thing we were not going to have a test on the video. Time passed incredibly quickly after that.

"Mr. Mors? Hold up a second, please," the teacher called to Aiden as the bell rang, ending class.

Sidelle and I shot out of the room.

"So?" I asked.

"Nothing," Sidelle grumbled. "I couldn't get a read on him."

"That's strange."

"Yes, it is. I'm thinking of joining Team Kieran. Something's off about Aiden. Kieran and I will compare notes."

We parted ways and promised to see each other at lunch after the next class. On the way Aiden joined me, and we headed to English class together.

"Are you okay now, after your girl time with Sidelle?"

I sighed. "Yes. I'm sorry I flipped out on you. I have no idea what has gotten into me lately. I'm usually not like this, I swear."

"That's okay. You're dealing with a lot. Adding me into the mix only made it worse." He smiled and eased the tension between us. "I know I'm a lot to handle."

I couldn't stay mad at him. Not when he smiled at me or made me laugh. Even though the others couldn't see it, Aiden reminded me so much of Shay. Even some of their mannerisms were the same.

"If you aren't okay with Quinn and me hanging out ... "

"No, no. It's fine. She's a great person. You'd be lucky to call her your girlfriend if it works out."

"Then," he said, moving his hand between us, "we're good, you and I?"

"Yeah."

When we entered English, it became apparent that Aiden's novelty had started to wear off. Most people had gone back into their little groups, gossiping about whatever. I hoped the rest of the day would be semi-normal, but I couldn't promise anything about the lunch crowd. Our school was small—the graduating class was only a little over a hundred and twenty students.

"I guess I'm not the shiny object of everyone's attention anymore," Aiden said when we entered the next classroom, and no one came up to ask him questions.

"You noticed that, too?"

"It's fine with me. I hate being the center of attention."

"What? You're not serious. And here I thought the world revolved around you."

He snickered. "Nope. Only some of the time."

"Figures."

Mr. Anderson cleared his throat. "Okay, class. Let's get started on group discussion. Please arrange the desks into a circle." He glanced at the new student. "Name please?"

"Aiden."

"Welcome to American English class, Aiden. We're reading and discussing *The Joy Luck Club* by Amy Tan."

The rest of the class had made a circle with their desks and were ready for discussion. Most of the students seemed to enjoy this class. Mr. Anderson didn't make us take tests, just actively participate in discussions.

"Who would like to give their overall comments about the reading? Their likes or dislikes and why?"

As usual, the whole class remained silent. No one wanted to go first and voice their opinion. No one ever volunteered anything around here—not until last week, when Shay had raised his hand to offer up the day's reading.

Mr. Anderson peered around the room. "How about ... Zoe?"

I took a deep breath. There was no point in refusing. "The whole dynamic of the mother-daughter relationships throughout the book was interesting," I said. "On the one hand, you have all the first generationers who are used to the old way. Then you have all their kids who want to be like everyone else, meaning more American. Each family has its own back story and ways to deal with what's happening in their lives. But you can tell they love each other, because ultimately all the daughters are trying to live up to their mothers' expectations. The mothers, in turn, love their daughters. They have made all kinds of sacrifices so their daughters could have better lives and futures."

"Wonderful, Zoe. Thank you. Anyone else?"

Aiden cleared his throat. "I found it interesting that the main daughter's character was telling her story, and she wanted to find her mom's other kin so they could become a family. The underlying plot was that your family may not be alive, and they may not even be your blood, but the realization of bonds can supersede the past." He leaned back in his chair and smirked.

"Wow. Very perceptive, Aiden. Thank you."

Everyone stared at Aiden, including me. He'd

apparently read the book. Had he read all the books on our list? If I asked him that, would he tell me truthfully, or would he lie?

Then I thought a little bit more about what he'd said. Had he been speaking directly to me, or had I just been imagining that? Because what if he was telling me I should seek my mom's kin—my angel mom's kin?

"I'm starving. Must be lunch next," Aiden said. "I assume I follow the herd to the lunch room? Or is it open lunch?" He waved his hand in front of my face. "Hello? Earth to Zoe?"

I blinked, trying to concentrate. "We don't have open lunch. They tried that a few years back, but some of the kids didn't return to school after, so they shut it down."

"Too bad. It's nice to be outside to eat. Gives the body a break."

"Oh, you can go outside. There are tables out on the patio. Just to warn you, though, Minnesota only has two seasons: winter and summer. It's either super cold or scorching hot. If you can stand either, by all means go ahead and sit outside."

He laughed, which I figured meant he didn't think I was serious. I probably should tell him he should also watch out for the state bird: the mosquito.

"So how does this work?" he asked as we entered the cafeteria. He looked around at all the food areas, ignoring everyone that stared at him.

I pointed. "Over there is the grill, and there's the sandwich line. That's the salad bar. Prices are listed unless you have the meal card, which basically means it's prepaid. You just go up and order and pay at the register."

"Got it. I can handle that."

"I sit at that table." I indicated the far table near the windows. I knew Kieran and Sidelle wouldn't approve, but I couldn't brush off the Minnesota niceness that had been instilled into me for my whole life. "If you want to sit with us, come on over."

I headed over to make my daily salad, selected my regular diet pop from the cooler, and then I proceeded to the register to pay for my lunch. Aiden stood on the other side of the cashier, pulling out a thick wad of bills.

"I got hers, too," Aiden said, smiling. "My treat for showing me around today."

"That's nice. Thanks."

Then I headed to my table. I placed my tray next to

Sidelle, leaving the spot next to me open for Kieran.

"The seating is all messed up," I said. "Where's Jackson?"

"He can't sit here," Sidelle said. "Not with the juniors. He's over in the sophomores' section. So what's going on? Are you better?"

"Maybe. Yes. No. I want to know where Shay is."

Kieran finally arrived from the lunch line, and he sat next to me. We squeezed Rena between Quinn and Sidelle. Kieran placed his tray next to mine then tilted his head, wondering how I was doing.

As soon as Aiden sat with the basketball team at the next table over, the guys around him all started talking at once. The rest of the cafeteria was quiet, all needing to hear Aiden's story. The boys peppered him with questions about California, so I guessed Noah had spread the word. Aiden was courteous to everyone and answered all the questions, maybe even embellished some of the stories. Everyone listened intently. Quinn was obviously enamored with him. She stared at him the whole lunch period, and I saw him glance over at her every few minutes.

The lunch shift ended with a shrill ring, and all the students shuffled back out into the main hallway and headed off to class. Aiden and I stopped at our lockers to exchange our books, and I dumped my backpack. I only needed one book for chemistry class, and then it was just gym class.

"Everyone's nice," Aiden said when I asked how he was doing. "I'll fit in well."

"I love these people," I said. "There isn't anything I wouldn't do for them. Most of us have known each other since kindergarten. Small towns, you know?" I smiled at him as we walked the flight of stairs to the second floor. "And yes, you're fitting in fine. Most of the girls think you're hot."

He wiggled his eyebrows. "I am, aren't I? It's the California tan."

"Aiden ..." I was going to tell him he wasn't as tanned as he thought. I decided against it. "Turn left. This is the chem classroom. It has the best view because it overlooks the wooded area."

Once we were in the room, I pulled him over to the windows, so we could look outside as the rest of the kids filed in. When they were all sitting down, I started to turn around, but Aiden grabbed my sleeve.

"Hey, sorry about earlier. You know, with the phone number? I thought about it, and I think I understand what that looked like to you. So here." He handed me a folded slip of paper, but his fingers pinched the edge of it, like he was being careful not to touch me. He kept ahold of the paper as I opened it and revealed his number.

"Oh! You didn't have to do that," I said, embarrassed. Why wasn't he releasing the paper? Seemed odd to hang onto it like this. "I could've asked for it, too. And I had no right to get all weird about it." *What is wrong with me?*

"Well, I also figured that since we live next door to each other, you should have it in case of emergencies or something. I bet Sarah would feel a lot more comfortable having the neighbor's number."

"Mr. Mors?" the instructor asked. We both glanced up.

"Yes?" Aiden replied, and then he smiled. "I'm here." He looked back at me and dropped his eyes to the piece of paper in our hands. He quickly let go and took a step back. "Sorry. Um, I'll just ... uh ... go."

I took my seat, all the time watching Aiden as he talked with the instructor about the seating arrangements and the itinerary. He wouldn't look at me, and I wondered what might be going through his head. I wasn't quite sure what was going on in mine. *Remember Shay?* It's not like I was pursuing Aiden or anything—far from it—but I guess it just felt good for him to connect with me. Every girl in school wanted to be near him, and he'd chosen to give me his phone number. Okay, I was second to get his digits. He was my neighbor, which meant it was almost a practical thing, but it still felt like something more. Like he thought I was special amongst all these sighing girls.

When the final bell rang and the last of the students took their seats, I caught Rena looking at me with questioning eyes. I was sure she'd noticed my expression, but I wasn't sure if she had any idea why I looked like that.

"Class, I'm sure you know who this is by now." The teacher waved her hand in Aiden's direction. "Aiden will need a lab partner for the rest of the year. Who would like to volunteer?"

All the girls' hands flew up, except for mine. I looked back at Rena to see if hers was raised, but she frowned at me.

"Rena," the instructor said, choosing my friend. "Thank you for volunteering to be lab partners with Aiden." She turned back to the teacher. "Rena will catch you up on things."

"Thank you," Aiden said.

"Rena," I said, whispering loudly so I'd be heard over the groans of girls who had not been chosen. "What's with the look?"

Her eyes went to Aiden as he made his way to a seat. "I saw you guys holding hands," she whispered back.

What? "But I didn't!" What was she talking about? "We weren't holding hands. Anyway, just don't tell Quinn you saw that."

"What does Quinn have to do with you holding Aiden's hand?"

I sighed. She didn't believe me. "Because she likes him."

"I didn't see him holding *Quinn's* hand," she said, regarding me skeptically. "I saw him holding *yours*. Don't you have a boyfriend?"

She turned away, and my stomach churned. She was mad at me. "But we *didn't*."

It didn't matter. She wouldn't even look at me.

"Okay," the instructor said. "Let's turn to page one fifty-three in the lab books and get started. Find your partner, then follow the instructions. If anyone gets stuck, please come to me for assistance."

The instructor sat at her desk while the rest of us proceeded to the back of the classroom.

"Hey, lab buddy," Aiden said to Rena. "You're Quinn's friend, right?"

"Yes."

I smiled and tried to get Rena's attention, but she still wouldn't look at me. She actually turned her back to me.

"Have you done this lab before?" she whispered to him, but loud enough for me to hear.

He looked the lab over and nodded. "Yeah. I um ... I did it a few months ago. I guess my old school was a little further ahead of you guys." He browsed through the book. "We had a different book, but most of the labs are similar."

"If you don't want to do the lab again, I can do this one alone."

"No way. You're the lucky one who got me as your lab partner since I've done most of these before. You'll get all the answers correct."

I worked in silence with my lab partner, Heather, measuring out various chemicals and dumping them into vials, glasses, and flasks. We watched how chemicals reacted differently when mixed with other liquids, changing when heated or cooled. The room was filled with chatter, laughing, and glasses clanking together. It almost sounded like a party. Aiden and Rena were the first to complete the assignment. They handed in their papers and sat back in their regular seats, waiting for the rest of the class to finish. I felt eyes on me and looked up. Rena watched me while she chatted with Aiden. *What's going on?*

The bell rang, and we all walked to gym class, though no one spoke to me. Once we were all there, Coach blew her whistle, and we quickly assembled around the grass center of the track. I stood next to Cali.

"Whoa. Get a look at Aiden," someone exclaimed in a noisy whisper. "He must work out, like, all the time!"

We all gawked. Yes, I'll admit it. My mouth dropped

open, too.

Aiden wore all black, with an Under Armour muscle shirt and shorts that showed off his tanned and muscular arms and legs. But my eyes had gone directly to the tattoo on his right upper arm.

A Triquetra symbol with red wings.

I was right.

None of this had been a coincidence.

"Okay, class," Coach said. "Today, we'll work on our golf game. Go on over and grab a putter appropriate for your height, and go to it." She held up one hand. "Now, please be mindful that this is *putting* and not *driving,* boys!"

She blew the whistle, and we went to the golf bag holding the many putters. We each randomly selected one.

"Hey—Cali, is it?" Aiden asked, stopping by us.

"Hi."

"Do you play golf?" he asked smoothly. *Could the guy even help himself?* "I play a wicked game of mini golf. We should go sometime."

She lifted one eyebrow. "Maybe we can double sometime with my boyfriend, Vash."

"Nice tattoo." I pointed at his arm. "Does it mean anything special?"

It did to me.

All Enlightens received a tattoo like that when they

turned eighteen. It marked them as a fighter for God. If Aiden was evil, he wouldn't have one, would he? I wished Kieran were there to see. He'd have all the answers.

Aiden had the good sense to look thrown off guard. "Uh, well, the wings symbolize ... um ... being free. And well, the triangle ... well, you probably don't know the technical name—"

"It's a Triquetra symbol." I shocked him into silence. "Does that mean something to you?" I asked again, looking directly into his eyes.

He hesitated. "No. It's just something I had the artist mix with the wings. It sort of reminds me of the Celtic symbols."

"Oh, I see. I'm curious. Why did you pick red for the wings? That's an interesting color choice."

He shrugged. "I thought most people would choose black or gray. There were some drawing samples of them. I wanted something unique to me, so I chose red."

Coach walked up behind us, clearing her throat. "Less talking and more putting, please," she said.

The rest of the students were practicing, but some were talking, too. They were also watching us being chewed out. To get out of the spotlight, we walked out toward an open area of the track and field area and started practicing. Cali, Luke, and Caden hit the golf balls as a threesome, which was fine. What *wasn't* fine was when Caden and Luke thought it would be funny to hit our golf balls with theirs. We ended up joining with them after a few strokes.

"How's your first day going, Aiden?" Cali asked.

"Great. I've met almost everyone in our grade, and all the teachers seem nice." He looked at me and smiled. As a result, everyone else looked at me, too. "I have to say, I don't think it would've been the same if I hadn't had the best babysitter ever to show me around."

I rolled my eyes. "Well, I sort of *had* to be the babysitter today since we have all the same classes."

"Hey, dude," Caden asked. "What's with you and Quinn?"

We all stopped what we were doing and stared. This could get interesting.

Aiden looked genuinely surprised. "Nothing. Why do you ask?"

"Well, I heard that you and her hit it off in your poly-sci class. And if I heard about it, I bet Morgan has, too. I'm warning you, dude. She has a mean streak—and by mean, I mean *crazy*. The last guy who broke up with her had his car keyed."

Aiden shrugged. "I met Quinn in class, but nothing else happened."

Caden stopped putting and leaned casually on his club.

"So you didn't give her your phone number?"

"Oh. That."

"Yes, *that*."

Aiden waved his hand, as if it really didn't mean anything. "Sure I did, but it's not a big deal. She asked if I was doing anything this weekend, and I told her I didn't have any plans yet. She told me to call her if I wanted to hang out or something."

Caden's gaze hardened. "You know she and I are dating, right?"

"No, I didn't, but I do now. She didn't say anything about it."

"We're going to prom together."

"Sorry, man." He shrugged.

Cali shook her head. "She'd better not get hurt by either of you, or else you'll be answering to us," she said. "We'll *all* be gunning for you, right, Zoe?" She elbowed me in the stomach to get my attention.

"Uh, yeah. So be nice to her."

After the final school bell rang, Kieran and I waited by my locker for Sidelle, Cali, and Vash.

"Going someplace fun for the night?" Aiden asked, sauntering over.

"Maybe. We always meet here after school," I told him. His gaze was suspicious. *What's that about?* I didn't need his permission to go anywhere. I didn't answer to him—or to anyone.

"We have plans," Kieran said.

"Oh, I didn't realize you were busy. You didn't mention it last night."

Something about his tone made me bristle. "Yeah, well, I didn't exactly think you needed to know. Besides, I'd just met you." I looked away, uncomfortable. "Maybe you can ask *Quinn* to hang out with you or something. I'm sure she'd love it."

Whoa, where had that come from? I liked Quinn. This wasn't her fault.

"Okay. Maybe I will," Aiden fired back.

"Kids, kids, kids. There's no need to fight," Sidelle scolded, glancing between us. "You guys can hang out another time. After all, you live next to each other. We've had this girls' night planned for a while. No boys allowed." She yanked my arm and whispered, "What's going on with you?"

"Kieran. Vash. Are you ready to go?" I asked, impatient. "We're waiting on you."

"I thought Sidelle just said 'no boys allowed,'" Aiden objected.

"Who, Kieran?" Sidelle giggled. "He's one of the girls."

He stared at Kieran, wide eyed. "Wow. Tough to be you. And Vash?"

Vash grinned. "Yeah, well, I'll be hanging around a bunch of beautiful women, and I plan to be the only man in the group." He draped one arm around my shoulder and the other around Cali's, and then he ushered us away. I didn't dare glance back, but I could feel Aiden's eyes on me the whole time.

Kieran, Sidelle, Vash, Cali, Jackson, and I gathered in Kieran's living room. A smile crept onto my face when I saw a Silico had been installed, just like the one at Vash's house. That meant Cali and I could continue our training.

Since I'd been busy as Aiden's babysitter, the day had gone by in a blur. I hadn't gotten the chance to ask Vash or Jackson how they were holding up, though I suspected they would both say they were fine and that I shouldn't worry. But still, I'd be a basket case. It'd be hard to lose a parent, never mind both at the same time. They were my friends. And friends were always there for each other.

"Sidelle came up with a brilliant plan for this weekend, including the two days off this Thursday and Friday," Kieran said, grinning. "She's even managed to cancel school by putting together a"—he curled his fingers into air quotes—"'teachers conference' in the Twin Cities. Smart move, Sid."

"Thanks," Sidelle said, but she frowned, deep in thought. "I was thinking we should go visit my father in Fairyland. We may or may not need the extra time, but once we enter Fairyland, we won't know how much time has passed until we get out. It could be a few days, or it could be a few weeks. We'll deal with that if it happens, and come up with some sort of story." She paced the large room. "We have to focus. We still don't know how the demons got onto pack territory, but the borders into Fairyland are all guarded by glamour, so no one can simply stumble into it. You have to know your way, and the Marqs don't. The DKs for sure won't."

"Cali," Vash said. "I want you to stay at the compound with Jackson and Era. That way I'll know you're safer being with the rest of the pack. Jacks, you'll be in charge while I'm gone, so you'll have to continue to monitor the lands and watch for strange behavior. The demons shouldn't have been able to penetrate the property but they succeeded. That means they had help. Find the traitor."

"Yes, Alpha," Jackson said gravely.

"Okay, Vash," Cali said with reluctance. "I'll go, but I need you to promise me something."

"Anything."

"You need to keep Zoe safe."

"Of course."

"Promise me, Vash. Say the words."

"I promise I will keep Zoe safe."

"Sidelle, Kieran. You need to do everything in your power to bring her back. She's my girl, and if anything happens to her—"

"We promise, Cali," Kieran said. "That's been our job all along."

"We need to come up with a story to tell your parents, Zoe," said Sidelle. "You stayed at Kieran's house last weekend, so maybe if you tell them you're staying with me, it'll be better. Let's tell them we have a huge final project to do. That isn't too much of a stretch, because the end of the school year is in six weeks. When we get back from the long weekend, the teachers are going to start piling on the homework and projects. I have it on good authority that we'll get a ginormous English project soon, and it'll require tons of research and writing. So you and I would be joined at the hip, even if we weren't going to my real home."

"That should work," I said. "My parents take school seriously, so they won't deny me study time, even if it's at someone else's house. Plus, they've met you a few times now. And if I bring Cali into the fold, the three of us can work on it together. That gives Cali an excuse, too. What do you think, Cali?"

"Yeah, but we have to come up with some sort of project, so we can describe it to them."

"Agreed," I said. "So let's think on it tonight and see what we come up with tomorrow. I'll tell my parents we haven't picked the topic yet. I'll say we still need clarification from the teacher." I smiled at Sidelle, already anticipating Fairyland. "Hey, Sid. What's it like? Your home, I mean. I've never asked you about it."

She shrugged. "Home is home. I live in Summer, which is like the weather in Minnesota during the summer months. Warm weather, flowers in bloom, rolling prairie grasses. We don't actually have a concept of time, so we count sundowns. The sun rises and falls when it wants to, which is why time passes in unequal intervals—"

"Let's talk about Aiden," Kieran interrupted. "Who else thinks there's something strange about him?"

"I will concede that there might be something a little bit off, but You just don't like him, for whatever reason," I said. "You've never liked him. I'm giving him a chance. Minnesota is far from California. A new person in a small town where everyone grew up knowing each other. I can imagine it's hard being new." I turned to Vash. "Right?"

"Zoe, it's just a feeling I get when he's around. Like he's hiding something."

"I don't trust him either," Sidelle added.

I shrugged. "So he hid the fact that he's an Enlighten. That's not enough to hate—"

They all stared at me. "Stop," Kieran said. "What do you mean by that?"

"He has the Mark."

"What? On his arm?"

"Yeah." I pointed at my own arm. "Where the angels get it. Right, Cali? You saw it in gym class today, right?"

She nodded. "It's a gold triangle with red wings around it."

Kieran's mouth snapped shut. "He's not a Nephilim, that much I'm sure of."

"He's not?" I asked. "Then he's an angel."

Kieran looked concerned. He shook his head slowly. "No. He's not that, either. Not as far as I can tell. And ... that's what worries me."

"What do you mean, he's not an angel? If he's not Nephilim or an angel, then what is he?"

"That's what I can't figure out, Zoe. And that's why we shouldn't trust him until we know for sure what he is."

"He's not a fairy?"

"No," Sidelle said. "He's definitely not a fairy."

"And he's not a wolf," Vash confirmed.

Sidelle frowned. "Plus, I couldn't Mind Walk him. I tried in class today. It's like he's blocking me. Just a little different from Zoe, but I don't think she's doing it on purpose. There's something similar in the way their minds works. I don't know for sure. It's strange."

That brought silence to the room, and we all considered what this might mean. I wondered—and not for the first time—if I could be wrong about Aiden. He obviously had a split personality that I couldn't figure out. When he was around Morgan, he didn't speak to me, but at home and during the rest of the day, he was pretty nice. Was that enough to not like the guy? Shouldn't I give him a chance to prove himself?

"Well, we aren't going to solve all the world's problems in one night." I got up from the soft leather couch. "Cali and I should get in some more training time."

"Yes," Cali exclaimed, grinning. "I totally agree."

"You guys practice. We'll keep talking about this," Kieran said.

"What's there to discuss?" I asked, selecting a helmet from the display shelf and strapping it onto my head. "I figure we have three things to do: one, get the pack to join us—done, two, go to Fairyland this weekend to visit the Summer King, and three, find out who Aiden is and what he's hiding."

I reached for another helmet, wanting to get started. Lucky for me, I'd chosen to wear yoga pants and a hoodie to school again today. Cali was only in a little pink sundress.

"I don't have anything to wear for this," she sulked, placing her helmet in her lap. "I didn't bring spare clothes with me."

"No worries," Sidelle said. "You're a size small?" She balled her fist as green glamour circled around her hand, and when she opened her palm, a pair of black pants hung from her fingertips. "Here you go. This should fit you. If not, I can adjust the size."

I never quite got used to how amazing glamour was, and Cali's jaw dropped. "That's amazing, Sidelle. Thank you. Now, Zoe can have a sparring partner."

She buckled her helmet into place and stood next to me on the floor mat Kieran had rolled out for us, and Vash and Jackson pushed the furniture to the outer walls. Sidelle took her usual spot on the couch so she could watch us. We started with a ten-minute warm-up exercise then launched into the program. Even though it had been a couple of days since we'd last trained with the simulator, my body moved like it had never skipped a day. Every move was right on, meaning I was no longer flailing around, like a massive swarm of bees was attacking me. I moved with surprising grace, though it was nothing like what Kieran looked like when he was in full battle mode.

"Level Three is more difficult," Vash said as he pushed "Pause." "First, remember everything you've learned so far. Core strength is found in your center." He patted his stomach. "Move from here and not your back. Second, remember the stances from Level Two, as this level you'll put them into longer sequences. As soon as the moves become second nature, we'll take you off the simulator and practice against real people. So maybe tomorrow we can start that." He grinned. "You guys have been doing a fantastic job, by the way."

With that, Vash pressed "Play." Our simulated bodies appeared on the screen, and I concentrated on doing the routine. I blocked out the real Cali standing next to me because I had to learn this. Like, *really* learn it.

My life had started making sense to me when I realized death could be right around the corner. I'd already witnessed the deaths of Vash's parents. This quest, this passage, had been tasked to me, so I needed to get going on my kick-ass plan. Not that I hadn't been taking it seriously before, but I hadn't fully comprehended the consequences until Keegan died. Sometimes, it takes a death before we truly understand we must live for something. And my something was to save the world.

Tuesday morning I decided to lay out the groundwork for the upcoming long weekend, hoping my trip into Fairyland would only take four days. I had no idea how I'd explain a month-long absence. Like Sidelle said, we'd cross that bridge if and when it came to that.

I walked down the stairs and into the kitchen where Dad was sitting at the table, reading the newspaper. I heard Mom in the laundry room.

"G'morning, Dad." I opened the cupboard, took down a bowl, then walked to the fridge.

"Morning, sweetheart." He peered over the paper. "Haven't seen Shay in a while. You still seeing that boy?"

The milk carton almost slid from my hand. "Gah, Dad.

Really?"

I didn't need him to remind me that my boyfriend was missing—or rather, taken by demons. At this precise moment, Shay was probably being tortured for information about me. I hoped he wouldn't tell them what they wanted to know, but I was painfully aware everyone had their breaking points. Especially under that kind of stress. I hoped he could hold on until we could find and rescue him.

"Whoa, there." Dad threw his hands up, dropping the newspaper onto his lap. "I'm just asking. If you're not, that's okay, too."

I shouldn't have snapped. "Sorry," I said. "I've been stressed lately. It's the end of my junior year, I've been thinking about colleges, and the teachers have realized that there are only six weeks left, so they're piling on homework with projects and final tests. Cali, Sidelle, and I have a huge project in English that the instructor announced yesterday. We haven't selected a topic yet, because Mr. Anderson needs to provide the parameters and—"

"Stop right there. Sorry I asked. I understand you're busy. Don't worry about it. Take one thing at a time. The rest will fall into place."

"Okay." I took a deep breath and sat at the table, cereal box in hand. "Since this week is a short week, the plan is to go to Sidelle's house so we can start on the project." I poured the round peanut butter balls of cereal goodness into the bowl, pleased with the story. After all, we *were* going to Sidelle's house. Only it wasn't actually in this world.

"Oh? What project is that?" Mom asked, entering the kitchen with a laundry basket.

"Zoe was telling me about an English project."

"I was explaining to Dad that we need more information before we can pick a topic, but Cali and I are planning to be at Sidelle's house this weekend, so we can get it started. Maybe even finish. Can I go?"

"Of course." She tilted her head, smiling. "I suspect that when you say 'Sidelle's house this weekend' you mean to say that you're planning to stay there the whole time?"

If she only knew. "Uh, yes. That's exactly what I mean. Is that okay with you guys? We'll either be there or at the library doing research. We might even take a trip into one of the larger libraries in Minneapolis."

"All right, but remember to eat ... and actually sleep some of the time."

"We will." I checked the wall clock and realized Kieran would be here any minute. I placed my bowl in the sink, grabbed my backpack, and ran out the front door.

Kieran's Cadillac sat on the driveway, and he was

leaning against the passenger side door. When he saw me, he smiled and slid his cell phone into his back pocket.

"Hey Z. I have some great news for you."

"You do? What?"

"We might have a lead on where Shay is."

It was good to hear there was at least *some* news. I ran to Kieran and gave him a hug.

"Where is he? Are we going to go get him? Is he hurt? He's still alive, right?" My stomach dropped from his silence. Sure, it was great news, but it wasn't what I'd hoped he was going to say. He had said the word "might."

"Hold on. I know you have lots of questions, but I actually don't know anything. Michael just told me that they have a lead, and they are taking the Reperio Team to check the authenticity of the source. We won't know anything until later today, but I thought you'd want to know."

"I do. Thank you, K." I hugged him again. "What's a Reperio Team?"

He grinned. "It's like the Green Berets of the angels. They find things."

That sounded positive. I nodded and moved on. "So it's all good for this weekend. You're coming with me, right?"

"Of course. Where you go, I go. It's always been that way and always will be."

I knew what Kieran said was true, but I didn't like what he was implying. Consciously or unconsciously, he was reminding me that the Orders of the Enlightens don't mix. Both Kieran and I were angels. Shay was a Nephilim. That meant we were not allowed to be together. It was just one more obstacle that Shay and I would have to overcome.

Kieran drove us to Coffee Grind, and we met up with Cali, Vash, Jackson, and Sidelle. I told them I was good to go for the weekend, and Cali said she was, too.

"Oh, and I have some great news," I said. "Kieran told me the angels might have a lead on Shay."

"Oh, Zoe," Cali exclaimed. "That's wonderful. I knew they'd find him."

"They haven't yet, so I'm trying to not think about it too much, or the shape he'll be in when they do rescue him. But it's a start."

"He'll be all right, Zoe," Vash assured me. "He's strong."

"And he'll come back to you," Sidelle said. "Because he knows you'll kick his ass if he doesn't."

I smiled as I headed over to order my caffeine fix. Shay had to be okay. He just *had* to be.

"You doing all right?" Jackson asked, sidling up to me. I hadn't heard him approach.

I nodded. "I'm better now, knowing the angels are

actually looking for Shay."

"My guess is Kieran is the one who nudged them to continue to look for him. He'd do anything for you."

"I know."

He cleared his throat and looked down at the floor. "It's not my place," he said quietly, "but I see the way he looks at you. He loves you, you know."

"I know, but I don't see him like that. Shay and I were meant to be together."

He shrugged. "Can't comment on that one because I've never met Shay. All I know is what I see in front of me."

"Thanks, Jacks. I appreciate you stepping up and saying that." The girl behind the counter smiled at me, and I ordered my usual chai tea latte before turning back to Jackson. "Hey, how are you and Vash doing? I haven't asked you since ... you know."

"It's tough, but we'll get through it. Vash will be a great Alpha. He *is* a great Alpha. And it's better now because he has Cali. It would've been harder if she hadn't been here to support him. If he hadn't found her when he did, I don't know if he'd be where he is today. She makes him stronger."

"How are *you* doing?" I touched his arm.

He sighed. "One day at a time. We all know this life is hard, but to see my father beaten like that? To have the demons kill him in front of his own pack and on our own property, well, that was brutal. And they *will* pay for it."

"I'm here for you if you ever want to talk or whatever."

"Thanks, Z."

"Order up for Zoe," the barista called.

I picked up the large white cup, and we walked back to our group.

"Some of the pack should go with the Reperio Team," Vash was saying. "If they run into Marqs—and I bet there will be some wherever they are holding Shay—we can distract them enough to get Shay out."

Kieran was nodding. "So instead of a recon mission, a rescue; we'll skip a step."

Vash nodded. "Plus, I'm betting some of the pack would welcome the opportunity to knock off a few more Marqs as a tribute to Keegan."

"I'll let Michael know. They can swing by the compound and pick up whoever you want to go."

"Why don't you and I go to my place to coordinate efforts? Jackson can stay here to watch over Cali and Zoe. It's easier than all this go-between."

"Sure. Zoe?" Kieran asked. "You okay if I'm gone for the day?"

"I'll be fine," I said. "Sidelle's here, too."

Sidelle crossed her arms. "Yeah. What am I, chopped

liver? The pup and I can handle things for a few hours. Today, we'll continue as normal: school, then we'll go to K's house to run another simulator level."

"All right. It's settled." Kieran nodded.

We piled into our respective vehicles to go to school, and on the short drive over, I let myself dream that I might see Shay that night.

"Oh, hey, K," I said as we pulled into the parking lot. "You know that red car at the far end?"

"Yes? What about it?"

"I've seen it before. Maybe last week. There's something familiar about it, but I can't put my finger on it. It's been driving me crazy."

He shrugged and pulled into his usual spot in the last row. "It has to be someone new. Maybe it's Aiden's because Jackson doesn't get his license until this summer."

"I've seen it around town, but that was *before* Aiden moved in next door."

"Maybe you saw a car like it?"

"Yeah, maybe." I shook my head. "But it's pretty unique. We don't get high end sports cars in town, this far out of the cities. They all look the same to me."

"It is a super special edition. Audi only made one hundred in that specific model of the R8 GT V10 Spyder."

I stepped out of the passenger side seat, swinging my

bag over my shoulder. "Of course you'd know what make and model it is. Boys and their toys."

Kieran escorted me into the building and to my locker. He leaned against the wall until Sidelle arrived.

"Okay," he said, smiling at her. "Changing of the guards. I'll be back as soon as I can."

I watched Kieran leave the same way we'd come. My stomach had tied itself into knots, so I tried not to think about Shay. There was no way I was going to work myself up when the mission was based on a lead, not facts. I wouldn't get excited until I held Shay in my arms.

The day progressed like any other. As Sidelle had warned, the teachers piled on the homework, apparently forgetting that this was a short week and the year was almost over. Nothing strange or out of the ordinary occurred, and I didn't have to babysit Aiden. In fact, he wasn't even at his locker in the morning. He was in all of my classes, but the teachers kept us busy the whole time, so I never got an opportunity to talk with him.

By lunchtime, a massive headache muscled its way in, so I was glad I had this one hour to relax and not worry about equations, reading assignments, or the history of whatever. Our table members were noticeably fewer than yesterday. Aiden sat with the Triangles and the other preppies, which was fine with me. He needed to branch out and make his own friends. Then I saw him lay his hand on Morgan's thigh, which confused me. I thought he liked Quinn. That two-timing, no good—

"It's not like that, Zoe," Quinn said, following my gaze. "We're not dating or anything. He's free to do whatever he wants and be friends with whomever." She glanced around. "Where's Kieran?"

"He had to stay after in one of his classes." I took a bite of my sandwich. "I just thought that you guys kinda hit it off yesterday."

"We did, but it's not like you can fall in love the first time you see—Plus, I'm dating Caden."

She stopped when I gave her a sharp look. Shay and I had known. Well, maybe not the *first* time. It had taken a few days, but the first time I'd seem Shay fighting off those two DKs, I decided he was the hottest guy I'd ever laid eyes on. When we found out what the electrical current between us meant, that had sealed it.

"Oops, sorry, Z. That's yours and Shay's story. But for others, it's different. That's all I'm saying. Yes, there's something there, but I didn't see stars. So don't go over there and make a scene."

I tried to look shocked at the suggestion. "Me? Make a scene in front of the Triangles? Never."

She giggled. "If it's meant to be, it'll happen on its own.

Besides, I heard that Caden told him we were going to prom together."

I decided to drop it since she apparently wanted me to. "Do you guys think Aiden looks like Shay?"

"You still on that?" Sidelle asked.

"Yes, because you and Kieran don't think so."

"Maybe a tad," Cali said. "It's the eyes and hair, but different, you know?"

"That's what they both said." I tilted my head toward Sidelle. "But I—"

"It's been a while since I've seen Shay," Rena said. "Is he out sick?" She frowned. "Zoe, I'm sorry I was being a bitch to you. I don't know what I saw between you and Aiden and I know you wouldn't hurt any one of us intentionally."

"Let's just pretend that lab never happened." I nodded to her.

Pushing thoughts of Shay from my mind, I enjoyed the rest of lunch. Just hanging with the girls did small wonders for my mind and spirit. It was a nice change from all the heaviness going on in my life. But I felt guilty for trying to ignore my heart's pull.

At the end of gym, I was finally able to snag Aiden's shirt. "How was your second day of school?" I asked.

"Good. Getting to know everyone."

With that he headed into the boys' locker room, leaving me dumbfounded. Wow, was that a brush off or what? I'd have to ask him about that if he was at his window tonight. A little miffed, I entered the girls' locker room to change, reminding myself that in a few more hours, Shay might—I erased that thought, unwilling to get my hopes up only to have them dashed. Shay was still missing.

I met Sidelle outside the gym doors. "You ready to go to K's?" she asked. "Did you bring clothes to change into?"

"Yep, I'm all set," I said. "Is Cali meeting us there?"

"No. We'll swing by her locker after this. Vash would have Jackson's hide if he wasn't with her at all times. If anything were to happen to Cali on his watch—"

"I get it." I stuffed notebooks and textbooks into my purple backpack. We walked down toward Cali's locker as the school emptied for the day.

Endless screams and groans echoed into the halls, but I couldn't see the agonized sources. I had no idea where I was or how many days I had been chained here. The room was dark, and I could barely see, even with my enhanced vision. I managed a few steps forward but was soon jerked to a stop by the thick shackles wrapped around my wrists and ankles. Reinforced metal, probably dipped in the River Styx. There was no way I would ever escape from here. Not without help.

Help.

They would come for me. Someone would. I was a warrior, and warriors leave no man behind, leave no comrade behind. In this case, it was leave no Nephilim.

A deep voice penetrated the darkness, reverberating against the cold walls. "I see you're finally awake."

"Is this the point where you say you're going to torture me?" I kept my voice low, not wanting my fear to show.

His smug laughter rumbled through the cell. "Your stay here won't be pleasant, Nephilim. Not at all. Now, sit back and relax, and I'll let you ponder things for a bit while I go topside and scout things out for myself."

In the next moment, a figure appeared inside my cell. I couldn't make out any distinguishable features, except that he was around my height and weight. Before I could say a word, an arm shot out from under his long, black robes, and his fingers curled into a ball. Even though he wasn't touching them, the chains constricted suddenly, slamming me back against the cold stone wall.

"Rumor is," hissed the voice, "there's a pretty young thing out there with green eyes and brown hair. They say she could be the one the Eternals have been looking for. The buzz around town is that she's been hiding in Minnesota ..."

He found her?

A finger pointed in my direction and twitched. My body slammed face first into the hard cement ground. I gritted my teeth, holding in my pain, but when I clenched my hands, the chains rattled.

"I see that got your attention," he said, his confident voice slithering over my skin. "I might have to go check this little bombshell out for myself, find out if she's worth all the hubbub I'm hearing. Maybe I'll make her an offer she can't refuse." He bellowed. "Well, she could try, I suppose, I have ways to make *her* accept my offer. I have you to barter with. Think she'll trade?"

Damn it. It is about Zoe.

I shook my head, then coughed when a metal collar suddenly appeared and clamped around my neck. It squeezed until it became a perfect fit, slowly drawing the chain into the wall until it was taut. I had to stand on my tiptoes to take some of the pressure off my neck.

"Still nothing?" He shrugged. "No problem. I don't actually need you to be alive for this. *She* might want her soul mate to still be breathing, but that's not in my plan."

"Leave Zoe alone!" I screamed, though my voice was muffled by the collar. I tried to move, but the metal barriers kept me in place. Another bracket wrapped snugly around my waist.

"Ah, there it is." He sounded pleased. "I've been wondering how long it would take for you to connect the dots. Yes, I know what's going on. You, an angel, and a fairy have been protecting a seventeen-year-old girl."

He turned away from me, and I saw a long sword

strapped to his back. The sheath was made of obsidian from the deepest places of Hell, and it carried a reddish hue. With deliberation, he withdrew the hilt and extended the long silver tip until it scratched my throat.

"She's nothing, you know."

"She's not nothing," I replied thickly, feeling fury beat in my temples. "She will beat you. You will fail at whatever plan you have. We will stop you from unleashing demons onto Earth."

"Oh, really? How do you expect to do that if you're here in Hell, and she's up there without you, unprotected? I've sent many minions to capture her, you know. Or kill her. Makes no difference to me."

The sword's tip scratched, and I felt a warm trail of blood trickle down my neck. My skin burned from the blade, and I gasped. He had dipped it into Hell's river. *Bastard.*

"They'll come for me," I managed. I tried to wrench my body away from the blade, but he didn't move. The searing cut went a bit deeper.

"You sure about that, Shay? Listen, before I leave you, I've decided I'll give you a parting gift. Something to remember me by." He scorned. "Not that you'd forget about me any time soon. After all, I *am* memorable."

He held the sword up at my eye level, bringing it just

close enough that I could see waves of heat rising from the edge. Suddenly, he pressed the flat side of the sword against my cheek. I screamed but heard nothing, saw nothing, but red behind my eyelids. The stink of my burning skin filled the air. When the iron finally left my face, I collapsed against the chains, but the stranger wasn't done with me. He thrust the tip of the sword deep into my shoulder, giving me a souvenir to remember him by. Twisting the blade and easing it in, scorching my insides as it dug through, shredding my muscles. All at once he withdrew it, and I gasped in what breath I could—just before he slashed my chest, slicing through my T-shirt and leaving a giant, burning X on my skin. White stars shot through my vision, and my legs gave out. I slumped forward against the shackles. My sweat and tear-slicked chin dropped to my smoking chest, and my breaths came in jerking, strained gulps.

From behind my closed eyes, I realized the room had lightened, casting a reddish hue over everything. The figure finally emerged from the shadow, and I squinted, needing to determine who stood in front of me. A pair of shiny, black combat boots stepped toward me, and I used every bit of remaining strength to lift my face to see his. I stared in disbelief at the man before me: young and blond ... with eyes just like mine.

I climbed out of Sidelle's Mini Cooper and stepped onto Kieran's driveway. "Zoe," Sidelle shouted, slamming her door shut. "The angels. They know where the demons are keeping Shay!"

"Nope." I shook my head. "Not listening. I can't get my hopes up then hear it didn't pan out."

She beamed. "I know, but this time they do know where he is."

My eyes narrowed. "How?"

"Kieran just told me." She tapped the side of her head.

"No. I mean, how do they know the intel is good?"

"Remember when Kieran told you that not all demons are evil? We initially thought they all were, but some are tolerable. Sometimes DKs aren't so bad. Especially, when they aren't trying to kill you. We've made peace with a few of them over the centuries. We trade favors when it's needed, though angels don't have much to offer them. Anyway, one of them said that Shay's being held in the dungeons."

I felt sick. "Is he alive?" I whispered.

"I don't know."

Moving like a zombie, I walked into Kieran's house, tossed my backpack onto the kitchen floor, and continued to the den, my favorite room in the house. The floor-to-ceiling windows overlooked the backyard and gave a clear view of the angel statue that kept watch over the house. All I could think about was getting Shay back, but what condition would they find him in? *Please hold on, Shay. Just a little longer. We're coming for you.*

"Zoe?" Sidelle asked.

Sidelle placed a comforting hand on my shoulder but didn't speak. With that small touch, she knew what I was thinking and feeling, even if I didn't—or couldn't—express it.

Jackson and Cali entered the small room while Sidelle and I gazed out of the window. No one spoke, and that was all right—for a while. Eventually, the silence got too heavy even for me. Fortunately, Cali sensed that as well.

"Zoe?" she said quietly. "I brought your bag from the kitchen. I thought you might need it to change clothes."

"Thanks, but I don't feel like training. I'm too worried about Shay."

"We understand," Jackson said. "But there's nothing you can do to help him right now, so you might as well do another level."

"Or," Sidelle suggested, "she could practice her angelic powers."

I plopped down onto the love seat. "But I don't know any others except for the protection orbs."

"That's why you'll practice, silly. So let's see what else you've got in there."

I let out a long sigh. They were right. I could do nothing for Shay from here anyway. Sulking wouldn't bring him back to me sooner, so I might as well do something productive.

"All right. Let's do this." I tilted my head and heard my neck pop. "If you want to practice more and go onto another level, you should," I said to Cali. "Jackson can be your sparring partner."

"Nah," Cali said. "I'll watch you for now. I can do levels this weekend at the compound. And maybe I'll be kicking some puppy butts."

I laughed, and she curled into the corner on the opposite

side of the couch while Jackson paced the room.

Sidelle sat in the wingback chair across from me. "Let's start with something simple," she said. "Focus. Zoe, I want you to close your eyes and listen to your inner self. Visualize the times when your protective orbs came out. You need to understand what you were thinking and feeling when your Angel Light appeared."

Those times were easy to recall. The first had happened unintentionally after the DKs had chased Kieran and me into the warehouse. That was also when I'd first met Shay. No. Not now. I shook my head to clear him from my mind. The second was in the woods in the back of Cali's house; the same night I learned Sidelle was a fairy. Then I thought back to the third time, which was the night when the Marqs had come to my house and killed Cali. The fourth time the orb had appeared was when the demons had attacked the pack's compound.

During the first episode, I'd been scared to death. The second time, well, yes, I'd been scared, but I was mad, too. And the last one? Oh, anger had rolled off me. She asked me to concentrate on those feelings, try to bring those emotions to my mind. She wanted me to produce the orb again, so I tried to clear my mind, and imagined being scared and angry.

It only took a moment for me to realize that wouldn't

work. Sitting here, safe in Kieran's house, I didn't have any worries. I wasn't mad, and nothing could hurt me.

"Okay," Sidelle said with a sigh. She leaned forward and placed her hands on the sides of my face. "Let me read you. Open your mind up to me."

A vivid motion picture began to play in my mind, and I saw again the first experience I'd had with demons. Sidelle hadn't even been there, but when she lightly tapped my ears, a flood of sounds rushed in—screams, battle cries, and the clanging of swords. Everything became terrifyingly familiar. The coppery smell of fresh blood heightened my senses even more. Everything about it was so real. Then the memory rolled right into the next one.

My body started to tremble. Experiencing the attacks firsthand had been one thing: reliving them was a whole other story. Everything came roaring back, and I became emotionally overloaded with the sights, sounds, and smells.

I lost myself.

When a DK ran at me, my arms lifted, and my hands grew warm. I thrust them out, shooting purple Angel Light from my palms and hitting the demon's center mass. The light enveloped him then imploded, taking him with it.

"Zoe!" Sidelle's voice echoed in the distance. "Zoe, it's not real. They're not here. Open your eyes!"

I did, blinking at all the stunned faces staring at me. I tried to focus, but I felt exhausted beyond words. I slumped back into the couch.

"Whoa, there," Sidelle said, giggling. "Rest a bit."

I calmed my breaths. Inhale. Exhale. When I was ready, I leaned forward and looked past Sidelle's shoulder. Where the fireplace had been, there now existed a massive hole in the wall, giving us an open view of the outside. Brick and mantle lay in a pile of rubble. How did that happen?

I sniffed, confused. "Why is there a burning smell in the air? Did I ... did I do that?" My eyes widened.

"Yeppers," Sidelle said. "You sure did. It's safe to say that when you're scared, you release your Light. But you can't control it yet. You need to figure out how to call it when you're calm." She walked over to the hole and peeked outside. She grinned back at me. "Kieran will never know." As soon as she placed her hands on the wall, the room vibrated a little, and the brick and wooden mantle started to reassemble.

I stared at Sidelle, in a kind of trance. "Whatever you did, it seemed so real. I got lost in it."

"Then I did it correctly. Good thing no one was in your way when your Light shot out. That'd be a bigger mess. Kieran might have noticed that."

"What happened?" I asked.

"Z, you were awesome," Cali said, sounding impressed. "You should have seen yourself. You stood, and we could tell something was happening around you. We watched your transformation. Your body seemed resolved, like you were ready to fight back. You were all calm. Then it was like electricity—the air around you actually crackled. Then you raised your hands, and a purple light streamed out, smashing the wall."

"It was cool," Jackson agreed.

"So," I said slowly, "I need to work on that. Is there something else I should try?"

"Let's do something easy," Sidelle said.

"I thought you said that last one was supposed to be easy."

"It was." She frowned. "Well, maybe not for you. Anyway, do the same thing as before. Close your eyes and focus. Listen to my voice and search within yourself."

When I was ready, Sidelle lightly pushed a finger on my forehead. "What do you see?"

"Nothing."

"You're not focusing. You're speaking."

I snapped my mouth shut and folded my hands in my lap. Suddenly, I saw what she meant. It was like I had eyes traveling around my brain. They moved to my arms and down to my legs, wildly spinning. I spotted a silver spark floating behind my right knee. It flashed and zipped up toward my head, and I jerked back, momentarily losing my focus. When I reconnected, I found the flicker near my left ear, and I had the strangest feeling it was leading me to where it needed me to be. When it burst out of my body, the expression "seeing stars" came to mind. I opened my eyes and stared as it pulsed in the air, bouncing all over the room. I had no idea what it was or if anyone else could see it.

I caught Cali's expression. Yep, they could see it, too.

"What is that?" I whispered.

"Beats the heck out of me," Jackson said.

Cali shook her head.

"I think ... I think it's part of your Angel Light," Sidelle mused.

"But my Light is purple." I rose from the couch and cornered the spark. "That is ... "

I didn't know how to explain it, but the tiny piece of energy felt like a safety blanket, wrapping around me. I extended my hand, and the little white light landed on my palm, spreading warmth through my body. As we all watched, the Light sank into my skin, almost burning me.

Suddenly, a silver Triquetra symbol appeared on the inside of my wrist. I traced a finger over the mark, and it flared, settling into a shimmering, iridescent color. No tattoo artist could ever have made a color that sparkled like that.

"Look!" I showed them all my hand. "I've got the Mark of an Enlighten."

Cali frowned at it. "But where are the wings?"

I stared at my wrist. "I don't know. Maybe I don't get them until I turn eighteen." I craned my neck to check my back. "I don't, right?"

"No, Zoe, you're not sportin' any wings back there," Sidelle assured me. "I do have to say, though, that you aren't getting anything in the order that everyone else does. First, you can create protective orbs, and now, you have only part of the Heaven's Mark."

"Maybe this means that I'm *not* an Eternal?"

"I doubt it. You'll still be an angel."

I knew she was indirectly reminding me that Shay and I couldn't be together. Fact was, he'd have to live out the rest of his life, and I'd watch him die of old age.

"Oh, my gosh." All heads snapped in my direction. "I just remembered something that happened in the kitchen when you were telling me about ... well, never mind. That's not the important thing. What I wanted to say was I think I moved a pop can that night."

"What?" Cali asked.

"Really?" Sidelle squinted her eyes.

"Yes, so maybe I should try moving things."

"Yeah. Can you do that?" Cali asked, clapping her hands.

Sidelle shrugged. "Sure. Let's—"

A loud crash came from the kitchen, and we all stared at each other in alarm. No one besides us should have been in the house. If someone was coming, the angel statue should've warned us somehow.

Urgent voices floated toward us, and we bolted toward the kitchen.

"Here. Lay him down."

Kieran?

"Move everything off the table," someone else said.

We arrived in time to see someone swipe an arm across the kitchen table. Two other men—or rather, angels—laid a body on top, and I caught the sight of familiar blond hair.

Shay!

I shoved someone out of the way to get to him, and then I gasped in horror. He wasn't the same young man he'd been before. A blister from some kind of terrible burn swelled on one cheek, and there was a cut on his throat that looked inflamed. His clothes were shredded, he was missing a boot, and an angry welt had formed across his chest in the shape of an X. A blood-soaked bandage had been wrapped around his shoulder. He wasn't conscious.

With trembling fingers, I stroked his matted hair. He

twitched, and I stopped mid-stroke, afraid to hurt him more.

"Shay. What did they do to you?" I whispered.

"Zoe," Kieran said softly, his eyes sad. "He's been through a lot. We should let the angels fix him the best they can, then let him rest. When he's ready, we'll move him to his bedroom, so he's more comfortable."

He placed his hand on the small of my back and tried to usher me away. I knew what he said was true; I needed to let them do their work, but I also needed to make sure Shay was okay.

At least he was alive.

"Okay." I leaned in and placed a kiss on Shay's cheek. "You're safe now," I whispered and stepped away.

Vash came crashing through the back door, almost colliding with Sidelle, Cali, and Jackson, who were gathered behind me. He stopped, looked around, then scooped up Cali and hugged her.

"You okay?" he asked. "I felt Jackson's panic through the pack bond."

"She's fine," Jackson said. "Nothing happened today. Well, nothing that we couldn't handle, anyway."

"What?" Kieran asked. "Come on. Let's go into another room and talk."

"No," I said softly. "You guys go. I'm staying here."

I watched Michael and Gabriel work, watched their hands fly over Shay's battered body. Every now and then, Shay would groan, but he never opened his eyes or said a word. Michael dissolved Shay's T-shirt and removed all the dried blood from his face and chest. Gabriel unwrapped the gauze and tried to clean the wound, but he shook his head.

"It's not working," he said. "Whatever they used on him to make this cut, my grace isn't healing him like it should."

"I can't fix his chest, either." Michael scratched his forehead, looking confused. "We'll know more when he wakes. He should be able to tell us something then."

"When will that be?" I asked.

"I don't know," Gabriel said. "I guess when he's ready to face whatever it is he's hiding from." He dressed both wounds with new bandages and then outfitted Shay in a comfortable pair of pajama bottoms. "We'll take him to his room to rest. You can watch over him there, if you'd like."

I nodded because I couldn't get anything else out. The damage would leave awful scars. Shay's perfect body would always be marred, and it would be a constant reminder to him of his time in whatever hellish prison he'd been kept in. I didn't care that his chest wasn't flawless anymore, but I was worried about how the memories would affect him.

By the time I had figured out which bedroom was Shay's, his dad had already tucked him under the covers. Gabriel nodded then flashed out of the room, leaving Shay and me alone. I trudged over, afraid to wake him, but also afraid he might never awaken. He looked so peaceful, tucked under the blankets, but I knew better. His arm muscles twitched, a silent indication that he was anything but. Behind the burned cheek, he ground his teeth. Every so often, he'd groan, making me think he was remembering what I suspected was some kind of torture.

I lay on the bed, facing him, wishing he could just open his eyes and smile at me. Very, very carefully, I placed one hand on his cheek, to avoid the awful blister.

"I'm not sure if you can hear me," I said, my voice cracking. "I've missed you so much. Tons of stuff happened this past week that's been important, and I wished you were there with me. I thought of you every day and hoped you were okay."

I sniffed, but I was determined not to cry. He needed me to be strong. He needed to hear my voice, know I was there for him.

"I asked God to keep you safe. Kieran kept telling me to have faith, that they'd find you, but I was afraid to believe him. I'm just so happy you're here now. You're safe. And that's what's important."

I rambled on, hoping my voice might somehow reach him, bring him back. I told Shay's sleeping form about the demon attack on pack land, letting him know who had died and informing him that now Vash was the Alpha. I told him how I'd used my Angel Light, about the new guy at school, and about Kieran's misgivings about Aiden. I told him about my brand- new tattoo, but teased that he'd have to wait to see it. I told him we were planning to go to Fairyland this coming weekend, and how Sidelle's brilliant suggestion to the school had made that possible. I even talked to him about mundane stuff like homework, of course that led to the topic of prom.

"You'd better be well enough to take me, Shay." I snuggled my body closer to his. "I won't let you back out of it."

"How's he doing?" Kieran whispered, tiptoeing into the room. "Any better?"

"He hasn't woken up, but he seems more relaxed." I motioned for Kieran to come closer, though I was cautious not to move the bed too much. "At least he's stopped twitching."

"That's a good sign."

"Yeah, maybe." I let out a long breath. "He's been through a lot. I can see it in his face."

"Zoe, you should prepare yourself. Shay might not want

to share whatever happened to him while he was in Hell. My guess is it's traumatic and—"

"Is that where they found him? In Hell?"

"Yes."

"He should talk to someone about it. He can't keep something like that bottled up. It's not healthy. When he's ready, and if he doesn't want to talk to me about it, will you?"

"Of course."

"Thanks, K."

Kieran patted my shoulder and left the room. I stayed next to Shay for a few more hours. When the moon started to peek through his window, I knew it was time for me to go. I wanted to stay, to be the first person Shay saw when he awoke, but I had to get home by ten for my parents. Reluctantly, I lifted my body away from Shay's then stood and stared down at his soft blond hair. I moved a strand away from his face and imagined his aqua eyes opening. I backed away from his bed, still watching, not wanting to miss any movement, no matter how small. That's when I noticed his body cast a slight glow, and I began to wonder.

People seemed to think I'd eventually develop even more abilities than the Archangels. After all, I had brought Cali back from the dead.

What if I *could heal Shay?*

I bent over the bed, focusing like Sidelle had said earlier, looking deep inside myself. I had no idea what I was searching for. I had to hope something would show me the way. And just like that, there it was: a faint purple light, flickering in my chest, pulsing in time with my heartbeat. *Thump. Thump. Thump.*

I held thoughts of healing and calmness in my mind. I expanded them, imploring Shay to open his eyes. As my thoughts expanded, so did the light. It moved toward my arm, and when I extended my hand and laid it on his chest, something magical happened. Purple Angel Light shot out from my fingers and created a glow in the room, and this time it was so intense that I stumbled back. Determined, I placed my palm against Shay's chest, refocused, then forced my Light into him. His white Nephilim Light connected, then mixed with mine, creating a swirling effect.

I could do this. I could heal Shay, take away whatever those demons had done to him.

Feeling more confident, I pressed my forehead against Shay's and opened my mind to his. The experience was shocking, like climbing over a brick wall that divided a calm meadow from a war zone. His thoughts were in turmoil. Pictures flashed, showing me a darkened cell, silver chains, black blood, and yet my face kept appearing in his memories. Every time my image appeared, his body and mind stilled, but it wasn't long before the gore would start up again. I realized he was trying to find his way back from the darkness using thoughts of me.

"Follow my voice," I whispered mentally. *"I'm here with you, Shay. Come back to me."*

His body appeared in my mind, as clear as if I'd opened my eyes. I reached for him, and he sprinted into my waiting arms. His fingers twined through a fist full of my hair, and he breathed me in. A slight tremor ran through his body. Pain or joy?

"Are you here, or am I imagining this?" He inhaled again. *"Or maybe I don't care. I think you are, and that's good enough for me."*

"Shay, I am here. I'm in your mind, and I am physically standing over your body at Kieran's house. You just have to open your eyes. Open them, Shay. Come back to me."

"Don't go." He shook his head, burying his face in my hair. *"Stay with me a little longer. How are you here?"*

I stepped back. *"I love you, Shay, and I will always find you. But you have to wake up now. I need you, Shay."*

I took another step away from him, then another. Inch by inch, I walked backward with my arms extended in silent encouragement. He followed me, and we joined hands when we neared the swirling Light.

"Are you ready?" I asked.

He nodded.

"Don't worry, Shay. I will be with you."

I felt his absolute trust in me as I guided him through the barrier. It was warm and secure in my heart.

Back in the real world, his chest heaved under my palm. I lifted my head, waiting. All at once, his body arched, and then he lay still.

"Wake up, Shay."

His eyes twitched then opened. Without moving his head, he glanced around, and when he saw me, he smiled, though it looked like a painful effort.

"Hi." I blew out a deep breath and tried desperately not to cry. "Don't try to move. How are you feeling?"

"Like I've been to Hell and back." His voice was husky and exhausted, but it was his voice.

"So you're ready to run a marathon with me, then?"

"Yeah. Just give me a few hours."

He reached up, cringed, but still managed to touch my cheek. I could barely breathe through the emotion swelling my throat.

"Thank you, Zoe. I've missed you so much. I'm so sorry I wasn't there for you when you needed me the most. I heard what you said while I was out of it, though, and it was your voice that helped me when I was there. You pulled me back. You have no idea what it was like—" His voice caught as he tried to rise. "But I don't need to burden you with that. I'm just happy we're together."

"Me, too." Very carefully I embraced him, then forced him to lie back. He felt so good against my body, but I pulled away. Surprising me, he grabbed the back of my head and brought it down for a kiss—and not just any kiss. In it I felt all his swirling emotions: rage, happiness, and sorrow. I had almost forgotten the electrical shock that raced between us. With his good arm, he tossed the covers off. He also accidentally ripped his bandage.

"Your chest looks better," I said, impressed. The giant X was already scabbed over and had turned pink. "Well, okay. Your chest always looks good. I meant your injury."

He lowered his chin. "Really?"

"It's not as red as it was before when the angels first brought you here. In fact, I'd say it's almost healed." Then I remembered. "Look!" I squeezed his hand and turned them both over, so he could see my tattoo. "We're not sure why I only got the Triquetra symbol, though."

"It's beautiful on you." He kissed my Mark. "This is special to receive this Mark from God, and that's why you got it now, instead of having to wait until you're eighteen."

He winced, reminding me that the best thing for him right now would be sleep.

"I have to get home." I dug out my cell and checked the time. "My parents are going to have a cow. I was supposed to be there already." I tilted my head, gazing into those beautiful eyes I loved so much. "But I want to stay here."

"No. You go. I don't want you to get in trouble on my account." He attempted another smile. "How're we going to go to Fairyland if you're grounded?"

"You're in no condition to go to Fairyland, Shay. You need to stay here and rest."

The smile disappeared. "I'm not leaving you again." He tried to rise once more but stopped when the pain got to be too much. He grabbed his shoulder and grunted, then collapsed back onto the bed.

"See?"

"Oh! You're awake, Bull's Eye." Sidelle bounded into the room. "I thought I heard kissing sounds."

"Be nice, Sid," I said quietly. "I have to get home. Will you watch over him?"

"I'm not an invalid." Shay clutched his stomach and sat partway up. "I'm almost as good as new."

"Listen here." Sidelle pushed him back down. "Don't make me become Nurse Meany. You wouldn't like it. Now, do as you're told and rest."

I gazed down at him, reluctant to go. "I'll leave you in her capable hands." I leaned over and kissed him again.

"Behave."

"Love you, my Angel." Shay blew me a kiss.

"Loves ya back." Not wanting him to see my tears, I turned and walked out of the room.

I didn't bother telling Sidelle how Shay had recovered so quickly; I didn't quite know myself. He had once told me the Nephilim had better vision and enhanced speed, but he'd never said if that included healing. I assumed it did. In that case, the fast recovery could be his own body's doing, and not me at all.

As I walked home with Kieran, a great weight lifted from my heart. We didn't speak since I was wrapped in thoughts of Shay. He was back and in one piece, though I'd have to wait and see if his mind was still the same. I couldn't imagine what being kept in Hell would be like, but I'm sure if it had been me, I'd be a changed person.

"Be safe, Zoe," Kieran said as I unlocked the front door. I noticed the table wasn't set, and the kitchen was cleaned. My family's rule was dinner would be served at five-thirty, and if you weren't there, you were on your own. I broke an English muffin apart and popped it into the toaster. The few minutes it took felt like a lifetime for my grumbling stomach. In all my haste to practice my powers and tend to

Shay, I'd forgotten to eat. Rummaging through the fridge, I took out jelly and cheese, and when the toaster chimed, I made a sandwich and sprinted to my room. After dropping my backpack on the floor, I went to the window and peeked out. Aiden's shades were open, but he wasn't there.

I sat at my desk and ate my measly dinner. The rest of the house was empty, which meant my sister probably had soccer or volleyball or some other school event. I was glad of that, because I needed quiet so I could process everything that had happened. I also had to start thinking of a plausible English project topic. I dug out my homework, pushed my empty plate aside, and booted up the laptop. When the homepage opened with the cursor blinking, waiting for me to enter something in the search engine, I stared blankly at the screen. Each flicker reminded me of Shay's heartbeat. After a few minutes of staring at the cursor, I conceded that I wasn't going to get any homework done.

I cleared a space between my bed and dresser, unrolled my purple yoga mat, popped in a video, and stretched. After an eight-minute warm-up, including a few downward facing dogs and warrior poses, a familiar *tink* hit my window. I paused the DVD, opened my white wooden blinds, and saw Aiden's smiling face. He motioned that he wanted to talk, so I pushed up the window and sat on the ledge. Recalling the brush-off he'd given me earlier, I crossed my arms and glared at him.

"Yes?"

"Hey, Zoe," Aiden said. "How's it going?"

"Fine."

"Are you mad at me?"

"What gives you that idea?"

"Oh, I don't know. Maybe it's your tone, or maybe it's your posture." He leaned against the windowsill. "Maybe you feel like I blew you off after gym class."

Precisely. "Did you need something?"

"Nothing important. Just got back into town and wanted to see a familiar face."

I couldn't keep quiet, though. "What's with you flirting with Quinn then buddying up to Morgan?"

"Morgan's not so bad once you get to know her."

"Yes, she is. I've known her since grade school, and she's always been horrible to me. But Quinn is special. I couldn't care less if you like Morgan, but don't string Quinn along."

He shrugged. "I'm testing the waters. Calm down. I'm not dating either of them. Quinn's going to the prom with Caden, so they might have a thing going on anyway."

"All I'm saying is that you better watch yourself. Quinn doesn't play dating games, so you're either with her or you're not."

He grinned. "Aren't you feisty today?"

"Gotta go. I have to get back to yoga, unless you have some other pressing matters?"

"Nah, it's all good."

I closed the window and blinds and resumed my workout, lying on the carpet in pigeon pose then moving to the plank position. A few more stances, and my body was coated in a shiny layer of sweat. Yoga was supposed to have a calming effect, and usually it did, but not tonight. Instead, perspiration dripped onto the mat and my anger flared. I huffed and stopped the video.

I needed to shower. After that maybe I'd try to get some sleep. Since we were going into Fairyland tomorrow night, who knew when I would be back in my familiar bed. I grabbed fresh boy shorts and a tank top and ran into the bathroom for my nightly ritual. When I was done, I checked my cell phone for any messages. The tiny blue light indicated I had a text.

Shay: Howdy

Squealing with joy, I jumped into bed with my cell phone in hand and typed.

Me: Hi

Shay: I miss you.

Me: I miss you 2. You should be resting!

Shay: I am. Sidelle says the X mark is, and I quote, "SO not worth calling you Bull's Eye anymore." It's fading fast.

Me: Does your shoulder still hurt?

Shay: I barely feel pain. Can move my arm well enough.

Me: You must heal faster 2?

Shay: Yes.

Me: Good. Glad you're better. I want to stay up and chat, but you need rest, and I need sleep. Loves ya

Shay: OK. Love U 2. CU tomorrow

The next morning, I awoke with a jolt. I couldn't exactly remember what I'd dreamt, but a shudder vibrated through me. After stretching across the bed, I started my morning routine—checking for all my books and homework, setting out clothes and coordinating shoes—then I hopped into the shower. After all, Shay might be coming back to school.

When I was done, I meandered down to the kitchen where my parents waited for me.

"So, now you don't even bother texting us that you'll be late for dinner?" Mom demanded. "Where have you been?"

"Honey." Dad patted Mom's shoulder then sat at the table.

I was startled by her unexpected outburst, but she was right. I'd been a little ... distracted.

"I'm sorry. I got caught up with a new game simulator at Kieran's house. I lost track of time."

She sighed and pulled me into a tight hug. "Zoe, I worry about you. When you don't call, I get all these bad ideas in my mind. I mean, have you seen the news lately? I'm sorry I snapped, but please call or text one of us and let us know you're okay and where you are."

I kissed her cheek. "Sorry, Mom. You're right."

"Spending more time at his house these days, huh?" Dad said. "I remember when you kids were little and played leaf houses in the backyard for hours." He shook his head. "Where does the time go? It seems like only yesterday you were a baby. But now, you've grown into a somewhat responsible adult."

"I have? I mean ... I am." From behind, I wrapped my arms around my dad's shoulders. "I love you guys. I can still go to Sidelle's this weekend, right?"

"Yes," Mom said. "But remember to keep your phone on so we can reach you."

"Okay. Thanks." I grabbed my backpack, kissed them both, and headed out the front door.

Kieran waited in the driveway, drumming his fingers on the steering wheel. As I neared, my chest pounded along with the bass of the stereo. When I opened the door, classical music blared from the speakers. Not what I'd expected. I knew Kieran listened to all sorts of music, but even for him this was rather odd.

"Hi," Kieran said, turning down the volume. "You ready?"

"Yep. Let's go. Last day before a long weekend." I shut the door and tossed my bag in the back seat.

"You ready for that, too?" He backed out of the driveway and glanced in the rearview mirror at Aiden's house.

I shrugged. "I've kinda grown used to just rolling with the punches and not expect anything."

"Not a bad plan."

"Is Shay ... He's probably resting today, right?"

"Yes, he'll go back to school next week. He seems pretty much healed, but he's probably being stubborn and lying about the pain. He wants to come with us this weekend."

"What do you think? He has to be one hundred percent just in case—"

"I know. I told him that, but he still insists on going with us."

I'd seen a little of that stubbornness last night before I'd gone home. He was determined to be with me, and while I wanted that more than anything, it was more important that he recovered first. "Let's see how he is by this afternoon," I said. "At the rate he heals, maybe he really is fine."

Kieran pulled into an open parking spot at Coffee Grind. "Speaking of Shay's healing ..."

I'd been wondering if he was going to ask. "Yes?" I stepped out of the car, needing a few extra seconds to gather my thoughts.

"Anything you want to share about that?"

Busted. "Well, actually, I tried using my Angel Light on him." I twisted my hands together, oddly nervous. "Sidelle had me practice angel stuff instead of doing the Silico, so I thought I might as well try it on Shay. Oh, hey. I forgot to show you. Look!" I turned my palm up, so he could see the silver Mark.

He grinned, looking impressed. "Congratulations. Did you get wings, too?"

"Bo wings, yet, but it was so cool how I got the tat. There was this white light pulsing in my body, and then it shot out my fingers and darted all over the room. I was scared it would escape, so I trapped it."

Kieran laughed as he held the glass door to the shop open.

"What's so funny?" I stared at his profile.

"It can't escape. It's a part of you."

I frowned. "Well, I didn't know that, and you weren't there to tell me about it. And I still did just fine." I inhaled the buttery aroma of freshly baked treats inside, lowering my voice. "Anyway, the light shot back into my wrist, and then this appeared. We were working on telekinesis when we heard you guys in the kitchen."

"Telekinesis? Why that?"

"It's just something I wanted to try."

I ordered my usual chai and waited in the pick-up line with Kieran beside me. He was my anchor in life. We'd had our ups and downs these past weeks, especially when he declared his feelings for me a few weeks ago. But I'd explained to him the strange phenomenon that happened between Shay and me. Kieran said that it was because Shay and I were soul mates. And now as we stood in line at my favorite local spot, it felt good. As if all was right between us again. When we had our drinks in hand, he looked for a place to sit. We spotted Vash, Cali, and Jackson.

"Hey, guys," I said, sitting with them. "You ready for the weekend?"

"It'll be a learning experience," Cali said. "And I'm up for it." Vash looked unhappy, so she kissed his cheek. "Jackson will be great company. Besides, eventually I'll live there with them, so I might as well get the swing of things now."

It didn't look like her kiss had helped him much. "I'm sorry, Cali," I said. "I don't mean to take Vash away from you. He could stay, and Jacks could come with us."

Jackson's eyes widened. "Yeah, I could go—"

"No," Vash said. "It'll be how I said. Cali and Jackson will be at the compound with Era, and I will escort you this weekend. I honor my promises. On the rare chance that DKs or Marqs break into the fairy realm, you'll need a more experienced fighter with you since you can't control your powers."

"Thank you, but I'm just—"

Vash held up his hand.

"Okay," I conceded. "Is Sidelle meeting us at school?"

"Yeah," Jackson said. "She said something about double checking the conference stuff."

"I see." I didn't miss the fact that he knew where Sidelle was. "Well, let's get the day over with, so our mission can start."

We filed out of the coffee shop and loaded into our respective vehicles. It was a somber drive to school since the gravity of the situation was really sinking in now. Leaning my head back against the car's soft leather, I closed my eyes and said a silent prayer.

23
Zoe

The halls were alive with excitement about the long weekend. When Kieran and I arrived at my locker, Sidelle already stood there, looking spectacular in her signature stilettos, a black and white striped maxi skirt, and a sparkly black tank top.

"Who's ready to par-tay?" she asked, beaming at us. "No school for four glorious days."

"Morning, Zoe," Aiden said, approaching us. "You got plans?"

"I'm going to Sidelle's, so we can work on our English project."

He looked disgusted. "Schoolwork the whole time? That blows."

I nodded, shrugging.

"So we won't get to have our evening chats?" he asked.

"Nope. I'm staying at her house."

The familiar sound of Morgan's clicking shoes echoed down the hall as she sidled up next to Aiden.

"Well, have fun with that," he said to me. "I'll be off looking for a good party to crash. Someone's gotta have one."

"Or we could find something else to do that's fun," Morgan purred. "We have four days to get to know each other better." She skimmed a well-manicured fingernail down his chest.

"I'll see you in first hour," I mumbled, not wanting to hang around and witness any more.

I didn't bother to tell Aiden that the person who normally hosted parties would be in Chanhassen, tending to pack business. As far as parties went, I wasn't sure if anyone else would step up to the challenge or not. Maybe one of the seniors.

The morning passed by in a blur. Teachers handed out assignments like they were going out of style. By lunch time, the staff was also looking forward to the extra days off. I overheard some of them talking about how they must have forgotten about the conference, and complaining that the topic wasn't clear. It didn't matter, because they all seemed united on the idea of going anywhere to get away from the students.

After school let out, we met at my locker, and we all headed out. Sidelle needed to drive her car home and then come to my house. Cali would drive to her house with Jackson, pack for the weekend, and continue to the compound. Vash planned to park his car at Kieran's for the weekend. After all the logistics were handled, I hugged Cali and Jackson, because I didn't know how long I'd be gone. I was bummed that I wasn't able to say bye to Quinn or Rena.

When Kieran dropped me off in front of my house, he smiled. "Pack lighter than you did last weekend, okay? Whatever you forget, Sidelle can get for you anyway."

"Should I bring food? I mean ... Can humans eat fairy foods? I'll grab some protein bars and nonperishable stuff." I answered my own question. "I suppose I should pack a dress or something, since I'm meeting royalty."

"Probably not a bad idea," Kieran said. He got out of the car and walked me to my front door.

"I'll bring this backpack just in case. It's better for hauling my crap than a suitcase. It's practical." I knew I was rambling.

He grinned. "You're nervous." It wasn't a question.

"A little bit."

"It'll be fine. One step at a time."

"Do you know how we're going to get into Fairyland?"

"No, but Sidelle will. So hurry and pack, so we can leave before your parents get home. Text me when you're ready, so Vash and I can meet you here."

"Okay. See you in a bit. I won't be long."

I unlocked the front door, pushed it open, and watched Kieran drive the short distance to his house. Vash's vehicle was already parked in his driveway. I closed the door and sprinted up to my room, dumped my school supplies onto the bed, then remembered I'd told my parents I was doing a project. Not wanting to carry the thick books around with me in Fairyland, I stuffed some of them between the mattresses and a few others in drawers. I laid two pairs of yoga pants, a tank top, a T-shirt, and a hoodie on the bed, then headed into the bathroom for toiletries. When I emerged, Sidelle stood in front of the walk-in closet, shaking her head.

"What now?" I asked. Was she planning to pack for me again?

"You won't need any of that. We need to travel light. Besides, Oberon doesn't like human clothing. Actually, it's the pants. He doesn't like them on females."

"Oh! I don't want to disrespect him, so I'll pack all dresses if—"

She shrugged, looking unhappy. "It's not that." She waved a hand. "Bring whatever you want. I'll fashion anything else you might need."

"Sid, what's wrong?" I wrapped my arm around her shoulder. "I've never seen you like this before."

She sighed. "I haven't been home in a long time. I mean, I've been there, but it's been a quick in and out visit. This is going to be different."

"Are you nervous?"

"No. It's my home, but ..." She looked at me. "Okay. Maybe a little."

"It's all right. I'm nervous, too. I have no idea what to expect. When I was at the pack's compound, all my previous notions were shot out of the window."

She took a deep breath. "Zoe, when we get there, you're going to see things that you don't see here. And ... you'll see me as I truly am."

"Sidelle, you're my friend. I don't care what you look like. Friends don't judge each other."

She smiled. "Okay. But I want you to be prepared. This hot body you see in front of you will not be the same once we're there." She swept her hand from head to toe. "Even though I'm still hot as a Summer fairy."

"Even if your face was covered in warts or something ..." I frowned. "It's not, is it? Because I say this now, but when I see them, I might have to take it all back."

That seemed to lighten her mood, so I got back to packing. I folded the yoga pants and tops, tucked my undergarments between them and stuffed everything into the backpack. I grabbed extra socks, took out my purple Converses from the closet, and exchanged my footwear. Finally, I selected a pair of black sandals and added them to the bag. I left Sidelle sitting on my bed, staring into space, and ran to the kitchen. Throwing cupboards open, I rummaged through and grabbed as many granola and protein bars as my arms could carry. I tossed the whole lot into the backpack's side zipper pocket.

My cell buzzed, so I swiped my finger over the screen and read the message.

Kieran: U ready?

Me: Yes. Come on over.

Kieran: OK

A few minutes later, the doorbell chimed. I opened the front door, and there stood my three glorious-looking boys: Shay, Vash, and Kieran.

"I hope it's okay I brought your boyfriend with us," Vash said with a smirk. "He wouldn't take no for an answer."

I was secretly overjoyed to see him there. "If he thinks

he's up to it, he can join us." I stepped forward and hugged Shay. "You know your body the best."

"I'm fine." Shay lifted his black T-shirt, and I was shocked not to see an X marring his skin. He tugged on the collar to show his healed shoulder. "See? Now let's get going. Is Sidelle here?"

"Upstairs."

I led the boys to my room, and they waited in the hallway. I grabbed my backpack, zipped it up, and we all headed downstairs.

"So how are we getting into Fairyland?" I asked as we passed the living room.

"We're going into your backyard," Sidelle said, opening the sliding glass door.

"Uh, okay."

"You'll see." We stepped out onto the cement slab patio, made our way around the Adirondack chairs and a bistro-style table, then onto the lawn. "Over this way."

Sidelle lead the group to the little flower garden in the back corner of the yard. Little solar lights lit the garden's sprouting wildflowers, as if highlighting its inhabitants: a pair of calico-colored porcelain cat statues. A white picket fence surrounded two sides with a stone pathway leading to a two-person marble bench. Handmade cedar arbor encased the seating area. I remembered when my dad had made the arbor. I'd been about three or four that summer, and he'd been on a woodworking kick. He'd come home from work and started making birdhouses and lawn decorations, and then this arbor was constructed. It took him the whole weekend to build, assemble, and stain it, but the end product was breathtaking. My mom had absolutely loved it. The next day, green morning glories had grown on both sides. Neither of my parents ever owned up to planting them.

"And here we are." Sidelle stopped on the last paver leading to the bench. "This is a porta."

"A what?"

"Entrance."

"Where?" I asked, looking around.

"Here." She pointed to the ground then rested one hand on the cedar trim. "Beyond this archway is one of the ways into Fairyland."

I inspected the arbor for anything that might seem to be out of place, for anything that might shed light on the process, but I came up empty. "So, how do we go through?"

"Just walk under the arch."

"But I've walked under this many times, and so have my parents. How come we've never been zapped to Fairyland accidently?"

"You need a fairy with you, silly. Now ... your first time might be a little disorienting. You know that sinking feeling in the pit of your stomach you get on a roller coaster when it drops? It's like that, kinda." Sidelle smiled, waving us forward. "Who's going first?"

"Where exactly in Fairyland does this lead to?" Kieran asked. "Should we be ready to do battle against Winter fairies or some beast from the Mist?"

"No," Sidelle said, scowling at him. "I wouldn't do that. That would be something a Winter fairy might do. This'll lead to the outskirts of Summer."

"I'll go first," Shay said. "Then you guys quickly follow, so we don't get separated. Sidelle, you go last, in case something happens on this side of the porta." He held out a hand toward me. "Ready, Zoe?"

"I am." I reached for his hand and squeezed it. He stepped forward, releasing our fingers, and disappeared from my view. It was a shocking thing to see, even after all the shocking things I'd already seen. With him gone again, I could barely stand still. "Okay, I'll go next." I took a deep breath, gripped the straps of my backpack, and walked under the arch.

Darkness enveloped me, and the ground was gone. I lost all sense of direction, free falling into Fairyland, and when I tried to scream, no sound came from my mouth. My hands grasped at anything to anchor me, but my fingers found nothing. A wave of intense heat blanketed me, and a second later I caught a hint of lilies and honey. Light pooled below me, and I landed with a thud on soft green grass, my breath shoved from my lungs. I fought to breathe normally as I adjusted my vision to the sudden brightness of the sun.

"Are you okay?" Shay asked. I nodded, still catching my breath. "That was interesting, huh?"

"The others should ... should be here soon," I puffed. Shay extended his hand, and I got to my feet. "I can't believe it was that simple. And right in my own backyard."

"There's a reason for that, silly," Sidelle said when she appeared beside me with Kieran. I'd been expecting her, but I still jumped. *She needs a cat bell around her neck.*

"We thought it'd make great garden art for your family, plus it served a purpose for us. Easy access. Now look around. Welcome to Fairyland!"

The landscape before us was spectacular. Waist-high, rolling green prairie grass tickled my skin, and vivid yellow birds flew over our heads. In the distance I saw a pond, and every once in a while something splashed on the surface. But everything was too bright. It was like I needed sunglasses to look at it. The colors in the Ordinary world were so muted compared to the blue of this sky, the white of these clouds, and the brown of these tree trunks.

"Pretty, isn't it?" Sidelle asked.

I stared at her. She was now dressed in something that looked like a dark green ball gown from England in the 1800s. Long, black hair draped down her back. Her bright, green eyes Asian-like. She seemed taller than usual, too.

"Come on. Let's go to the castle." She stopped mid-step. "Oh, Zoe. You'll need this from now on, per Oberon." She tossed me a golden sphere the size of a baseball. "You're to keep this on your person at all times, as a token of being Oberon's personal guest."

I blinked at the ball. "How am I supposed to hide this thing? Can't I just put it in the backpack and carry it?"

Kieran regarded me with disappointment. "That isn't on your person," he said. "Just make do."

"So there isn't anything you can do to make it smaller? Like actual coin size or something?"

"Nope," Sidelle said. "Oberon used special glamour for it that I can't break."

I held the ball in one hand and Shay's hand in the other. Without a pocket big enough to store it in, I had no other choice. This was going to get old, fast. Besides, what if I needed both hands to do something?

"We need to make it to the castle by sundown," Sidelle reminded us.

"Can't you poof us there?" I asked.

"I tried. I can't take all of you. And if I transport you one at a time, then I'm leaving those left behind in possible danger. You never know who or what lurks around here. Don't worry. We aren't that far."

If we weren't far from the castle, and we needed to be there before sundown, then why was the sun still so high in the sky? Something didn't add up. I pulled out my cell phone, but the screen was blank.

"Dang it," I shouted.

Everyone halted.

"What's wrong?" Shay asked.

"My cell phone is dead, and I forgot to pack the charger."

"Doesn't matter. Those won't work here anyway," Sidelle called from the front of the line.

"How am I supposed to know when sundown is?" I demanded. "What if we don't make it out in time?"

"You don't. No one does. The sun and moon rise and fall when they want to."

I let go of Shay's hand and trotted up to Sidelle. "You have a beautiful home, Sidelle, even if it's kind of weird. Very you."

"I'll take that as a compliment."

"You should. I can understand why you like Summer,

the warm weather and all that. You *are* this." I waved my hand around. "And Sid?"

"Yes?"

"You're beautiful, too."

She lowered her eyes then glanced my way. I beamed at her. How she'd even imagined I'd think anything less of her now that we were in Fairyland was just plain dumb. The Sidelle standing beside me now was still tall and thin, but there was also a grace to her that didn't project when she was in her human form. Her hair was black and surprisingly long, not cut in the pixie style I'd grown to love. The features on her face seemed sharper, more angled, the slant of her eyes almost Asian-like, and larger, taller ears poked through her hair. I checked her shoulders for the wings I knew she kept hidden, but I couldn't see any. As we walked toward her home, I kept checking to see if maybe they were back there. They never appeared.

The boys quietly chatted behind us as Sidelle and I took in her homeland. She never talked much about her time here in Summer, which made sense. No one would have understood, except maybe Kieran if he had been here before. Maybe now that I'd been here, she'd open up and tell me about herself.

Eventually, the landscape changed from prairie land to woods.

"This is called the Wild Forest," Sidelle whispered as she stepped into the tree line. "Be careful and quiet. We don't want to awaken anything that lives here. The Mist surrounds Summer and Winter, moving like a living, breathing creature."

I tried to step where Sidelle stepped. She didn't make a sound with her feet, nor did Kieran, Shay, or Vash. I was the only one making enough sounds to raise the dead. Then an eerie silence stopped us in our tracks. Even the wind stilled. The air was perfectly quiet.

"Come on," Sidelle whispered, a slight tremble in her voice.

As soon as we took a step, the wind picked up big time, making the treetops bend and sway. Sidelle quickened the pace, her long, black hair whipping around in the wind, and I trailed behind her.

It happened again. The wind stopped as if a door had been shut. Everything was dead still, and we were hot and sweaty as air pressed in on us.

From the distance came a terrifying roar, the bellow of a furious beast. Sidelle closed her eyes, looking like a child who'd been caught sneaking away. Well, it was understandable, really. It was difficult to keep five beings—okay, one person and four others—perfectly quiet while they marched through a forest.

I grabbed Shay and Kieran. Panic surged through me. My body shook.

When it came again, the sound was closer. No one had to tell me twice. We raced through the evergreens and brush, ducking under branches and pushing others aside. We needed to get out of the way of whatever was trailing us, but the noise of splintering wood and the thundering of running feet was getting louder. Everyone tore through the woods, never looking back.

"This way. My home!" Sidelle panted, leading us into a large flower garden. She cocked her head listening for whatever was hunting us.

Sidelle's home wasn't what I'd thought it would be. Somehow, I'd pictured a huge house with a terracotta roof, brightly colored walls, and flowers everywhere. Something like a home in Italy.

I definitely hadn't imagined a castle.

Lush gardens surrounded the castle's stone walls, and flowers stood tall over the grounds. Even the tree branches were thick with overly large leaves. The castle itself was something straight out of a Disney movie, its brick and boulder walls seemingly impenetrable. Turrets soared into the sky at least five stories tall, and green flags flapped at the top of each one. The windows were as tall as anything I'd ever seen, but there was no glass in them.

"You live in a castle?" I asked.

"I haven't lived here in a long time," Sidelle said.

"Not what I expected."

She looked surprised. "Where did you think I lived?"

"Uh, not something like this. I'll leave it at that."

We stopped at the wooden gates, and Shay and Vash stared at the castle with awe. Kieran couldn't seem to care less. He'd probably been here before, or nothing amazed him. The heavy gates cranked open and out stepped four guards. Each was dressed in a full metal chest plate and tan breeches, and each held a wooden shield, which displayed the castle's crest: a thorn crown wrapped in green wings. The guards formed a single line and bowed in unison.

"State your business, fairy," one said.

Sidelle nudged me forward.

"We wish to speak with the king." I held out the golden token. "He gave me this."

"I wasn't speaking to you, Ordinary." The lead guard looked past my shoulder. "And you're accompanied by an angel, a werewolf, and a Nephilim?"

"Yes."

His gaze shifted back to Sidelle. "I ask again, fairy. State your name and business."

She lifted her chin. "My business is my own, but my name is Sidelle."

He appeared immediately sorry. "I apologize! I ... I did not recognize you. Please accept my humble apologies." He dropped to one knee, and the other guards quickly followed suit. "Welcome back to Aestas Castle. I'll personally escort you to the throne room."

We followed him into the castle, and even though the guard kept glancing back with pleading eyes at Sidelle, she looked anywhere but at him. I'd have to remember to ask her about that. Once inside the potent aromas of lily of the valley, wisteria, and jasmine mixed with the sweet fragrances of honey, ripe strawberries, and fresh pineapple. It was a sensory overload to my nose. I had to hold my breath until we reached the throne room.

After a few turns of a large wheel, a set of floor-to-ceiling double doors ground open. More guards were stationed inside, creating a line to the throne. A fairy stood a few steps away, holding a long trumpet. He held the instrument to his lips and sounded a couple of short blasts.

"Welcome to Aestas Castle," he shouted. "Approach! The king has informed me that he will not see to your business now, but he has requested you all stay in the southern wing. He'll summon you when he's ready to hear your business."

"But—" I started.

The guard held up his hand. "The king has spoken. The guards who brought you here will escort you to your rooms. Now go." He waved us away.

I stared at her. "Sidelle? Can't you do something? We came all this way. We're on a time crunch, you know. We only have four days."

She shook her head. "I know, but there isn't anything I can do. He has spoken. Let's go to the rooms, freshen up, and wait. If it's too long, then I'll try to seek a private audience with him."

That was the best we could do. We followed the guards to the southern tower, which encompassed more than one floor. One of the guards said it was where honored guests of the court stayed. The windows overlooked gardens, rolling pastures, and cascading waterfalls, providing one of the best views.

We each had our own room, but the boys opted to stay together. The room they selected was large enough that they were able to move a second bed from another chamber. Since Kieran didn't sleep, Shay and Vash only needed two beds. Sidelle said she would stay with me, so I wouldn't be alone. She suggested that we change into the clothes supplied in the cabinets.

My room had a four-poster, king-sized bed, a couple of chaise lounges overlooking the windows, a seating area, and a private bathroom. Fresh flowers decorated every surface, and a platter of fruits, cheeses, and meats sat on one of the tables. Curious, I walked over to a tall cabinet and pulled open its doors. I stared in disbelief. Hanging on the bar were ball gowns of every color. After great deliberation, I selected a lavender one. It was the most beautiful dress I'd ever seen. In it, I could really look the part of a princess in my own fairytale. For a few moments, this magical gown distracted me from the real reason for our being here. Maybe that was Oberon's objective.

"Come on, Zoe," Sidelle said. "I'll help you change. These things can be a bitch to get into. Especially if you try to lace up the back by yourself."

I was no longer shy undressing around her. She'd seen me naked—or close to it—more times than I'd care to admit. But just as I was about to pull off my top, the hairs on my arms stood straight up, and I froze.

"Uh, Sid? Do you know her?"

A young, beautiful female fairy with short brown hair sat on the windowsill, a pair of giant, iridescent green wings hung loosely on her back. Her distinct, almond-shaped eyes were the same incredible color as Sidelle's.

"Brea? Is that you?"

"Oh, my fairies," the fairy squealed. "Rumor was you were back in the castle." She flew off the ledge and wrapped her arms around Sidelle. "I can't believe you're back. After all this time! It's been how long?" She stepped back.

"A few centuries in human time since I've seen you, but I've been here for a report to my father just a few years ago."

It had been centuries since Sidelle had seen her friend?

"Zoe," Sidelle said. "This is my best friend, Brea. Brea, this is Zoe."

Brea looked at me curiously. "So she's the one, huh?"

"Yep."

"Hi, Brea." I extended my hand, but she didn't take it. Instead, she drew me into a hug.

"A friend of Sidelle's is a friend of mine." She leaned back and gazed into my eyes. "She must think highly of you if she calls you her friend, Zoe. She doesn't have many. Or at least she didn't when she was here."

Sidelle cleared her throat. "We don't have to talk about that."

"Fine," Brea said, giving me a wink. "I get the message loud and clear. Listen, in honor of your return, the king has declared a ball tonight."

"Of course he has," Sidelle said with a sigh. "I wouldn't

expect anything less."

"Ah. So you still hate having a good time?"

"What do you mean?" I asked. "Sidelle loves to party! In my world, she's the one at school everybody wants to hang out with and *be*." Dropping my shyness, I slid the rest of my clothes off and stepped into the gown.

"School?" Brea shouted at Sidelle. "You're in *school*?"

I turned, holding the front of the bodice up, and watched the best friends banter. Sidelle came around behind me and started to lace the dress up my back.

"Yes. It's something I had to do while interacting with the Ordinaries." She nodded toward my bag, and Brea went to get it.

"Well, wonders never cease." Brea opened the zipper and pulled out my black heels. "These are what?"

"Stilettos. Very fashionable but take some getting used to."

Brea shrugged and placed them on the floor in front of me, waiting for me to step into them. It was like having handmaids attending to my every need. When I was ready, Sidelle clasped her hands over my eyes, spun me around, and guided me toward the floor mirror. Then she pulled her hands away.

Staring back at me from the mirror was a plain looking girl with long, brown hair in an absolutely glamorous lavender ball gown. My hand went to my hair, and I twirled a strand around a finger, feeling completely out of place. I even pinched some color into my cheeks. But Sidelle and Brea knew what I was thinking. They stood on either side of me and raised their arms.

"Close your eyes, Zoe," Brea said.

A wave of shimmer swept across my face and my head tingled. When the two of them told me to open my eyes, I did. I stared at the gorgeous, practically unrecognizable—to me, anyway—young lady in the mirror, standing next to two stunning fairies. My hair was in an up-do; the stylishly braided cords had been wrapped around the crown of my head and adorned with tiny white flowers. Lavender shadow accented my eyes, giving them an almond shape. Pink, glossy lips and mauve cheeks gave definition to my face.

A knock on our door broke my stare. Brea's eyes snapped toward door, and she hid her wings.

"Enter," Sidelle sang.

The wooden door opened and in strolled three handsome men. All were wearing brown breeches and white tunics, and each tunic was embroidered with the Aestas castle crest. They looked dashing. Then they noticed me, and the heat from Kieran's and Shay's eyes was enough to melt my insides. I knew Vash appreciated beauty as well, but his eyes were only ever on Cali, so I didn't take any offense.

Shay stepped forward and wrapped his arm around my waist, planting a sweet kiss on my forehead. Smart man. He knew not to mess with my makeup.

"You're stealing my breath," he breathed into my ear, sending heat to my cheeks.

Kieran walked farther into the room, and I noticed his eyes never wavered. Now, I saw what I'd failed to notice a few seconds ago: he wasn't staring at me. His gaze was entirely on Sidelle. She looked fantastic, but she always did. Her green gown was timeless, and her hair was styled in an intricate up-do similar to my own.

"Someone is head over heels for a certain fairy?" Shay whispered. I could only shrug. This was definitely new.

"The guards at our door said the king has summoned us to the throne room," Vash said, holding out his arm for Brea. He gave her a wink. "I guess that leaves you and me tonight, Beautiful."

"My name's Brea." She linked her arm in the crook of Vash's, then giggled. "Do you mind if I ... um ... show my wings?"

He howled. "By all means. Let 'em fly."

Her iridescent green wings unfolded, extending tall and upright. As Vash led her out of the door, I heard him ask if she knew where we were going, and her response was, "I know this castle like my own wings. Trust me, Wolf-boy, I won't lead you astray."

"We should go, too," Shay said. "We don't want to keep the king waiting." Following Vash's lead, he bent his elbow, and he escorted me out of the room.

When we entered the throne room, its energy was charged with something ancient and powerful. King Oberon was perched on his throne, a glowing, pale bluish-green scepter in his hand. His green robes lay spread around him, reminding me of a prairie, and giant, dark green wings draped loosely across his back. White branches twined through the crown on his head. He was the perfect picture of royalty, casually draped in his throne. He rose and stood on the dais while he waited for us to come to him.

"Welcome, Zoe of the Ordinaries' realm," the king proclaimed. "I hope you have found your stay here at Aestas Castle to be a pleasant one?" His eyes went to my hands, and a slight frown creased his brow. "My guards informed me that you had brought my token of goodwill."

Oh, no. Was I supposed to bring it? No one had mentioned that before we'd left. "I did," I managed, "but ... but I didn't bring it with me for this meeting." Taking a deep breath, I stepped forward and released Shay's warm hand. "I left it in my chambers. I hope that's all right. If you want, I can go back and get it."

"That will not be necessary." He waved my friends forward. "And who are the rest of you?"

"I'm Shay Curator, a Nephilim sworn to protect the Redeemer." He smiled and bowed.

"I am Kieran Auduro, Zoe's Guardian angel."

"I am the Alpha of the Spiritus pack of Minnetonka. My name is Vash Bellator."

"You're young to be an Alpha, yes?" the king asked, frowning.

"I am." Vash nodded and sighed. "My father was killed last weekend while protecting our pack and Zoe. Our compound had a surprise attack by DKs and Marqs. We lost the Alpha, the female Alpha, and two members."

The king placed his hand on Vash's shoulder. "I am sorry for your loss, Alpha. But I am pleased to meet all of you. And step forward, my daughter. Now that she is home and has brought the Redeemer to me, we will celebrate!"

I didn't want to interrupt, but something had to be said. I curtsied. "I'd like to discuss the situation at hand, if I may, Your Majesty."

But the king was all smiles now. "All in due time, my dear. First, we must celebrate the return of my daughter to

Fairyland, to the Summer lands, and to me. It's been a very long time since I've seen her properly." He cocked his head toward Sidelle. "That last one doesn't count since you were only here a few sundowns."

Sidelle nodded.

"Then let's not waste any more time."

On cue the double doors opened, and fairies filed in playing flutes, fiddles, and drums. The throne room exploded into song, and I stared with wonder at the beautiful fairy couples who danced, fluttered their wings, or cocooned themselves. Smaller fairies streamed into the massive hall bearing plates of candied fruits, breads, and meats, which they set on the royal table. The delicious aroma of cheeses and buttery pastries filled the air. Freshly cut flowers appeared in tall vases and lined the tables.

The candle lights dimmed, and that was our cue. Our meeting with the Summer King was officially over. He dismissed us but motioned for Sidelle to stay. The group of us shuffled across the floor, trying not to bump into anyone, and the boys landed directly in front of the food table. Brea and I waited for Sidelle at the side.

"Is any of this stuff safe for us to eat?" Vash asked. "I'm starving."

"Zoe brought granola and protein bars," Kieran said. "But this food should be fine for you and Shay."

"How do you know?" Shay asked.

"I don't for sure, but it's just fruit and meat. You could find this out in the Wild Forest."

Shay and Vash exchanged a glance. Vash tentatively grabbed a hunk of meat. He sniffed it, ripped off a small piece, and placed it in his mouth. Looking thoughtful, he chewed then swallowed. He shrugged.

"Not bad. Kinda dry and tasteless, but it's food."

"If you get sick, don't blame me," I said, grinning.

Vash and Shay didn't say a word as they loaded up a wooden board with meat and a few fruits. My eyes went to Sidelle.

"Brea, will everything be okay for her?" I asked. "She's been over there a long time."

"Don't worry about it. She can handle her father."

"Is she really his daughter, or is that a figure of speech?"

"She's definitely his offspring. We grew up together, did everything together, but she was always a little odd. She didn't like doing normal fairy stuff. She hated dances and all the dressing up. She preferred to be alone."

I shook my head, amazed. "Sure doesn't sound like the Sidelle I know."

"I guess centuries can change a fairy."

Eventually, Sidelle strolled over toward us, looking annoyed. "Oberon will meet with us after the party, but the question is when this party will actually be over in his mind. They have been known to last many sundowns."

The room vibrated with happy fairies, and the mood was contagious. "So for now, I guess let's enjoy the night." I tugged on Shay's hand. Grinning, he set his plate of meat down and led me to the dance floor.

I was so grateful to have him back with me. I'd sworn from the moment he returned that I'd cherish all the times we had together, and that definitely included this dance. Our bodies became one as we swayed to the odd music, our friends left us alone, and I loved them for that. Shay and I danced in each other's arms until my feet couldn't stand any more.

When I awoke, the sun was high in the sky. Sidelle and Brea sat on the window ledge, chatting quietly. I didn't recall when we'd gotten back to the room, but my throbbing legs and feet felt like they'd run a marathon. I snuggled deeper into the soft blankets and pillows, hoping to sleep a bit more, but my body—and now my mind—wouldn't have it. I groaned and rolled onto my side, letting my friends know I was awake.

"Morning," Sidelle said cheerfully.

"Or should we say ... good *late* morning?" Brea asked.

"What time is it?" I stretched my back and threw the covers off. "I can get up and be ready in a flash. Probably not as fast as either of you, but for a human I can be speedy."

"No worries. The boys are still zonked out." Brea jumped down from the sill and hopped onto the bed. "That Vash sure is handsome ... for a wolf." She raised her hand. "I know he's off the market; I saw his tattoo. And I know what he has with Cali is real and can't be broken." She lifted her shoulders and dropped them, gentle as a sigh. "I'm just saying he's cute."

"Still haven't found your Prince Charming, Brea?" Sidelle asked as she joined us on the bed.

"Nope. The pickings are slim here. I've been seeing that guard, Galen, off and on. Remember him? He was stationed outside this room, as a matter of fact when—"

"Yes, I know who he is."

Someone knocked. "Lady Sidelle?" a male voice called.

"Yes?"

"The king will see you and your party now," he said through the closed door.

I jumped off the bed and scrambled to gather my belongings. The dress I'd worn last night was tossed across the back of a chair, and my shoes had been left by the foot of the bed. I grabbed my bag from the floor and dug out clean jeans and a shirt.

"Tsk," Sidelle said. "You can't wear that. Go to the wardrobe and pick another dress. When we leave Aestas,

we'll come back for your bag."

I did as directed and selected a soft, buttercream gown from the rainbow of materials. As beautiful as it was, it wasn't too difficult to maneuver into. Both fairies helped me slip the silky material over my sore shoulders and then used glamour to straighten my hair and clean my face. *No wonder Sidelle hated doing this every day.* The two fairies changed into fresh gowns, and we banged on the boys' door, hoping the guards had already told them about the meeting. Then I remembered the token, and I ran back to the room to grab it.

When we entered the throne room, Oberon was not there. We waited near the dais ... and waited and waited. Vash looked half asleep; Shay was a little more awake, and Kieran, well, he looked spectacular. As always. I drummed my fingers on my thigh when the oak doors flew open, and the king waltzed in.

"I hope I have not kept you waiting long." He didn't give anyone a chance to answer. "Good. I trust everyone is fully rested and ready for the day? Let's begin." He waved us forward, using glamour to make some chaise lounges appear. "Tell me everything from the beginning as you know it, Zoe."

I did exactly that, going back to how I'd learned what Kieran was, how I'd met Shay, and about the DKs who had chased me into a warehouse and proceeded to explain how Sidelle had saved Shay and me from the Marqs, then how Vash came into my life. Vash expounded on the attack on the pack's land, and between the three boys, they filled in details of Shay's kidnapping and rescue.

"I see." Oberon stood, then paced as if deep in thought. "Zoe, did you bring the token?"

"I did." I held up the golden ball.

"Do you know how I know what you speak is the truth? Do you know how I know that you are, with certainty, the Redeemer?"

I shook my head.

He plucked the token from my hands. "There is old glamour infused into this. Only the one who will join the Enlightens, as the prophesy states, is able to actually hold it on their person."

"But Sidelle can hold it."

"Yes, and that's because she is of me, just like this token. Her glamour is derived from mine. You don't believe me? Tell me, has anyone else tried to carry it for you?"

"No. Sidelle said I had to, so I did.

He folded his arms across his chest. "But you went to the pack without any proof and asked them to join you?"

"Yes."

"Well, here is your proof to me." He tossed the token to

Kieran, who moved with lightning speed and tried to catch it. But the ball passed through his hand like it wasn't there, landing on the floor with a loud *thud*. Shay leaned down and attempted to return it to me, but like Kieran, his hand passed through it.

The king smiled. "Zoe? Please."

I walked over and picked up the token.

"Excellent. Now, I'd like to see what you can do with it."

"What do you mean?"

"I mean, I want you to use your Angel Light and try to do something with it."

No pressure. "Okay, but I'm not actually very good at that. I've only recently started practicing—"

"Do what you can." He placed a hand over mine, which held the token. "Listen to your heart and mind."

My eyes drifted shut, felt the warmth of Oberon's large hand, the coolness of the metal from the ball, and called forth my Light. The more I practiced, the faster it came to me. Purple light glowed between the token and my palm, its rays extending outward like the sun. Oberon had said this trinket was infused with his glamour, and he was as ancient as the earth itself. In this moment, old magic was being mixed with Angel Light. Green and purple. The possibilities in my mind were endless.

I chose something simple. When Sidelle had first given

me the token, I had asked if it could be made smaller, made into something more manageable to carry—so that's what I did. A brownish color swirled in the air, encasing the ball. I pressed the Light down, and it flattened the sphere. When I opened my eyes, a palm-sized golden coin lay in my hand.

Oberon smiled; then he turned and walked out of the throne room leaving us wondering what he knew that we didn't.

Before we left Oberon's court, we returned to the room to pick up my backpack. While we were there, I changed into jeans, a T-shirt, and my Converses. Confusion wracked my mind as to what just happened in the throne room. We headed back to the outskirts of Summer, but I still didn't know if Oberon was going to send fairies to help us in the upcoming battle or not. He hadn't said a word since I'd created the coin.

In order to get back to the gateway, Sidelle said we had to pass the Mist, which would open into the Ordinary's plane. We were all walking behind Sidelle when she suddenly stopped and cocked her head.

"What is it?" I whispered, scanning the area for any threats. I had no idea what they could have been, though.

For all I could have guessed, the grass was dangerous. Then a figure appeared ahead of us, blocking the path. It was running awkwardly toward us, waving its arms ... er, *branches* at us. Once it got closer, I realized it was a miniature tree. A *talking* tree.

"Do not use this porta," said the tree.

Sidelle glanced at our expressions, smiling. "Uh, don't worry guys; it's only a nymph. They're harmless." She turned back to the tree. "Thank you, Tree Nymph. Do you know why the porta is being guarded? And who's guarding it?"

One of the branches swung my way. "I would assume because of her."

"All right. Is it just this one being guarded?"

The branches shook from side to side. "No. *All* the portas leading to her realm."

"Oh, that's bad." Sidelle lowered her head and shook it. "We're trapped in Fairyland. What's guarding them, Tree Nymph?"

"Demons and hell hounds."

"That's not good. How do they know where they all are?"

"What're we going to do?" I cried. "We need to get back. Could this be part of Sammael's plan? To trap us here?"

"Could be," Kieran said. "Doing this takes you out of

the Ordinaries' world, thus rendering you helpless to prevent his escape." He drew in a long breath. "Sidelle, are there any other gateways that Sammael wouldn't know about? Ones that are super-secret?"

"I used one many eons ago when I came to earth. Oberon created a portal on the spot for me to walk through, so I don't know if there are any others. With my father, you never know. He's powerful and may be able to hide them."

"There's another porta."

Our heads snapped in the direction of a new voice, but I couldn't see anything. I looked to the others since their eyesight was much better than mine. Branches cracked and leaves rustled. Someone or something approached, and as the noise grew closer, the temperature fell. As we watched, ice crystals formed on low hanging branches and grass areas.

"Get back to the Summer's edge right now!" Sidelle screamed.

We turned and started to run down the path from which we came, but hadn't moved far before it turned to a sheet of ice, making it extremely difficult for us to make a quick escape.

"Sidelle, is that you?" the voice asked. "Just where do you think you're going?"

Sidelle glided to a stop, and we bumped into each other.

"Leave this to me," she told us, her voice as cold as the frost that now crept up my legs. "Keep going to Summer's edge. It's just up ahead." Turning back, she shouted, "Finn, show yourself!"

We kept going like she instructed and eventually crossed an invisible line back into Summer, where the ground was soft and green. From there we turned to watch a tall man with jet-black hair step onto the path, wearing brown breeches and a dark blue tunic.

"What do you want, Finn?" she spat. "Why are you here?"

"What I always want, Sidelle. You."

She coughed out a laugh. "You blew that chance twice now, Fairy Boy. You're wasting your time."

"Maybe, but the good thing is I have forever to change your mind. Again." He advanced on her, and Sidelle took a few steps back toward us. "Heard you were in the area, so I decided to check up on you. It's been a few weeks. I missed seeing your smile, Delle."

"I don't need you to check up on me. I don't need *anything* from you."

"We'll see about that."

He took a few more steps, and she retreated more. He peered over her shoulder at us—which wasn't too much of a stretch since he was a good three or four inches taller than she was—and looked straight at me. Kieran placed a protective arm around my shoulders, which was sweet. I wasn't sure what he could do against a Winter fairy, but I was grateful for his touch.

"I see you brought her here to your court."

"So? Oberon wanted to meet her."

"Hi, Zoe."

When he smiled, I recognized him as the Winter fairy who had helped us with the Marquises demons when they'd surrounded my house a few weeks ago. Sidelle had brought him back when she'd visited her father, although her version was different from his. She said Finn had invited himself to escort her to the Ordinaries' realm. But after the fight, he had just disappeared and Sidelle was tight-lipped about it.

"I hear you're looking for a way out," he said, still watching me. "I may know some that are not as widely known and may not be guarded."

I moved out from under Kieran's arm and took a step toward Finn. Shay grabbed my wrist and shook his head, but if the Winter fairy knew of a way out, I had to at least hear it. We needed to get out of here. Seeing resolve in my eyes, Shay let go of my wrist but walked with me when I approached. Kieran and Vash joined us.

"Is that true?" I asked Finn.

"Maybe. I can't guarantee it's not being guarded, but very few fairies know of it or are stupid enough to use it. Only those who need to know of it."

"And how do you know about it?"

He smirked. "Because I am one of those who needs to know."

That still didn't answer my question. Could we trust him? Sidelle obviously did not. Motioning for her to join us, we walked a few steps away from the Winter fairy and got into a little huddle.

"Can we trust him?" I asked her. "If he does know a way out of Fairyland—"

"I wouldn't trust him farther than I could throw him." Her eyes narrowed. "He has to have an alternative motive for helping us get out."

"Do you know of these other portas?" Kieran asked.

"No, but our courts are different. He knows more about this kind of stuff than I do. It could be a secret one in Winter, or at least that's where I'm guessing it is." She looked directly at me. "Zoe, you realize what it means if we have to go into Winter?"

I nodded, so she explained to the others. "There's a high probability that we may not survive. Besides the dangerous temperatures, there are other nasty creatures that will kill us on sight—especially me, if I am caught trespassing. This would be extremely treacherous." She glanced quickly at Finn. "Oberon would not be pleased if I was captured. I could be tried as a traitor or worse—"

"I won't let them have you, Sidelle. We would all fight for you," I exclaimed. "Besides, I'm from Minnesota. Cold doesn't hurt me."

Kieran nodded. "Sidelle, I have your back."

"They'd have to go through me, too," Vash added.

It always amazed me when Sidelle was surprised by how much we loved her. "Thank you. All of you," she said, as a tear rolled down her cheek. "Okay. Sounds like we're going. We'll need some winter gear."

"It's not in Winter," Finn said, overhearing. "Not the one I'm thinking about."

"Then where?"

"It's in the Mist."

We walked for miles, and I was glad I'd chosen to wear my Converses. We skirted around the edge of the Wild Forest, not wanting to run into anything like last time. A small clearing opened before us, leading into a vast canyon, and the other side of the ravine was covered entirely by a cloudy haze. Sidelle had told us the Mist surrounded Summer and Winter, moving almost like a living, breathing creature, able to mess with our minds and make us lose our sense of direction. She warned us that it was possible to get lost in the Mist and never be seen again. The swirling clouds felt eerie, and the hairs on the back of my neck stood straight up, screaming at me to leave this place. When I looked at Finn and Sidelle, their wings kept fluttering erratically.

"We're going into that?" I whispered.

"Yes," Finn said. "No fairy travels into the Mist intentionally, and glamour can't be used there. Imagine us without magic?"

Sidelle shuddered.

"How are we going to get to the other side?" I asked.

"We'll fly," Sidelle said. "Our wings still work because they're a part of us. They're not glamour."

"Does Angel Light work, K?"

"I don't know. I've never been in the Mist before."

When Sidelle, Finn, Kieran, and Shay all opened their wings, it was like I was standing next to a green, blue, gold, and silver rainbow. The fairies' wings were different from those of the angels'; they were smaller and iridescent, but each of my friends' wings was beautiful in their own unique way.

Shay stood behind me and wrapped his arms around my waist. "Ready?"

I couldn't help beaming with anticipation. I leaned my head back against his muscular chest, pressed my hands over his, and stepped onto his boots. Closing my eyes, I remembered the first time he'd taken me flying the night I met him, and what a thrill it had been.

"I'm ready whenever you are," I said.

He whispered softly into my ear. "We're already moving, Zoe."

I hadn't sensed him taking off, but now I could feel the wind his wings created, moving my hair against my face. I opened my eyes, looked down, and gasped. Heights never scared me, but staring directly into the misty pit did make my stomach heave.

"It's okay," Shay said, tightening his grip. "I've got you."

"I know you do." I turned my head and placed a kiss on his cheek.

From the corner of my eye, I spotted Kieran and Finn behind us. Behind them, Sidelle carried Vash the same way Shay carried me. I peeked over at Vash's face and gaped. His eyes were unnaturally wide, showing only a faint sliver of white. His arms floundered, forcing Sidelle to hold him tight against her body.

"Stop moving!" she yelled at him. "I'll drop you if you keep squirming."

"I was never meant to fly, Sidelle. Wolves like their paws on the ground."

"Puppy."

With a soft *thud,* she landed on the other side of the canyon. Shay set me down but didn't release me from his arms.

"Remember?" he whispered.

"Yes," I breathed. "I was thinking about that as we crossed."

Sidelle snickered. "Get a room, you two. Sheesh. Even in the gray and dreary Mist, you can't keep your hands to yourselves."

"Be on your guard," Finn said, sobering us. "We don't know what's out here." He turned to Kieran. "Maybe you should see if your Angel Light works, just in case we need to see or something."

"Good idea." Kieran cupped his hands, and a white light appeared. He opened his palms, and it intensified. "Looks like it works."

"Nice to know. I bet whatever else you can do will also work here."

Vash, no longer in human form, shook like a wet dog then trotted ahead of us.

"I guess he doesn't like flying," I said.

"Or maybe," Sidelle said with a smirk, "it scared the fur right off him, and he's getting back to his inner self."

I turned to Finn. "So, if no fairies ever come into the Mist, how do you know where it is?"

"I've heard rumors."

"Hold up." Sidelle stopped walking. "We're going based on a rumor? Isn't that a little, oh, I don't know ... dumb? I mean, if you know of another one, and you know exactly where that one is, shouldn't we be going there instead?"

"This one's safer, trust me."

"But we could walk in circles or never find it." I shook my head. "How're we going to find our way back if this doesn't pan out?"

"I don't think you have to worry about that, Zoe," Shay said, pointing ahead of us.

As Vash passed through the trees, he rubbed his body on the bark, leaving a scent. He'd stop, sniff, then trot farther ahead and repeat.

"He's marking the way for us."

"Maybe it's a good thing he came with," Sidelle said with a shrug. "I guess puppies do have a use after all."

Vash growled as if to say, *"I heard that."*

The perpetual gray atmosphere weighed heavily on me, and I doubted myself more with every step. How could a seventeen-year-old girl save the world when she didn't even have a license to drive? How could someone as good-looking as Kieran be my best friend? How could a plain-looking, average girl snag a gorgeous boyfriend like Shay? The answer? *She couldn't.* My pace slowed as the questions swirled in my brain. *Shay doesn't love me. How* could *he when he looks the way he does, and I'm ... this?* I dropped his hand.

"Zoe?" Shay asked, frowning. "What's wrong?"

"Stay away from me." I took a step back and folded my arms, sulking. "You're lying when you say 'I love you.'"

Sidelle turned back and stared at me. When I wouldn't say anything more, she crossed her arms as well. "What's gotten into her?"

"I don't know," Shay said. "She just started talking nonsense."

"So now I don't talk about anything important?" I yelled. "See? Just proves you don't love me, since you apparently think I don't have anything worthwhile to say."

"Zoe?" Kieran stepped in as he always did and shook my shoulders. "What's going on with you?"

I practically snarled at him, "Like you wouldn't love to see Shay and me break up."

He blinked. "I won't deny that."

"Why didn't you ever ask me out? You had all the time in the world, and you let him beat you to it."

"Hey, he's not any better for you," Shay objected. "I can make you just as happy as an angel could." He stepped in, shoving Kieran to the side. "Besides, he'd probably try using Persuasion on you."

Kieran shoved him back, eyes narrowed. "You know Guardian angels don't have that ability."

"What the heck is going on with them?" Finn asked.

"Stay out of it," Sidelle snapped. "This has been a long time coming for them. Plus, it's not like you know anything about love."

Finn's jaw dropped, looking as if she'd just smacked him. "What? I know plenty, Delle."

Before I knew what was happening, Shay had punched

Kieran square in the mouth. Kieran faltered, massaged his chin, then barreled into Shay, taking him to the ground. Fists punched, and legs kicked, but this time it wasn't the beautiful dance I'd once seen them perform while fighting the demons in the warehouse or at my house.

Then Shay's Nephilim Sword appeared in his hand, ready to strike. Kieran ducked in time to avoid getting hit in the head. He retaliated and shot Angel Light toward Shay. I watched them fight, doing nothing to interfere. Sidelle and Finn stood off to the side, no longer talking to each other. Vash hurried to my side and nuzzled my leg. *"Zoe?"*

"What? Have you come to pick on me now, too?"

"No. What's wrong with them? Why is everyone fighting?"

"Like I have any idea."

My sharp tone caused Vash to step back. *"Zoe, this isn't like any of you. Something is messing with your minds. It's creating doubt, heightening fears."*

A sharp pain pricked the meaty flesh near my thumb, and I glanced down. A tiny stream of blood oozed out of my skin.

"You mangy dog. You *bit* me!" I stared at the tiny red river making its way into the center of my palm. I shook my head, and suddenly some kind of curtain opened in front of my eyes, and all was better in my mind again. "Wait. What's happening?"

"I think it's something to do with the Mist. It's making everyone crazy. I had to shock you out of it."

"But why not you?"

"Maybe because I'm in my natural form."

I nodded. "Go help the others."

While Vash nipped at the rest of our friends, snapping them out of whatever strange hold the Mist had on us, I sat on a boulder and looked around, searching for something different from the endless gray. Out of the corner of my eye, something shimmered. I rose to my feet and went to stand under a willow tree. Its branches bobbed and danced, though there wasn't even a slight breeze. One by one, my friends stood by my side. No apologies were said; there was no need for them. We understood it hadn't really been us saying those awful things.

"Why are we here?" Shay asked, looking up and down at the willow tree.

I held my palms up; a strange tingle danced across them. "I think this is what we're looking for." I said. "Can you feel the energy?"

"She's right," Sidelle said, eyes wide. "It pulses with a force that dwarfs my glamour."

Without thinking, I reached for one of the lowest branches, wanting to feel its power, but Shay pulled me from my trance-like state.

"Don't."

"This is definitely it," Finn said. "The leaves' coloring isn't right. There's something off about it. And with our odd behavior ... yes, I'd say this is definitely the place."

"I don't know where this porta will take us," Sidelle said, "but we should link hands and touch it together, so we don't get separated." She took my hand, and I grabbed Shay's. The rest followed until we had our fingers locked, and we stood in a loose circle around the trunk. The last two of us grabbed a healthy handful of Vash's fur. "So. You'll get the same free-falling feeling as before. Are you ready? Finn? Do you want to or should I?"

"I'm not going with you. I agreed to get you to a porta, so I have. I didn't know you wanted me to come." He stepped back, out of Kieran's reach. "You guys go before I change my mind."

I looked at Sidelle. Her typical cheery expression had grown somber. "Fine, if that's what you wish."

"Can't he come with us?" I whispered, squeezing Sidelle's hand.

She sighed, obviously battling with her emotions. After a moment she gestured with her chin toward Finn. "Whatevs. Just get over here, would ya?"

She waved him forward, and after only a slight hesitation, he joined us and linked hands with Kieran. With his free hand, Finn reached for the odd-colored green leaves—but nothing happened. I didn't get the sinking feeling, and the landscape was still in front of us.

"But I thought it was the porta." Sidelle slumped. "It has to be. I can feel it. It's just like the one in the field in Summer, right, Finn?"

He frowned. "Yes, but something's different about this one. It's like the porta is closed to this side and—"

A horrific sound shot into the sky, like thunder, only much louder. The draping arms of the tree parted and out stepped more than two dozen demon knights and Marqs. Vash charged the closest Marq, fangs bared, Shay brought forth his Sword, Kieran readied his Angel Light, and Sidelle and Finn called their glamour before remembering it didn't work in the Mist. I summoned my Light as we backed away. Shay sliced the first few DKs who ran in his direction. He grabbed my hand and tugged me away from the action.

"Stay here."

"Oh, no," I said, yanking my hand out of his grasp. "We're not having that discussion again, Shay. I've learned a lot since you were gone. I can handle myself." To demonstrate, I shot a ray of purple Light toward an advancing DK, and it burned a hole into his chest, right where his heart would have been. The DK dropped like a sack of potatoes. "See?"

One corner of his smile curled up. "I stand corrected. Okay."

Evidently, he didn't believe me. "Look, I remember how it was at my house. You three could barely contain the dozen Marqs. You need my help, and I'm gonna give it whether you like it or not. Now go kill a few demons before I do it all myself."

He smiled and did as I requested, running back into the fray with his sword swinging in all directions. Sidelle and Finn tag-teamed as much as they could, but without their glamour, they were useless against the Marqs. Over the centuries, Sidelle had obviously picked up some fighting skills, because I watched her neatly dropkick the nearest DK. Unfortunately, he was back up and gunning for her within seconds. But she was relentless, issuing kick after kick, punch after punch. Eventually, the DKs went down but not quickly enough. We needed to end this and fast. Vash couldn't take on this many Marqs on his own. Yes, some of the Alpha's strength had passed to him from his father, but it wasn't enough to allow him to kill two dozen of them by himself.

Kieran's Light shot across the area, finding its mark, and wrapping around one of the Marqs. I watched for another second then joined him. Gathering as much Light as I could, I watched Sidelle and Finn run past me and an idea hit. Just because their glamour didn't work in the mist, didn't mean I couldn't draw from it. I found her green spark and his blue one, and when I merged them with mine, I felt stronger. A dark violet Light overpowered everything, and I used my mind to extend and retract the wall. When Shay screamed in pain bringing me back to the fight, I refocused on him and my other friends.

The orb wavered and then blew out like an explosion, shoving me and the fairies backward. The blast radius managed to take out half of dozen of the Marqs, but it still wasn't enough.

"We can't fight this many," Kieran yelled. "We have to retreat!"

My Light was fading quickly. I wouldn't be able to hold out much longer. Fatigue overpowered my body, and I could feel my legs giving way. Someone grabbed me under my arms and dragged me back, away from the fighting. I felt a warm body carrying me. The sounds around me grew quieter, and my vision dimmed.

It was Shay who carried me away from the battle, leaving Kieran and Vash to hold off the enemy for a few more seconds, so we could get a head start. After hiding, dodging, and trying to outsmart and outrun our pursuers for what seemed like an eternity, we finally stopped to breathe.

"So we try the one in Winter now?" I panted.

"Yes," Finn said. "It won't be guarded."

"And you know this for sure ... how?" Sidelle asked.

"Because no one knows about it besides the Queen."

"And you."

Finn nodded but didn't say anything more. He continued to walk.

"How come we didn't go there first?" I asked, but I didn't get an answer.

After a few more hours passed, we finally stopped to rest and to find shelter. We were weary from the demon attack, and I was hungry. I imagined Shay and Vash were, too, but neither said anything. After Sidelle went to look for a place to hole up for the approaching night, I huddled next to Shay and fell asleep in his warm arms.

When I awoke, it was pitch black. My body jerked with panic.

"Shh, Zoe," Shay said. "It's okay. You're safe. We're in a cave. We didn't want to use any glamour for light, just in case the demons were tracking us."

I nuzzled into him. "Okay."

"Go back to sleep. I'll wake you when we're ready to leave."

The next morning we started back on our trek to find the Winter porta. At some point when the sun was high in the sky, we stopped, noticing how the landscape changed up ahead, transforming into a wintery land. Ice crystals hung from every tree, and a blanket of sparkling snow covered everything. Gray mountains dotted the horizon.

Sidelle looked back at Finn and nodded. He stepped closer to the invisible border—though perhaps it wasn't invisible after all.

"We'll need winter coats, boots, hats, and all that, Finn," Sidelle said. "And anything else the boys can carry in backpacks, like sleeping bags and blankets. That sort of stuff. Can you manage that?"

"Yes."

With a wave of Finn's hands, a snowstorm started to brew all around him, engulfing him until we could no longer see him. All of a sudden his arm shot out, and he motioned for us to step out of Summer and come closer to him. We glanced at each other, then at Sidelle, who nodded with determination. Taking the cue, I stepped out first. As soon as the first snowflake fell onto my head, I was covered in a hat, a scarf, a knee-length down jacket, and warm boots. Everything was in varying shades of dark blue. The outfit was nicer than any I'd had back home, and I appreciated Finn's good taste in clothes. One by one, my friends emerged, decked out in dark blue winter gear. And just like that, the snowstorm stopped.

"Okay," Finn said. "We should get started. It'll be sundown soon, and we want to make it to Winter's Pass before then. It's just beyond that ridge."

We stepped in line behind Finn, trudging through the snow, single file.

"Yeah, fine," Sidelle said, walking right in front of me. "But can't we just use our glamour to get there?"

"No. Mab would know, and we don't want that. Not if we're going to ..." He hesitated.

"Exactly where are we going?" she asked. "Where is the secret porta, anyway?"

"Um ... inside the castle."

Sidelle froze. She stopped so suddenly I walked into her back. "Um, Finn? Did you just say the *castle*? You couldn't have told us—*me*— sooner? How the heck are we going to get five of us into the castle and go unnoticed?"

"I haven't thought that far ahead," he muttered. "Come on. Keep going."

"Can't we go back to Summer and get Oberon to help get us out?" I asked.

"We're closer to Winter now, and we'd waste more time backtracking," Finn said.

"Should've told us that earlier," Sidelle mumbled.

We were headed toward Aesculus, home of the Winter castle. From Sidelle's reaction that was a bad thing. I didn't know how long it would take for us to get there, or what we would find once we did. I couldn't even be sure Finn wasn't leading us into a trap. How could have it come to this?

"Um, can one of you tell me what's with the castle?" I asked.

"It's where Queen Mab lives. She's the ruler of Winter,"

Sidelle replied grimly.

Finn slowed his walk to keep pace with mine. "It's where I live, too."

"You live in the castle?" I asked.

He glanced at me, smiling. "Yes, a prince generally lives in a castle, or at least they do in fairytales."

"You're a prince?"

He gave me a little bow as he walked. "Prince Finnegan, at your service. Delle is the only one who calls me Finn. You may, too, if you'd like. I apologize we weren't properly introduced the last time we met, but I guess we were all pretty busy fighting demons and such."

This was news to me. "You're a *prince*? Is that why you know about the secret porta? Because you needed an escape route?"

"It doesn't matter how I know about it," he muttered, "but I'll admit, I did use it to run away once."

"Probably because he needed to bolt from all the one-nighters," Sidelle said under her breath, but everyone heard her.

"I haven't been with anyone since you—"

"Save it. I don't want to hear your voice."

We didn't run into any demons along the way, so I hoped we had escaped them, though my gut told me that wasn't true. All was quiet on Winter's Pass. But the enemy was still in Fairyland. They were just biding their time.

The day had turned into another sundown when we exited the Mist and came upon Aesculus Castle, nestled between a snow-covered mountain and a bottomless cliff. A frosty mist blanketed the land, making it impossible to see more than a few inches ahead, so we had to be careful when we traveled along a strip of ice, the only road to get to the castle. The narrow pathway was suspended high above the canyon, which separated the frozen tundra from the city limits.

"I need to shield all of you, so you'll go undetected," Finn said as we neared the castle's gates. "Sidelle, whatever happens, do not use your glamour. Understand?"

She nodded.

"Okay. Here we go. Let's hope this works—I've never shielded this many. Delle, grab the back of my cloak and don't let go. All of you, hold hands. I won't be able to hold it long but hopefully long enough to get us inside." He raised his hood, dropping it low over his face.

"That'd be good." Sidelle's voice dripped with contempt, surprising me. They definitely had some ugly history between them.

"I'll make myself invisible," Kieran said, and then his body disappeared.

"Okay. Ready? Let's go."

A cold shimmer moved over me, but I could still see everything. As we approached the massive iced gates, two guards stepped out.

"State your business."

Finn lifted his hood and stared at each guard. "Don't ever question me again," he snarled, "or I'll have your head. Am I clear?"

"Your Highness! I ... I did not see—"

"Move aside!"

The flustered guards quickly bowed and stepped out of Finn's way.

We moved as one into the Winter garden of frozen trees, flowers, and fountains of cold bluish water shooting from spigots. The castle doors opened on their own, probably recognizing their Prince.

"My boy has finally returned." The shrill female voice echoed off the ice walls, capturing my attention. Finn stopped and jerked his cloak off, mumbling something. He threw it at Sidelle.

"You need to hide. Try not to even breathe," he said and shoved us into an alcove. "And keep this on as best you can." He left us there and turned back the way we had come. "Yes, my Queen?"

"I've been wondering where you scampered off to."

"Do you need something?"

"No, just checking up on you."

No wonder he ran away, to escape his overbearing mother.

"I'll be in my room if you need me."

I never saw the Queen. She'd been able to speak as if she were standing in front of me, but she'd never materialized. Maybe it was something to do with the castle itself.

After a few moments of silence, we poked our heads out of the alcove. "Can we come out now?" I whispered.

"Yes, but let's get to my room as quickly and quietly as possible."

Finn walked with his head high, a look of determination etched on his face. I could tell by the reflection off the mirror-like walls that no one dared smart-mouth him.

We hadn't made it far before a loud crash shook the whole castle.

"We've been breached," the Winter Queen shouted. A tall, elegant woman emerged from behind an ice wall, long, black hair flowing behind her and past her tiny waist. Despite my terror, I couldn't help noticing that her ball gown was an intricately embellished blue, the color of a glacier. "Everyone, to arms!"

"How in the fairies did *they* get here?" someone cried.

Blue flames lit torches along the ceilings, shining an eerie blue hue over everything. Winter knights in matching breeches and tunics appeared, carrying wooden shields and spears, and their chest plates glittered with something shimmery. Panic seized me; I assumed we'd been discovered.

Then I realized it wasn't about us at all. "*Demons,*" I heard in Vash's mind.

Guards ran through the castle while some went out to the courtyard to protect their home from the coming demon attack. I looked out a glassless window and gasped at the sight. Bodies of dead Winter fairies lay scattered across the white frozen landscape; the castle was overwhelmed by the demons storming through the gates. Judging by the sheer numbers of Marqs, Sammael meant business. He wanted no one left alive.

"We have to help them," I whispered.

"Zoe, we can't." Shay tugged on my hand. "We have to get you out of Fairyland. Winter can take care of them."

"Are you sure? Because it doesn't look like it."

The air sparked with electricity. A storm was brewing. The sky lightened as thick snow fell, blanketing the air in white. Blue charged ice spears flew directly at their targets and never wavered, but while packed snowballs thrust some of the DKs backward, the Marqs still advanced. Finally, an organized line of Winter fairies held the castle's walls, and I saw the Queen standing at its center, fighting side by side with her subjects.

"Yes, we can, and we will." Finn yanked my arm so hard I thought it might come out of the socket. "You're too important to die here, Zoe. You need to be back in your realm." He shoved me into Shay's waiting arms. "Go with him and Kieran."

"Can't Sidelle call Summer for help? Fairyland is their home, too!"

He shook his head. "Most of her powers don't work while she's here, in the heart of Winter. She needs to go with you to open the porta. Besides, she can't use her glamour out here in the open, or all of Winter will know that there's a Summer fairy in the castle." He shot another shard of ice down the hall at an approaching DK. "Zoe, *leave*. Don't make me shove you through the porta. It goes easier on the body if you go voluntarily. Trust me."

I hated the thought of leaving them like this; I knew I could help. But they were serious. I had to get out of here. "If I can come back, I will," I promised.

"Whatever." Finn turned Sidelle toward him. "Delle, follow this hallway to the end. There isn't any glamour on the door so just push it open. Once you enter the bedroom, look behind the door for an ice-encased mirror. That's the porta. *Go!*"

He stepped backward and resumed a fighting stance. Footsteps echoed down the narrow hallway, which was soon crowded with demons. We ran to the end of the hall, and I looked back, watching him battle his way forward, driving the demons back the way they came. His tactics were direct and precise.

He glanced back toward us one more time. "Delle, go."

But the split second cost him dearly as he didn't see the Marq on his right side. A black sword sliced through the air and scraped across his arm. Finn screamed in agony as blue vapor escaped the wound. I couldn't stop myself. I pulled my arms free of Shay and Kieran and summoned my Light. When it had charged, I sent it flying into the oncoming demons. They halted a few seconds, probably wondering what the new purple light was, giving Finn enough time to regain the upper hand. Whatever glamour was infused in his sword seemed to be sufficient to stop them.

Purple ribbons, like the ones that had appeared when the Marqs had killed Keegan, swarmed the hallway, weaving together to create a solid barrier between us and them. Finally, with no other options, we left Finn alone with the demons. Now, we stood outside giant iced doors that led to the queen's private chamber. Muffled shouts and grunts could still be heard from the other side of the purple wall.

Sidelle puffed out a breath. "Here goes nothing." She

placed her hand on the slab but nothing happened. Lifting one eyebrow, she gave it a shove and simply pushed it open. "Ha! He told the truth for once."

A floor-to-ceiling mirror stood in the opposite corner. A blue light pulsed from it, providing the only glow in the room. Sidelle called her magic and forced her magic to form into her palm.

"Sidelle," I whispered. "Finn said—"

"I just want to check that the queen didn't use glamour in here."

Her light cascaded to the floor, flashed once, then disappeared into a seam. The green spark traced its way up the walls and over the ceiling. I watched it dart around, searching. A moment later, the light shot out of the ground at my feet and hovered above her hand. It sprayed outward into the open space of the room; then the rays converged toward the mirror behind us, forming back into a ball. It pulsed three times and disappeared.

"So far, so good."

The mirror beat with an old energy, and an uneasy feeling washed over me, similar to the feeling I'd had when I'd manipulated the token from Oberon. My fingers glided up and down the sides of the ice encasement. I stepped around to the back side, expecting to see my straight brown hair and eyes. Instead, the glass-like sheet of ice shimmered, looking like a drop of water had created a ripple on the surface.

This was the porta Finn had told us about. This was our way out of the castle.

Something clicked in my brain. *Old magic.* I removed the coin necklace from around my neck and looked at it, wondering. *Mixed glamour and Angel Light.* I fiddled with the coin, turning it between my fingers, thinking about when Oberon had said it contained his glamour.

"I've got it."

"Got what?" Shay asked. "What are you up to?"

"I'll send Oberon a message through this." I held up the gold coin. "He said his magic is in it, and when I reformed it, my Light became infused as well. I can send him a message through this, so he will come and help Winter."

"Zoe, we need to go," Sidelle said urgently.

"I know, just give me two seconds. I need to get help. He needs to know what is happening here." I closed my eyes. "Watch the door ... just in case."

My body tingled, but even though the idea was mine, I had no clue what to do. I pressed my palms together, holding the coin between them, and thought about the message I wanted to send. In my mind, I saw the token and how it used to be a sphere, and I felt the energy of Oberon. Purple ribbons flattened into a sheet of paper, reminding me of a post-it note. I thought of an ink quill then started writing.

King Oberon,

We tried to leave Summer, but a Tree Nymph told us the portas were being guarded by demons. The Winter Prince told us of another way out, but it was risky. We found the porta in the Mist, and when we tried to open it, demons came through. We fled to the other porta the Prince knew of, but the demons followed us. Now Winter is under attack.

I know Winter is your sworn enemy, but it's time to join together and stop evil from spreading deeper into Fairyland. You can battle Winter another time, but right now your battle is against Hell. Sammael has managed to bring his followers to your realm. Will you stand beside your sworn enemy and help them survive this attack?

If you do nothing and Winter isn't able to hold them back, Sammael will come for you and your kind.

I believe you told me about the token for this purpose, and now I'm asking for your help. It is not for me but for your kind. Please send as many as you can spare. I fear the castle will be overrun soon.

Sincerely,

Zoe

I thought of an envelope and tucked the note inside.

Then I opened my eyes and stared at the coin in my palm. The envelope hovered above it. I infused the paper and the token, sending the package on its way to Oberon. Instantly, the gold coin disappeared from my hand.

We had sort of let the demons in through the porta. This was bad. Very, very bad. *How was I going to live with myself knowing I had caused Winter fairies to die?*

The whole way back from Fairyland to my house, I was haunted by images of the fairies we had to leave behind. I only hoped Oberon received my message in time and decided to send help. I'd have to get in touch with Sidelle later tonight and confirm.

When Kieran finally dropped me off at my house, it was nighttime, and I prayed my parents wouldn't be home to grill me. I couldn't handle them right now. No one was home. I trudged through the kitchen, picked up the paper, and read the date: Sunday, April 24. *Great, I didn't miss my junior prom.* I saw the note my parents had left on the fridge and then walked up to my room, relieved I didn't have to answer tons of questions. The clock on the wall read 7:34. The house would most likely be quiet for another few hours.

I didn't hear Shay calling my name—not until he touched my hand. The jolt pulled me out of my thoughts.

"Are you okay?" he asked. "I can stay, if you'd like."

"I don't know." I faced the window.

"Don't know if you're okay or if you want me to stay?"

He couldn't see my smile. "I *always* want you to stay, Shay."

"But ... ?" He stood next to me.

"I just need some time to process, if that's all right with you."

"Sure." He brushed the back of his hand down my cheek, and I closed my eyes, loving his touch. "Take all the time you need. I'll always be here."

I touched the warm electrical trail he'd left on my face. I grabbed a fist full of his shirt and pulled him toward me so I could kiss him. At first it was a little rougher than I was going for, but it then softened. My arms wrapped around his shoulders, and his hands moved to my waist, pulling me closer. He molded his body against mine, threading his fingers through my hair, kissing me back. Any thoughts of how horrible I knew I looked after this impossibly long day simply floated away. Kissing him made all my worries and fears dissolve.

Need tugged at my brain and heart. My emotions swirled around me, around us. Purple light shot out of my body, just like the first time our make-out session had turned hot and heavy. I led him to my bed, letting myself fall onto it and taking him with me. He kissed my forehead, my neck, my lips. With every kiss, I felt the pain of his torture while he'd been in Hell, as well as the longing he'd held for me that whole time. Worst of all was his fear that he might never see me again. I needed him to understand I would never leave him. My breathing became labored as I pushed his dirty black T-shirt up and ran my fingers over his chest. His skin, which had been so horribly disfigured during his capture, was perfect again. Soft. Our kissing broke off, and I ran my finger over the place where the X should've been. Then I inspected his shoulder.

"I wouldn't have fought if I knew I wasn't at one hundred percent," Shay assured me. "You don't have to worry."

"I still will."

"I worry about you, too." He ran his finger along my skin, near my belly button, and I shivered. "Are you always going to glow?" he asked, grinning. "It's going to be kinda hard to hide us making out if you keep telling the world."

My face was on fire. "I'm sorry. I don't know."

"That's okay. I'm just teasing. I'd shout it from the rooftops if you'd let me." He lowered his lips back to mine, making me forget temporarily about the Winter fairies' deaths, the upcoming battle between good and evil, and all the pain Shay tried to keep hidden from me.

A few hours later, I awoke in his arms.

"Zoe?" he whispered. "Your parents are home."

That got me moving. I rolled off the bed and ran into my walk-in closet, where I selected new clothes. I sprinted into the bathroom, scrubbed the dirt off my face, and combed the rat's nest out of my hair. My heart pounded as the steps outside my bedroom door drew closer. When I emerged from the bathroom, Shay was gone. I checked the window, and it was shut.

I heard a knock.

"Yes?"

"Are you decent?"

"Yes. Come in."

The door opened, and Dad walked in. "How was your weekend with Sidelle?"

I prayed he couldn't read my mind as I lied. "Oh, you know, busy. We had to do a lot of research and organization. I didn't sleep too much, and our eating schedule was off"—at least *that* wasn't a lie—"but you remember how that goes, right?"

"Sure. I remember pulling all-nighters at the U. But we always stopped working to have a little fun."

"Nope, didn't do that. Between running here and there for stuff, we didn't have a chance to have any fun at all."

"No late-night girly talks?"

"I'd zonk out most of the time."

He frowned. "Seems to me Sidelle would look out for you a little more."

"She does," I said, shrugging, "but you know I get my stubbornness from you."

He turned to leave, then stopped. "Oh, and Zoe?"

"Yeah?"

"You have a mark on your neck." He pointed at his own to show me where, then wiggled one eyebrow. "And I know she does a good job protecting you. All your friends do."

He left and closed the door.

Shay shot out of the closet. "He knows."

"Well, duh, he knows. He pointed out the hickey you left on my neck!"

"Not that. Well, yeah, that too, but he knows about all this stuff." He came closer to me. "Didn't you hear him?"

Now, he was making no sense. "Yes, but that doesn't

mean anything."

"Sure it does. I'm sorry, Zoe, but I don't think your parents are who they say they are."

What? I stared at him, shaking my head. "Don't be silly. Of course they are. Kieran and Sidelle would've known if they weren't. They've been in my life since I was born."

He tilted his head, thinking. He let out a long breath. "The next time you talk with Kieran, you should ask him." He stepped toward the window. "Well, I'll leave you to it, so you can rest and get ready for school tomorrow. I know you didn't get much sleep over the last four days. But I'll be back after I check in with Kieran."

After he left through the window, I got ready for bed, stunned by his parting words. I did need sleep, but my body wouldn't rest. Words tumbled around in my mind as I tried to replay conversations I'd had with my parents over these past few weeks. Why weren't they freaked out more? Did they really know about the Enlightens? And if so, could they be angels like me? Finally, exhaustion overwhelmed me, and I floated off to sleep.

I hadn't spoken to Aiden since last week. When I noticed the same flame-red car in the same parking spot on the school grounds, it jogged something in my mind.

"Come on." I pulled on Shay's sleeve, determined to get to the bottom of this mystery. I scanned the parking lot to make sure no one was watching us as we headed toward the sports car.

We peered into the dark tinted windows but couldn't see the interior. The car shined and was full of so much chrome we could see our reflections almost everywhere. The license plate read: HELBOUND. I *had* seen this car before. *When?* Here in the parking lot, some time ago. *Who drove it? Think!* The driver ... he wore a hat with a red feather. And ... and Morgan. She had been getting into the passenger side. *Bingo!*

"This car was here two weeks ago," I declared. "Now, I remember it. It was on the day Vash came to school. Didn't Kieran tell you that we had this conversation?"

"You sure?" Shay asked. "I haven't had a lot of time to regroup with Kieran."

"Yes, positive. It has to be the same vehicle. Cars like that are rare at the school, let alone this town."

The first bell rang, so we hurried to our lockers, ending our conversation. Later, when I saw Rena in the hall after first period, I stopped her. I felt bad for the way I'd treated her and Quinn the week before, and I needed to set things right again.

"Rena!" I called.

"Hi, Zoe. Hey Shay." She turned to me. "I've been trying to get a hold of you all weekend. Is your phone on the fritz or something?"

"No, why? What's going on?"

"Quinn went home Wednesday night after cheer practice and felt sick. Must've been bad because her parents took her to the hospital later that night."

"What?" My stomach ached. The last conversation I'd had with her left a sour taste in my mouth. "Is she all right?"

She shook her head, looking concerned. "The doctors don't know what's wrong with her. They ran the usual battery of tests, but as of last night, they're thinking of transferring her to the Mayo Clinic in Rochester to be seen by a specialist."

"That's horrible! I have to go visit her."

"I can take you," Shay said. Then the tardy bell rang.

Quinn didn't return to school, and I never had the chance to visit before the doctors moved her to Rochester.

By Thursday, my life had returned to a normal routine—or at least what I thought normal should be. No demons attacked, no one died, and I continued to attend school. The teachers still piled on homework, even though this weekend was prom, and no one would be doing anything except eating, partying, and dancing. Every afternoon I went to Kieran's and practiced the Silico with Cali. Her life became a routine, too. She had informed us that nothing happened while on pack land, and Jackson hadn't found out who helped the demons. So everyone was still on high alert. And every evening I hung out with Shay, or we sat in Kieran's backyard or mine, or we'd walk to Coffee Grind.

Today was no different. Cali and I had advanced to the next level, which was the actual hand-to-hand combat. She partnered with Vash, and I went with Shay since neither would intentionally hurt us. We decided that as soon as we were comfortable with our sparring partners, we'd switch. Vash and Shay each had their own fighting styles, so we would pick up new maneuvers or stances through working with both.

"Hey, Sidelle, did you hear that Quinn still isn't better?" I asked during a break.

"Yes, I heard. I wonder what she has."

"You don't know?"

She scowled. "I don't go poking around people's brains, so no, I don't know what ailment she has. Sorry, Zoe."

The last two days of school passed quickly, even though Quinn was MIA. Aiden seemed upset about something.

Maybe he missed her. The gossip of the week was about Aiden and Morgan. One of the seniors had thrown a party on Friday night during the long weekend, and they'd both shown up. Shortly after, they'd left ... *together*. Rena told me that on Saturday, he'd had a lunch date with Quinn, then a dinner date with Morgan. For me, that was the last straw. I decided that whatever ailed Quinn was Aiden's fault—or at least I'd blame him for it. Rena, after I badgered her for a full day, finally said that Quinn and Aiden had hung out together a couple of nights last week, too. Aiden had even gone to her house to check on her. How could he flirt with her and still date Morgan? Because on Monday, he and Morgan were inseparable, either joined at the hands or by the lips.

By Friday afternoon, I had managed not to say a single word to Aiden at school or at home. Hopefully, he got the message loud and clear. After Shay dropped me off at my house, I ran to my room, wanting to grab a change of clothes so I could get in one more practice before prom weekend officially started. I noticed the blue light on my cell phone flashing, so I checked to see who it was. I hoped it was Shay letting me know to come over ... but it wasn't.

Aiden: Are you mad at me

I punched at the phone's keyboard.

Me: What do you think?

Aiden: Where are you

Me: What do you want?

Aiden: I want to explain

Me: Why? Seems obvious

Aiden: Please

Me: Fine. My backyard.

I stepped outside and waited. It wasn't long before heavy footsteps approached through the grass. Not bothering to look up at his face when his black combat boots came into my peripheral view, my head eyes focused on the ground. Aiden didn't say anything as he sat on the swing beside me, and that bugged me. I wanted him to hurry and spit out whatever he wanted to tell me. By sitting here, I was losing precious time with Shay. We stayed silent for a long time, and I still didn't say anything. He'd called the meeting, and I wasn't about to break first. I watched him fiddle with his hands, like he was nervous or trying to figure out what to say.

"Zoe, I'm sorry," he eventually said, looking at me with pleading eyes. "It's not what you think."

"Whatever," I snapped.

"I didn't—"

"I said *whatever*. Say what you came to say. Then go away."

He blew out a sigh. "I ran into your friend, Kieran, earlier today. He asked me a lot of questions about my tattoo, so I showed it to him. It's no big deal. Then he drilled me about ..." He swallowed, taking a deep breath. "About the Enlightens, asking what I knew about the Orders. I didn't know you knew, and I couldn't figure out how to tell you about me. Now, I don't have to."

I glanced at him, surprised, but he was looking at the ground. This was totally not what I'd been expecting to hear about.

"You don't know what it was like for me," he said. "I hated the thought of moving to Minnesota. Then on the night before the move, I had a dream about a girl with brown hair and green eyes. There wasn't any storyline to the dream, but I kept seeing a face, like flashing images. Imagine my surprise when I saw you on your front step, next to the house we'd just bought, and you looked so much like my dream, except you were too far away for me to see clearly. Sarah wanted me to hurry up and pick out the bedroom I wanted. I literally ran into the house, so I could come back outside and meet you. I checked each room's view before I picked my room, and I hoped the purple one was yours."

He grinned, but he kept looking down. "Imagine my joy when I walked up and you smiled at me. I didn't want to scare you, but the truth is I had to make a conscious effort to slow my breathing. Because the fact is, it was *your* face I had dreamed. Then add to my surprise when you came to my room. You were so cute, especially when you got all huffy. I'm sorry, I didn't handle that moment well. I was ... I was shocked."

He finally looked at me, and I was struck again by so many things, like how incredibly hot he was, and how the color of his eyes was so like Shay's.

"I still can't believe I found you," he said. "Then that night we sat on our windowsills and talked? Man, I loved that and every night since. I wanted to get to know you. You, Zoe, *all* of you. I had to. I—"

I didn't like where this was going. It made my stomach churn. I changed subject. "Why are you dating Morgan and not Quinn?"

He shook his head. "Quinn's with Caden." He got off his swing and surprised me by kneeling in front of me. When I didn't move, he leaned back to sit on his feet. "Sure, we spent time together last week, but we're just friends."

His hand hovered above my knee, but he pulled back when he saw the look of warning in my eyes.

"Does she know that?" I asked.

"She knows now." He sighed. "Zoe, I didn't know you knew about Enlightens. How was I supposed to tell you that she's a Nephilim?"

"What? Quinn?" *What on earth*? "How do you know that?"

"I can tell." He tapped the side of his head. "She doesn't have a tattoo yet, so she hasn't made the full transition. She doesn't know about us, Zoe. About Enlightens, I mean. I had to tell her to help her prepare for it. She told me she was adopted, so I knew she wouldn't know about all this. I mean, who would teach or train her? So I took it upon myself to help her through the transition until she gets her tattoo. That's why she's been out sick. The transition is happening now."

I thought about what Aiden had said. Of course he wouldn't have known I knew about the Enlightens, and that meant all this had been a massive misunderstanding. He had checked on Quinn, testing the waters with her to find out what she knew. When he realized she didn't know anything, he'd helped her since there was no one else.

"Wouldn't Kieran know this?"

"Maybe. Have you asked him?"

"No, I've been busy this week and didn't have a chance. Sidelle didn't know, so I left it alone, chalked it up to some mystery disease."

That's when I noticed Aiden's expression was one of fear. He didn't know what I was thinking, and he seemed genuinely concerned. Realizing I'd been wrong about him felt like a huge weight lifted. My anger vanished. He grabbed the metal chains of my swings, forcing me to face him, and pulled me over until our heads were only inches apart. His beautiful eyes were wide. When they dropped to my lips, I smiled, and he closed the distance between us.

At the last second, he stopped, and my brain caught up with my body. I scrambled away, my fingers pressed to my lips. My stomach heaved with the knowledge that I'd almost kissed him. No, wait. *He'd* almost kissed *me*. What had come over me? Even though I hadn't done anything, I felt sick with guilt. Shay was the love of my life and my soul mate. We were meant to be together.

"I can't. Shay's my boyfriend. I won't betray him."

He cleared his throat. "Sorry."

"Look, I gotta get going," I said, waiting for him to release the chains of my swing. "I'm meeting him for a date."

Aiden completely ignored what I'd said. "Where did you and he meet?"

I guessed I could spare a few more minutes. I loved to talk about anything to do with Shay. "In a warehouse in the Void. It sort of blossomed from there." I sighed. "When we touch, we ... um, how can I say it? Um, well ... it's like an electrical current goes through us. As our relationship got more intense, so would the shock. Kieran said it was because we were soul mates."

"Wow, soul mates. Guess it's true then. It does happen." He sat back on the other swing. "So is that what this is?" He pointed to the inside of my wrist. "I've never seen one like that on another Enlighten."

I shrugged, words wanting to come out of my mouth. "I don't know what it means, but I guess I should tell you something else ... about me." I looked him in his eyes, hoping I was doing the right thing. "Do you know about the Prophesy?"

"Yes. Everyone knows it."

"Well, here's the thing—" A tingle shattered my mind, like a gateway being pushed open. "I'm the Redeemer." I couldn't stop the words even if I wanted to. And did I want to?

The next day was prom. I still had a few things to do before I could go to Cali's house and meet up with the rest of the girls, so I woke extra early and did laundry and then picked out clothes to pack for the weekend. The cover story I'd told my parents was that I planned to stay the night at Cali's, since we were all going there to get ready. But the real plan was to stay at Kieran's in Shay's bedroom. I really didn't think my parents would've minded if I'd told them a partial truth because they knew his parents—or at least they knew the two angels who portrayed themselves as his parents.

Finding a large duffle bag, I tossed in all my toiletries, a few items of clothing to change into over the weekend, and extra shoes. With great care, I laid out the white dress from Macy's. I cringed, remembering that was also the night of the demon attack at my house and when Cali died. Shaking those thoughts, I dug around in my dresser for jewelry.

I made it over to Cali's by eleven. Giggles greeted me. Squeals floated down the staircase. When I entered Cali's bedroom, clothes and make-up were spread out everywhere, and Rena walked out of the bathroom with her hair already styled. It looked like a tornado had landed.

Relief washed over me when I saw Quinn sitting on the ottoman, applying her eyeliner. She had been discharged from the hospital yesterday morning when more tests had come back negative. She'd insisted that she was not missing prom, and there was nothing the hospital could do to prevent her leaving since they couldn't diagnose her.

"Zoe, you made it," Cali said, jumping up to grab my bag. "Here, let me help you."

"Thanks. You guys. I can't believe prom is here already."

"I know!" everyone squealed.

"We're going to make this a night to remember, aren't we girls?" Rena said. "Hurry up, Zoe, get going on your hair and make-up."

"Where's Sidelle?" I asked, frowning. "It's not like her to be late."

"What are you talking about?" Sidelle asked, gliding into the room in a gorgeous olive-green dress peaking above her signature black stilettos. "I'm right on time."

"Wow, Sidelle, you look awesome!" Cali exclaimed. "Where did you find that dress?"

"In an old trunk I had shipped here from one of our properties overseas."

"It's gorgeous," Quinn said as she emerged from the bathroom. "Zoe, you're up."

"Okay, I'm on it." I draped my garment bag carefully over my arm. "Sidelle? Do you want to help me with my hair?"

"Lead the way."

I closed the bathroom door behind me then stripped out of my yoga pants and T-shirt. "It's been quiet for some time now, right?" I whispered. "Nothing has happened since we got back from Fairyland. Isn't that weird?" Taking out my dress, I unzipped the side and stepped into it. "Can you help me zip?"

My dress was made with chiffon and considered to be tea-length, cut in an A-line style with delicate capped sleeves. A three-inch white satin ribbon circled the waist, and it was tied into a bow in the back, its tails hanging as long as the hem. The back was cut into a heart shape with the point plunging to the waist, and the front had a large scooped neckline that showed off my silver wings necklace. The dress fit as if it had been made specifically for me.

"I agree it's been quiet," Sidelle said, zipping me up. "Maybe too quiet. We all have to be on guard tonight." She waved her hand across my hair, and it formed into a gorgeous up-do.

"Can you do my makeup, too, but maybe do it the traditional way?" I opened the bathroom door. "Hey, ETA on when we're ready?"

"About five minutes for me," Quinn said.

"Same here," Rena replied.

"I'll be ready when everyone else is," Cali said.

I sat on the small vanity chair while Sidelle applied my foundation, lip liner, and eye shadow.

"Pucker ..." she said, demonstrating. "Close your eyes ... and you're ready."

At noon the house bell rang, and we peeked out the window. A row of sparkling vehicles lined the curb. Doors slammed and the boys filtered out of the cars, all dressed in black and gray suits.

"They're here!" Cali shouted. "Come on. Is everyone ready for pictures?"

As the suavely dressed guys entered the foyer, we descended the staircase one at a time. Cali went first, and the look on Vash's face was priceless. Then it was Quinn, Rena, and Sidelle's turn, resulting in plenty of "oohs" and "aahs." I waited until the end, and then I wrapped my hand around the banister and headed down to the first floor. At first I could only see Shay's black shoes and pants; then a white shirt came into view. A silver tie peeked out from his buttoned sports coat.

"You look amazing!" Shay said, beaming at me. "Absolutely breathtaking." He extended his hand and presented me with a white orchid. "Here. This is for you."

"Thank you." I held out my arm while he stretched the band and placed the corsage on my wrist. "You're quite dashing in your suit, too."

We stepped outside into the bright sun. Quinn, Caden, Rena, and Noah said their goodbyes; they were off to meet up with the basketball team. The rest of us climbed into the caravan of vehicles and headed for my cul-de-sac. Shay pulled into the driveway, stopped the car, then helped me out. The others stayed on the porch while he and I walked hand in hand to the front door. My family waited for us in the living room.

"Oh, Zoe," Mom exclaimed. "Don't you look stunning in white! And Shay, you look handsome." She held up her camera and snapped a photo.

"Hi, Mrs. Jabril," Shay said.

"You guys must get in the habit of calling me Jackie or at least Mrs. J." Mom motioned for us to stand in front of the fireplace. "Tell everyone else to come inside. They don't have to linger out there."

Click. Click.

"Sidelle. That's a gorgeous gown," she said, beaming at my friends. "And Cali, that color is great on you."

"Thanks, Mrs. J," Sidelle said.

"Geez, Zoe," Stella said. "I didn't know you could walk in shoes like that." She giggled. I normally didn't; we all knew I preferred my Converses.

Click.

"Gentlemen," Dad said as he shook Kieran's and Shay's hands. "How lucky you are to escort these beauties today." Then he turned to Vash, smiling. "I don't think I know you, young man."

"Vash. I'm Cali's date."

"Well, you're a lucky man, escorting her tonight."

"We all are extremely blessed," Kieran said.

After Mom took a few more pictures of us as individuals and as couples, and some with the whole group, we were done. We piled into our respective escorts' vehicles for the hour drive to the Mall of America for dinner. Along the way, Shay and I rocked out to various music to get us in the mood for dancing. At one point my mind wandered, making me wonder for a split second if something bad was going to happen, but I pushed that thought away. Nothing would spoil tonight.

Once we arrived at M.O.A., we walked to CRAVE Restaurant. Kieran told them that our party had arrived, and we were told the wait was an hour. Sidelle suggested spending that time at Nickelodeon Universe instead of her using glamour to get us the table faster. I hauled over to the ticket counter and asked for the smallest ticket package, but Shay pulled out his wallet.

"Nope. This is a date, and the girl doesn't pay." He waved his hand at me to put my money away.

"That's so old school," I said.

"That may be, but you're still not buying the tickets."

We walked hand in hand around the indoor amusement park, trying to decide which ride to go on first. The Log Chute ride was quashed right away because no one wanted to get wet.

"Let's do the Avatar Airbender," Cali shouted, pointing toward the far end of the park. "I haven't been on that one since they built it."

"We don't all have to go on it," I said, eyeing the corkscrew blue support beams. "I'm thinking it's not the best one to ride in a dress."

"If the boys want to go, they can," Sidelle said.

"How about we all go on the carousel?" Vash suggested.

That sounded more like it. I glanced around, looking for Kieran and Sidelle, then saw them whispering in each other's ears. *Hmm.* Shay squeezed my hand, and I focused on the people standing in front of us, waiting for the gate to open for the carousel's next set of riders.

"You look beautiful," Shay said. "Just what I imagined an angel would look like."

I blushed. "You look handsome in your black suit. Just what I *know* a Nephilim looks like."

We moved up with the line and walked around the operator, and I selected a blue and pink zebra. I stepped back, looked at my shoes, and hiked up my skirt. I decided to sit side-saddle, like a proper lady would sit on a horse. There was no way I was going to attempt to straddle the thing in this dress. Cheesy circus music played in the background as the carousel spun. It was corny as all heck, but I loved every moment of it. Shay rode beside me, and Kieran and Sidelle were a few animals behind.

"We have time for one more ride," Kieran shouted to us. "Then we'll have to get back to the restaurant."

The ride slowed, and Shay lifted me off the zebra. After that, we chose to ride the Rock Bottom Plunge roller coaster. I've never been a huge fan of roller coasters, but I didn't want to spoil the evening, since it was just getting started. At least on this ride, our dresses wouldn't fly up and I could fix my hair. But with all the product in it, I doubt it would move. We sat in a yellow car and waited for the operator to press the red "GO" button. The ride started with a jerk, and my heart raced. Once it got going, it shot down the teal track then launched high into the air. The twists and turns meandered around the park, giving us a bird's eye view of the Mall, but I didn't care. I screamed like a banshee all the way through the ride. I didn't even notice when it slowed until Shay tried to peel my white-knuckled fingers from the shoulder bars.

"It's okay, you can let go now," he said, chuckling. "The ride has stopped."

"Zoe?" Sidelle asked. "Are you okay?"

I didn't move. "Y-yes. I'm totally fine."

"We need to go, Z," Kieran said. "The next set of riders is waiting."

Laughter and giggles snapped me out of it. They weren't directed at me, I didn't think, but the thought prompted me to let go. Shay helped me out of the death trap, but I wobbled on my stilettos.

Kieran was on my other side in a flash. "Maybe you should sit," he suggested.

"No, I'm fine. We can't be late for dinner. We still have to drive an hour to get back for the dance."

"Then buck up, Buttercup," Sidelle said. "Let's go chow, so we can get our dance on! And here, let me fix your and Cali's hair." With a wave of her hand, all was righted again in the same up-dos and not a hair out of place.

We were almost late for our dinner reservations, but then all six of us settled at a corner table with white linens. It had to be the most elegant place I'd ever eaten at. The atmosphere was dark but romantic; hushed conversations and the clinking of glasses and silverware permeated the air. Black-suited wait staffers bustled around the room, quietly taking orders and bringing out food. Everything on the menu looked spectacular, and at first I couldn't decide what to get. *Thank God for pictures on menus.* I eventually narrowed it down to either baked mac and cheese or filet mignon.

"Isn't this place awesome?" Sidelle asked. "I went to the one in Florida when I was on my way to South Beach some years ago."

A few rows over sat another young couple, also dressed in formal wear. The girl's back was to me. I couldn't see her face, but there was something familiar about her. Then she moved her chair to the side and revealed her companion. *Aiden*. He wore a black tux, a white shirt, and a red tie. The girl giggled at something Aiden said then turned in my direction. *Morgan*. She glared at me, turning back around.

Of course he'd taken her to prom. Aiden reached for his glass, held it up in a mocking cheer, and smiled. How could he take *her*, of all people? I clenched my fists, but Shay eased one of them open and threaded his fingers through mine. We ordered our dinners, and the conversation returned to normal. But something began to nudge the back of my mind, and the nudging got more persistent as the night continued. I felt *off*, and I couldn't explain why. The tiny hairs on my arms and neck still lay flat, so I was fairly sure no demons lurked in the area, but still ...

The drive back to St. Joseph was uneventful and long. I was too amped up and ready to dance the night away, and I refused to let Aiden and Morgan ruin my evening. This night had to be perfect. So far, so good.

But I couldn't help the nagging feeling in the pit of my stomach. Something wasn't right.

As Shay and I walked into the school, we passed under a white and teal balloon arch, and he squeezed my hand. I stood in the doorway, taking it all in. The decoration committee had done a fantastic job making the old gymnasium look and feel just like I pictured heaven would be. Everything was white except for the teal flowers strategically placed around the room. Tulle covered the rafters, giving the appearance of a low ceiling. Twinkle light gave the room a soft glow. Everything lived up to the prom theme: Heaven is a Place on Earth. In the center of the ceiling hung a giant disco ball, which reflected shimmering dots across the walls. Off to my right, about a dozen round, high-top tables had been provided where students could gather, eat, or rest. On my left stood a long line of prom goers who awaited their turn for their keepsake, where a photographer had set up a backdrop to snap pictures. Teachers stood watch over the food tables and around the perimeter of the gym, ready to interfere with any misbehaving students.

A band had been set up on a raised platform on the opposite wall from where we'd entered. Shortly after we arrived, the music started. Screams, whistles, and shouts erupted from the students, letting everyone know that the dance had officially started.

"Zoe, may I have this dance?" Shay asked, giving a formal bow.

I grinned. "You may."

Shay led me into the throng of dancers then placed his free hand on my waist and pulled me tight against his chest. I inhaled, breathing in his scent: musky lavender tinged with a hint of something as sweet as a strawberry. Even though the music had a fast, upbeat tempo, and Shay was an awesome dancer, he and I swayed to our own slow rhythm. We shifted back and forth for a while, and then he led me into a spin. People moved out of our way as we gradually created an open space. Other dancers stopped to look at us, then resumed flailing their arms and jerking their bodies around in their kind of dance.

"You're so beautiful," Shay whispered into my ear.

"You clean up nicely, too."

"I hope I can make this a night you will always remember."

"I won't forget any of this, Shay." I stood on my tiptoes and placed a kiss on his lips. "I'm so glad to have you back. I didn't know what I would do if you—"

"Shh. I'm here. I'll always be here for you."

We stopped dancing and just stood there, holding each other.

"Get a room," Sidelle muttered as she and Kieran waltzed past.

I smiled at her and waved. Everything was perfect.

We kept getting glares as people bumped into us, which meant we'd either have to start dancing or get off the floor. Shay kissed the top of my forehead, and then we broke apart. He loosened his tie and jammed out to the rock song the band was playing, and I followed suit. Sidelle and Kieran came back around to join us, and we made a circle as Vash and Cali danced toward us. I spotted Rena and Noah standing in line, waiting for their prom photo. They waved when they saw me looking in their direction, so I motioned for them to join us. Quinn and Caden stood with the rest of the basketball team near the food tables, so we shuffled our circle over to be near them. Quinn grabbed a reluctant Caden's hand and dragged him to the dance floor, even though his face was beet red. He kept looking back at his teammates with pleading eyes. Maybe he just didn't want to dance next to Shay and Kieran, who made dancing look like a breeze. Of course for them, it was.

The entire evening was just how I'd dreamed it would be. I was surrounded by my closest friends, my boyfriend's arms were wrapped around me, and there wasn't any place I'd rather be. I didn't want the night to end. A few songs later, I was breathless and needed a break. I tugged on Shay's hand, fanning myself.

"Do you want something to drink?" he asked.

"Yes!" I screamed over the blaring music. "I need to sit, too, and rest my feet for a bit."

He led me over to one of the high-top tables and pulled out a chair, and then he kissed my hand. "You rest those pretty little toes, so we can dance the rest of the night away."

"I'll be right here."

The song ended. The gym doors swung open and hit the walls, creating a loud bang. Everyone stopped and stared at the entrance as Aiden and Morgan strolled in, hands linked. He wore an impish smile across his face, or maybe that was him being happy. Morgan, wedged in a red, flowing gown, sashayed across the room like she owned the place. Her dress flared out behind as her two bookends, Ashel and Abby, flanked her with their dates.

My stomach churned, reminding me of the uneasy feeling I had in the restaurant and on the car ride here.

"What are you all staring at?" she yelled. "I'm fashionably late. The party can start now!"

I rolled my eyes and turned away, hoping she didn't see me. She and I didn't need to get into a fight tonight. Really, I didn't want to get into *any* fights tonight. As I watched my friends on the dance floor, I realized how much I loved them all. I'd do anything to keep them safe. We had to beat Sammael; that's all there was to it. Then we'd keep him locked in Hell with no way to escape. I had to find a way to get a Seraph's Sword. The sooner, the better.

"Hey, Zoe."

I turned and faced Aiden. "What do you want?"

"To ask you to save a dance for me."

"Why would I do that?" I glared at him. "I can't believe you took *Morgan* to prom. Doesn't our friendship mean anything to you?"

He held up one hand. "Whoa, hold on. I came to this school late in the year and didn't have anyone to bring. She was available, so I asked her. I know you two don't get along, but—"

"'Don't get along' is an understatement."

"I don't see why you gals can't be friends."

"Tell her that. I don't need friends who bully me."

"Well, don't do her any favors then. Do me one. Please save me a dance."

He had a point, in that most of the girls had already been asked. Of course, Morgan was one of the last ones without a date, so she for sure would have said yes if Aiden had asked her.

"Fine, I'll save you a dance." I folded my arms and lifted my chin. "But only if you can pry me away from Shay."

"That's all I ask. Thank you, Zoe."

He turned and walked away to find his date with his head down, passing Shay as he returned with a few drinks in hand. He watched Aiden's retreating back. Shay turned to me. "You okay?" he asked. "Who was that?"

"I'm fine, and that was no one." I raised the plastic cup and toasted his. "Thanks for getting these."

"No problem." Shay peered over the rim of his drink. "What did he want?"

"Nothing. Just a dance." I tossed back the cool blue liquid and slammed the empty cup on the table. "But I only agreed to dance with him if you and I weren't dancing."

"Then we'd better not let him have an opportunity."

"My thoughts exactly," I said, beaming.

We threw our empty cups into the trash can and headed

back to the dance floor. Hand in hand, we joined my friends and stayed out there until our legs wouldn't hold us up anymore. Shay was always by my side. Sometimes he reached for me, touching my arm, and other times, he grabbed my hand and twirled me into his embrace. Eventually, I flung my stilettos into a corner, and Cali and Quinn followed my lead. Sidelle, of course, kept hers on.

An upbeat song merged into a slow one, and Kieran appeared at my side. "Zoe?" he asked. "Dance with me?"

"Of course, K."

Shay let go of my waist, and I stepped into Kieran's open arms. My two favorite guys seemed to be on better terms lately, but even if they weren't, I couldn't imagine Shay denying my best friend a dance.

"I saw you with Aiden," Kieran said once we were on the dance floor. "Is he bothering you?"

"Nothing I can't handle."

He nodded, satisfied. "So? How is tonight? Is this everything you dreamed it would be?"

"Yes," I said, smiling at him. "Everything and more."

"Good. I'm glad."

Kieran was just as good a dancer as Shay, if not better. Our bodies flowed as one, like we were meant to always be with each other. Maybe it was because we'd known each other for so long. Kieran turned gracefully and whirled, leading me across the floor, and I was the envy of everyone—or at least that's what I liked to think. Truth was they were staring at Kieran because, well, how could they not? There was a glow about him tonight. It was as if he'd let out some of his Angel Light to shine around us.

"I wish ..." Kieran started, but he didn't finish his sentence. Instead, he rested his chin on top of my head. We slowed, and I looked up into his blue eyes. "I ... Zoe, I'm sorry. I have to say it. I think I'm in love with—"

"May I cut in?" Aiden stood next to us. "Please?"

We stopped moving, and I stared at him. I shook my head, knowing I was rude, and that I previously said I would. I tightened my grip in Kieran's hand. I need to hear what Kieran has to say. I have to know who he's in love with.

"I don't think so, Aiden." Kieran turned our bodies.

"Please? Zoe, you promised."

I looked into his pleading eyes. Kieran shook his head but didn't say anything. I slowly nodded, even though I really didn't want to end my dance with Kieran.

Aiden reached his hand toward me. Kieran obviously wanted to tell me something important about someone he had feelings for, but I'd kind of promised a dance to Aiden. Darn the Minnesota nice and promises.

Kieran extended his arm in a sweeping motion, and

Aiden stepped in. As soon as Aiden touched my hand, a jolt coursed through my body like an electrical current. I stared, quite literally shocked. I'd never felt anything so intense before. It was nothing like the shocks that Shay and I experienced. This was something entirely different.

Something menacing.

I looked into Aiden's aqua-colored eyes, the same beautiful shade as Shay's, and realized this was the first time we'd actually touched. We'd come close many times since I'd known him, but he'd always pulled away. It was like he purposely didn't want to touch me, like he couldn't bear it. But this dance had been his request, not mine. As we circled across the dance floor, we passed Shay. My heart ached—I wanted to be in *his* arms, not in Aiden's. Aiden kept his back to Shay and Kieran, and both glared at Aiden's back. Finally, *Ever the Same* drew to a close. It was one of my favorites by Rob Thomas, and I knew it well, and I wanted to return to Shay's arms.

Aiden spun me around, then dipped me low to the floor. I tilted my head back and saw Shay and Kieran upside down. Aiden lifted his head and finally looked at them. He winked at my boys, lowering his lips to my ear.

"Finally," he whispered. "You're mine."

Confused, I looked at Shay, whose eyes grew wide then narrowed. He leaned over to tell Kieran something and ...

then my world came to a screeching halt.

Shay moved with lightning speed, but he wasn't fast enough.

Kieran's body glowed, producing his Angel Light.

My vision dimmed, but I was conscious enough to see a pair of jet-black wings wrap around me.

My body gave in, and I collapsed into Aiden's arms.

"No!" Shay's voice rang in my ears.

Then Aiden and I disappeared.

Continue reading for a sneak peek at a few chapters of Zoe's final story in *Wars & Wings*!

Chapter One

My head throbs in time with my beating heart. At least there's that bonus; I still have a heartbeat.

I must be alive if I can feel my body. Or maybe this is what death is like.

Under my palms is cottony material. I run my fingers along the edge. My back is pressed on top of something soft. A bed maybe? I scrunch my eyes tight, refusing to open them yet.

There is no sound. No furnace running. No birds chirping. Only the *thump, thump* of my heart.

Is this heaven?

Thoughts carry me back to the last night I can remember.

Prom.

A white dress. Driving to the Mall of America. Dinner. Dancing in the arms of Shay, my boyfriend. Twirling across the gym floor with my best friend, Kieran. Someone cutting in.

Blackness envelopes me.

But not before I hear someone whisper in my ear: "Finally. You're mine."

Who was holding me?

AIDEN!

I bolt straight up, and my eyes fly open.

I'm in a room without windows or doors. How is that possible? I stare down and am sitting on a bed. To my right is a small love seat and table. To my left is a toilet, sink and a privacy screen. The walls are white, reminiscent of a hospital room. Gray cement is used as the flooring. I deduce that this could be a basement. But where?

How did I get in here? How did Aiden bring me to this room? I have no idea how long I've been out. Without the sun or moon to let me know the time of day, my only guess is that it's Sunday.

My cell!

I pat the sides of my hips and feel the smooth chiffon. Nothing. Remembering that my dress doesn't have pockets like how some styles do today, so I had to use the strap of my bra. Tacky, but it's a good thing I did. My fingers brush against the slim, metal of the devise. I clutch my phone and stare at the screen. It's missing the date, but the time is flashing: 10:34 am. That's not possible.

I check the battery life and it's holding at 60 percent. At least something is good now.

But I gaze at the bars of service. Nothing. This is bad.

I try dialing Shay's number anyway. The call doesn't go through. I quickly write a text. The stupid phone says it can't be delivered.

I am going to kill my neighbor as soon as I see the whites of his eyes. Or, I should say the black of his wings. My fingers curl into tight balls as the memories come crashing in.

The live band is ending the song *Ever the Same* by Rob Thomas. I'm on the dance floor with Aiden, but looking at Shay and Kieran standing off to the side. I spin in Aiden's arms, he dips me low to the floor. My heads tilts back and I watch upside down as Shay leans into Kieran and says something. Gold angel Light blasts from Kieran's body. Shay moves with lightning speed, but doesn't reach me in time.

Black wings wrap around me.

The guttural cry of Shay screaming *"NO!"* still rings in my ears.

I realize without a doubt this is Aiden's doing. Stupid me for trusting him. That lying back-stabbing no good angel with wings. And I don't mean figuratively. He's no angel with everything he's done to me: befriending me, taking my nemesis to prom and now adding kidnapping to his rap sheet. Oh no. He's no angel at all, that's for sure. I can't bring myself to think of him as anything worse than that. He's not a demon Knight or a Marquises demon. I'd know if he were. *Wouldn't I?*

Yes, I would. My demon radar would have gone off at

some point. I've spent time alone with him on many occasions and nothing about him seemed out of place. He screams bad-boy and loner, but demon? Kieran would have known if Aiden was an angel though, right? And Sidelle would know if he were a fairy. I guess I never bothered to ask either one of them, but they didn't let me know either.

He could be a Nephilim; he does have wings after all. Black ones to match his heart, if he even has one of those. I slam my fists against the bed.

Thankfully, I'm still in my prom dress so at least Aiden hadn't undressed me when he locked me into this prison. I wiggle my toes and my stiletto shoes are not strapped to me feet. A quick scan of the small room informs me that they are not with me. *Drats*. Remembering I left them in the gym, recalling that during the night I flung them off into the corner. Now how am I going to make my great escape in bare feet?

First, I need to figure out how to get out of this place that has no doors or windows. Sliding off the side of the bed, I stroll to the couch, but I stop right before I get to it. Like an invisible wall, I can't penetrate it to sit down. My hands run up and down finding a weakness in the force, but none can be found. Why put furniture there if I can't use it.

I saunter across the foot of the bed toward the make shift

bathroom. My fingers reach out to grab the edge of the screen and my fingers wrap around it. I drag it a couple of inches to make sure. Turning toward the sink, I flip the faucet to the hot position and immediately hot water flows onto my hand and down the drain. But what I find most interesting is that there isn't any piping running into the floor. It's as if the water empties into nothing. But at least I have running water. Now to check the toilet. While it seems new, I don't dare want to get sick from unsanitary conditions or anything. I roll out a panel of toilet paper and press the flushing handle. All looks to be in working order, but again, there are no plumbing pipes.

I edge around the toilet to examine how far the space is around the area and it's not much. Another invisible wall meets my hand about a foot further.

Walking back to the bed, I hop onto the mattress and jump up to touch the ceiling. I can't reach it, so I plop back down and wait.

Wait for my friends to rescue me.

Wait for Aiden to come back to answer a few of my questions.

Wait for me to come up with a plan.

Wait.

My tummy growls. Great. There is no sense of having a bathroom if I don't eat anything. I don't have my clutch either because why would I if I'm dancing? Usually I keep an energy bar or some other snack food in my purse everywhere I go.

I sigh.

There is nothing to occupy my mind with. I can't count ceiling tiles because there aren't any. I can't count wall cracks because they are smooth. I can't count patches on the lavender bed quilt because it's one large piece of material. The only items worth counting are the two-inch purple yarn ties that holds the top and the bottom together; there are 120 of them.

I worry about how long I'll be kept here waiting. I wonder if my friends are already out looking for me. I have a gut feeling I'll be here a long time.

It's only been a couple of hours and I'm bored out of my mind. This must be the worst way to die. I dismiss that thought because I refuse to acknowledge that this is my end. It's not.

It can't be. It's been prophesized that I save the world by uniting the Orders together to battle against evil. And Aiden, I have decided, is evil. The next time I lay eyes on him, he's going to wish he were never born. Figure of speech since angels are created and not born. I have yet to determine how I'm going to make him suffer if I'm in here and he's out there doing who knows what.

But still.

I check my phone for the time again; a little after six. I've been captive for under twenty-two hours. I must have dozed off at some point because now I'm beyond famished. It's still too bright in the room, which reminds me that I never recall seeing any lights or switches. I crawl off the bed and walk to the sink. Using my hand, I cup water into my mouth. At least I won't be dehydrated. I'll need all the strength I can muster if I'm going to kick Aiden's ass when he steps through the no door.

I let out a scream from everything that's been building up in my mind. Frustration that I trusted him. Anger for letting him kidnap me. Depression that I won't get out of here alive. Worried that the world will no longer exist because I have failed in my mission and Sammael escaped from his prison.

The non-lights dim and a silver serving tray with a turkey sandwich, a bag of FunOnions, a napkin, and a diet strawberry can appear on the bed. I note that no utensils are on the tray. At least he's being cautious and rightfully so. I'd use the spoon to stab him in his scrawny neck.

Ripping open the bag of chips, I inhale and savor the onion fragrance. I force myself to eat slowly, chewing everything carefully and fully; not knowing when my next meal will be. Plus, now I have something to do.

Powering down my cell phone to conserve the battery life, my thoughts go back to Shay. I know he's going ballistic searching for me. He'll leave no stone unturned. He won't stop looking for me. I bet he'd travel into the depths of Hell for me. Oh wait, he was already there when the demons kidnapped him and tortured him for information about me.

Since Shay and I are soul mates, could he feel my discomfort? I couldn't detect him but over the last few months, we've been through a lot with each other and we've grown. Maybe a plan is forming. I'll have to think more on that.

I toss the empty bag of chips on the floor, and pick up half of the sandwich, wishing for saran wrap so I could save part of it for later.

My BFF, Kieran, will move the heavens to find me. He waited centuries to discover the girl who would save the world. It's not in him character to stop.

And Sidelle went into her nemesis's territory to help me get back home. So, I know she'll look into every alternate world known to her to rescue me from Aiden's clutches.

A smile stretches across my face thinking of Sidelle and wondering what she would do in my place. She'd say some snarky comment about not letting this situation dampen any of my training. Of course, she'd probably use her glamour to get her out and I don't have that option. Or do I?

Carefully reaching for the can of pop, I crack the top open and savor my first sip. Just because my sparring partner Cali isn't here with me, doesn't mean that I should stop conditioning myself. It will take my mind of my confinement. I move the tray off to the side of the bed.

I wish I have shoes, and a change of clothes, but I make do. Raising my leg onto the bed, I stretch my calf muscles. Hold it there for ten seconds and release. Switching legs, I repeat. I reach one arm into the air and grab the elbow with my other hand, letting the arm dangle down my back. Rotating my head from ear to ear, I hear a much-needed *pop*.

Standing in front of the bed, I make circle motions with my arms and my legs. After a few lunges I'm ready. In prayer position, I clear my mind and start the fighting dance. With graceful movements that flow like water between moves, my arms and legs lengthen, stretch, and retract. It becomes a cross between yoga, ballet and karate.

I'm not sure how long my routine lasts because I won't make myself turn on my phone to check the time. Sweat beads along my forehead and the hindrance of my long skirt limits my movements, but I can't get myself to rip the bottom off. It is my prom dress, after all.

To cool down, I splash water on my face and I wish I had a bar of soap to scrub my face clean of makeup. Grabbing one of the pillows, I tug off the cover and use it as a wash cloth. Much better. I almost feel like a new girl. Almost.

I head back to bed and eat the rest of my sandwich and drink the rest of the pop. With nothing else to do, I lay across the bed, telling myself that every day no matter what I will do at least what 30 minutes of exercise feels like.

Eventually, my eyes close, dreaming of an aqua pair staring back.

ACKNOWLEDGEMENTS

Thank you to my family and to all the friends who have supported me through this whirlwind and crazy journey. Your encouragement means the world to me.

To my book club peeps and cheering sections: thank you!

A very special thank you to my beta readers: Kristi, Jennie, and Angela. You helped me make it shine.

To my friend Angie, who listened to my constant rants, both triumphs and complaints. You kept me sane whether you knew it or not.

To the Writer's Block, Dakota County, and The Loft Literary YA Writing Group who shared their wisdom and experiences with me: thank you.

To my critique partners, Ann and Niki, for providing insight, picking up on my echo words and cutting the way too many 'ing' words.

To my editors: Genevieve Graham and Jen Leigh. You helped me create better sentences, better scenes, and deeper characters.

A warm and heartfelt thank you to Angela for another superb cover. I get so many wonderful comments from readers that they love them!

Jessica, your eye captured exactly what I was going for.

Thanks for making the photo session really fun and entertaining. And who doesn't want a shoe chair as a prop?

And lastly, to my husband: without your support in this whole process, none of it would be a reality. Thank you for attending the many fairs, show, boutiques with me!

Thank You.

~ Kristin

Call to Action

I hope you've enjoyed Zoe's adventure: *Daggers & Dresses*. To find out what happens, check out the rest of my series available now.

Swords & Stilettos, Book One
Daggers & Dresses, Book Two
Wars & Wings, Book Three

Novellas:
Fires & Fairies, Sidelle
Arrows & Angels, Kieran

Short Stories:
Poisons & Princes, Finn
Ninjas & Nephilims, Shay

Follow me online
Website | Instagram | Twitter | Facebook | Pinterest

USA TODAY bestseller, Amazon bestselling, and award-winning young adult author, Kristin D. Van Risseghem grew up in a small town along the Mississippi River with her parents and older sister. Currently, she lives in Minnesota with her husband and a Calico cat, named Daizy. Kristin also loves attending book clubs, going shopping, and hanging out with friends. She has come to realize that she absolutely has an addiction to purses and shoes. They are her weakness and probably has way too many of both.

In the summer months, Kristin can usually be found lounging on her boat, drinking an ice cold something. Being an avid reader of YA and Women's Literature stories, she still finds time to read a ton of books in-between writing. And in the winter months, her main goal is to stay warm from the Minnesota cold!

Kristin's books are published by Kasian Publishing LLC.

Dear Reader,

I hope you enjoyed *Daggers & Dresses*. I have to tell you, I love the characters of Zoe and Shay. Though many beta readers and critique partners telling me: "What about Kieran?" Well, stay tuned because his story isn't over. Kieran will have his own Novella. How did he become the bossy Guardian Angel?

When I wrote *Swords & Stilettos,* and now *Daggers & Dress* I received many comments from readers thanking me for sharing Zoe's journey. Some had an opinion about her and Shay, while others rooted for Kieran. You are the reason Kieran's story is told in *Arrows & Angels*. So tell me what you liked, what you loved, and even what you hated. I'd love to hear from you. You can write me at KRISTIN@KRISTINVANRISSEGHEM.COM, visit me on the web at www.KristinVanRisseghem.com, follow me on Twitter @KVanRisseghem, and like my Facebook Page: https://www.facebook.com/KristinDVanRisseghem.Author/ to keep updated on the Enlighten Series.

And for all of you who are writing, I encourage you to keep at it. Keep going and looking ahead. You can do it! Find beta readers and critique partners, and join writing groups. If some aren't working out, don't be afraid to search out new ones. I found a slew of writers on Facebook, Twitter, and Meetup. These people will help you with your writing because ... well, let's face it, your friends and family just won't get what you're talking about if they aren't writers. Surround yourself with the people who are 'in the know' and who will understand what you mean when you say WIP, or MS, or ARC.

Finally, I need to ask a favor. If you're so inclined, I'd love you to write a review of *Daggers & Dresses*. Loved it, hated it – I just enjoy your feedback. As you may have gleaned from my book, reviews can be tough to come by these days. You, the reader, have the power to make or break a book.

Thank you so much for reading *Daggers & Dresses,* and for spending time with me.

Sincerely,
Kristin D. Van Risseghem, Author

www.ingramcontent.com/pod-product-compliance
Lightning Source LLC
Chambersburg PA
CBHW020601310726
48979CB00008B/1294/J

9781943207497